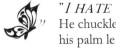 

"*I HATE* "
He chuckle
his palm le
your arms around me."

"No."

"Mmm." He hoisted me into the air with both hands on my waist. I grabbed his shoulders in response, gasping as he pressed his groin into the apex between my thighs. "Grip me with your legs, baby, or you'll fall."

"Put me down."

"Not a chance." He captured my mouth instead and took full advantage of my shock by slipping his tongue between my lips.

What is happening? Why is he doing this?

And oh, no, this... can't... be... happening.

Dizziness shot through my mind.

Adrenaline fueled my limbs.

I wanted to *hurt* him. Needed to fight. Because this couldn't be allowed to continue!

I clamped down on his tongue, only to be rewarded with the most beautiful taste in response. I froze. Then moaned. *Oh my...* Exquisite decadence filled our mouths, distracting me from my goal and throwing me into a whirl of oblivion that I couldn't escape from. Instead, I fell headfirst into it, allowing my instincts to take over.

My legs were around his waist in a second.

My arms encircling his neck.

And his essence coated my lips, my mouth, my *throat.*

I groaned, craving another swallow more than anything else in the world. He gave it to me with his tongue, sliding along mine, feeding me that delicious liquid I desired.

One hand remained against my hip while his opposite rose to my hair, his fingers entangling in my strands as he tilted my head to better receive his kiss.

Some part of me was screaming at us to stop. But I couldn't hear her over the roar of *need* in my thoughts.

Heat unlike anything I ever remembered feeling seared my insides, pulsing through my veins with one driving thought—*more.*

Midnight Fae Academy

Book One

MIDNIGHT FAE ACADEMY

USA TODAY BESTSELLING AUTHOR

LEXI C. FOSS

Midnight Fae Academy: Book One

Copyright © 2020 Lexi C. Foss

Editing by: Outthink Editing, LLC

Proofreading by: Jean Bachen

Cover Design: Lori Grundy, Cover Reveal Designs

Interior Designs: CyberWitch Press

Published by: Ninja Newt Publishing, LLC

Print Edition

ISBN: 978-1-68530-155-2

To Matt, Laura & Vicki, for your constant support and love and for allowing me to finish this story while on vacation. You've all always respected and understood my need to write. It is, after all, good for the heart. ;) Thank you for the memories. Xx

MIDNIGHT FAE ACADEMY

BOOK ONE

AFLORA

GLACIER WAS LATE.

Again.

This whole long-distance relationship thing where we met in the Human Realm for dates was just not working for me. The damn Water Fae never showed up on time.

Instead, he left me sitting in this coffee shop in the middle of Orlando with a mouse-shaped mug of inky liquid. How humans stomached this stuff was beyond me. One sip and I wanted to puke.

But I came here to make him happy. Because I hadn't seen him in over a month due to summer solstice break.

Things would be fine when we went back to the Academy in a few weeks. Maybe. Except we would always have this elemental problem hanging over our heads, what with me being the heiress to the Earth Fae throne and him being a regular old Water Fae.

1

I blew on my steaming liquid, more to mask my frustrated sigh than to cool the liquid. Because yeah, I wasn't going to drink this. I had some spritemead in my fridge back home, just waiting to be cracked open.

Another glance at the clock had me shaking my head.

"This is ridiculous," I muttered to myself. I should not have to wait over an hour for a boy to arrive. Especially one who proclaimed to adore me.

"It is," a feminine voice replied as a puffy, blue-dotted, edible thing appeared beside my mug. "Have a muffin. On the house."

I frowned at the *muffin* before glancing up at the woman who had delivered it.

My eyebrows lifted in surprise. "A Fortune Fae," I said, glancing around to make sure no one heard my admission, before noting her vibrant green apron. "A Fortune Fae working in a human coffee shop?" It came out as a question because what kind of fae chose to reside in this realm? Particularly one of her heritage. "That must be a daunting job, what with people touching you all day."

I took an entire course last year about Fortune Fae. While they loved to deal cards—to tell the future—they hated to be touched. It inspired visions, typically unwanted ones. And I imagined humans would have the same impact.

She tossed her long dark hair—similar to my own—over her shoulder and laughed. At least she didn't tinkle like some fae preferred. That grew old quickly.

No, this fae wasn't afraid to express humor.

A trait that endeared her to me immediately.

"Who are you?" I wondered out loud.

Her smile reached her blue eyes. "Gina," she replied, taking the seat across from me. "I thought you could use some company since your date is a no-show. Oh, but it's not through any fault of his own, I assure you. Fortunately, or perhaps unfortunately, it'll be the least of your concerns very soon." She blinked, her blue irises turning clear for half a second before returning to normal.

A vision, I realized. A notorious habit of her kind, as was the cryptic commentary.

I sighed. "I expected as much. I don't think his parents care for our relationship." I picked at the wrapping around the *muffin*, trying to figure out why a human would eat such a thing. It resembled fabric. "I'm Aflora, by the way."

"I know," she replied, her expression lighting up. "Sole heir to the Earth Fae throne. It's a pleasure to make your acquaintance, Your Highness."

The teasing quality of her voice had me snorting. "Yeah, somehow I doubt you mean that." I narrowed my gaze. "Which tells me you're here for another reason entirely."

"Oh, I am," she agreed. "However, our paths crossing is just a coincidence of happenstance. I only became aware of your destiny recently when I sensed the balance disturbance. It's going to be an interesting year for you, Aflora. Assuming you take the path left. Hmm, but if you go right, I suspect it'll catch you eventually anyway. You're in his thoughts now, after all."

"Uh-huh." This chick was proving all my textbooks right about Fortune Fae and their penchant for talking in riddles. "Well, that sounds fun."

"It will be." She smiled again, only to falter as her gaze flickered once more. "*Shit.*" She glanced at the clock and pushed away from the table. "I'd offer some advice for the road ahead, but I've gotta run. My future keeps finding me despite my deviations from the trail." She gave me a little finger wave and darted out of the cafe, still wearing her apron.

I gaped after her, as did several of the patrons around me.

From what I could tell, she was the only one on duty.

And this is why hiring a fae is a bad idea, I thought at the owner. *We're not the most reliable sort in your world.*

Case in point, my late date.

3

With a sigh, I pushed my coffee and muffin aside, done waiting. At least I'd understood that part of Gina's prophecy—*Glacier isn't coming.*

Fine. I preferred my spritemead over a date with a boy anyway.

Gathering my purse, I left my mouse-mug and the papery dough cake on the table and headed out into the early afternoon sunshine.

Orlando at least had the weather right. Muggy, hot, and oh-so bright. I smiled as I wandered toward the portal, absorbing the elements along the way. The tropical plants here wouldn't survive easily in my home world, but maybe I could manufacture a greenhouse to accommodate them.

I paused to touch a particularly beautiful tree with large green leaves sprouting from the top. *Mmm, this would be easy to—*

Pain shot up my side as something hard rammed into me, sending me several steps forward. "Sorry!" a human shouted as he pedaled by on a two-wheeled contraption.

A bicycle, my memory supplied, recalling a course on mortal transportation.

I glowered after him, ready to give him a piece of my mind, when a hand brushed my arm. "Are you all right?" a deep, masculine voice asked, the accent decidedly smooth.

"Oh, I, yes. Thanks." I glanced up into a pair of ice-blue eyes, the color and perfection of the irises stunning me into silence.

"Are you sure?" he pressed, his fingers trailing up my arm and leaving a trail of goose bumps in their wake. His lips kicked upward, revealing a pair of dimples that didn't seem to match his ruggedly square jaw or the dark brown stubble dotting his chin.

A proper five o'clock shadow, I mused. Then blinked. *Wait, why do I care about such a thing?*

"Careful, beautiful," he cautioned, his arm sliding around my waist. "You're swaying."

4

"I am?" I whispered, my throat going dry as his intoxicating scent surrounded me. *Mmm, a dark spice tinted with an earthy aroma.* I leaned into him, pressing my side into his hard torso.

Melting.

Falling.

Ensnared by his masculinity and grace.

That's not right, I thought, frowning. *I don't even know this guy.*

I attempted to step away, only my feet refused my mental command.

What's happening to—

"You're bleeding," he murmured, his hold tightening as his opposite hand drifted across my arm.

I glanced down to see the trickle of red oozing from my skin.

And blinked.

"How?" I asked, trying to shake myself out of this daze, to force my legs to work. But I felt spellbound, lost to the stranger's touch, as if being pulled into a dream.

A part of me recognized the magic, felt the dark tendrils of it seeping into my pores. With it brought memories of the time I nearly died, how I'd fought to cling to the source of my existence in a futile effort to save everyone but myself.

"The bike," the stranger beside me said softly, drawing me from the nightmarish image threatening to capture my mind. "He clipped you as he took the corner. Clumsy fool."

"Oh." I swallowed. "I'm... okay."

Minus the daydreamy state I'd lost my senses to.

The world shifted as he moved us into the doorway of a building, one I recognized as my destination. *Odd.* I could have sworn that was a block away.

Who is this guy? Why is he holding me?

His arm loosened, giving me a chance to flee, but I found my back pressed up to a wall instead, my vision lost to a haze of momentary darkness.

Something's wrong. A thought that had tried to appear moments ago, only to disappear beneath this strange magnetism. Whatever spell he'd cast over me had my mind short-circuiting, my body bending beneath his command.

Must... stop... this...

"He warned me you would be beautiful, Aflora," the voice whispered, his face far too close to my neck. "But I didn't expect you to be such a delicate little flower."

My lips curled down at the phrase. "Wh-what?" I stuttered, my breath seeming to escape me as he kissed my throat. *What are you doing?* I wanted to demand, but my mouth rejected the words, choosing to moan instead. *How do you know my name?*

This can't...

Oh...

His mouth touched my skin, causing my knees to buckle.

Holy Elements...

This was bad. I felt the illicitness of it crawling inside me, igniting my instincts, only to be tampered down by a seductive, dusky cloud.

Dark magic, I recognized, my heart skipping a beat. It swam all around us, infiltrating my ability to reason. To think. To *run.*

"Stop," I managed to say, my demand lost to the raspy quality of my tone.

He chuckled against my neck, his tongue darting out to tease my racing pulse. "I wish I could, delicate flower. But I've been given a task. *You.*"

My fingers curled into fists, my limbs locking up as I fought to break the spell he'd woven over my form.

Which only earned me another chuckle from the powerful Midnight Fae before me. "Mmm, yes. More of that, please." He nipped the tender skin behind my ear, his amusement palpable. "I was beginning to wonder if perhaps I'd found the wrong fae, what with your easy acquiescence and all."

Easy acquiescence.

I'd show him *easy acquiescence.*

Just as soon as I could find my will to freaking move.

But his magic swathed me in a sea of black, cutting off my access to the element I relied upon for survival, and sank harsh claws into my soul.

I gritted my teeth, furious that I'd allowed him to trap me so effortlessly. That bike had momentarily stunned me, allowing this Midnight Fae jackass to hook me in his dark web.

Fortunately, it wasn't my first date with his kind of magic.

Closing my eyes, I ignored the inky strands floating around me and focused on finding the core of my strength.

Earth.

It was dangerous to access the source of my element, but my royal bloodline enabled me to seek it out, to see the original World Tree. Its massive roots resembled a tangle of life reaching out to every living Earth Fae, the thickest band connecting to me—the last Earth Fae heir.

I crawled along it, absorbing its strength and readying my attack.

The Midnight Fae wouldn't know what—

His canines sank into my flesh, eliciting a scream from my throat. Dread, darkness, and desire flooded my senses at once. A denial parted my lips. My soul screaming at the wrongness of his bite. While my body melted into him in a stark betrayal of my mind.

A tear slid from my eye, the pleasure from his embrace cutting deep into my spirit while my mind recognized the absolute horror of what this meant.

Midnight Fae were not meant to consort with other fae in any capacity. And that included tasting the blood of an elemental or any other fae.

This defied every rule I'd ever learned, and not just because of his teeth in my neck, but because of the very visceral need his touch elicited from within me.

"Stop," I demanded, but the moan underlying the word belittled my intention.

He captured my hip with one hand, his chest a solid wall of muscle at my front. How could my assailant feel so good? Every part of him seemed to line up perfectly against me, including the impressive erection digging into my lower belly.

Wrong, I reminded myself. *But feels so good.*

I wanted to crumple into a pile of agony and ecstasy at the same time. But with every pull, I felt my connection to the elements faltering, the life energy I adored slipping from my grasp.

To give in to him, to lose myself in this way… *No.* I couldn't. I had to fight. My fae brethren would understand. They'd prosecute him for this. Because it wasn't my fault. They had to know that.

I hope.

However, if I didn't at least make my displeasure known, they'd assume me to be complicit in this crime. And then we'd both be punished.

My limbs began to cool as my blood flowed in the wrong direction—toward his mouth. There wasn't much time. I had to make my stand now, while the feed distracted him.

Closing my eyes, I allowed myself to go limp, feigning submission. *Come to me,* I called to the source of my elemental power. *Fill me with the vitality I need.*

This would be easier in the elemental world, the Human Realm far away from the core of my energy. But it heeded my call, recognizing my royal bloodline and filling me with enough strength to rock the foundation of the ground below.

It knocked the stranger's footing out from under him, causing him to lose his grip for just a moment.

I sprang out of his hold, grabbed the nearby rocks of the walls, and commanded them to pelt him.

Only, he deflected them with a flick of his wrist, his icy gaze glowing with his dark essence. "You're going to regret that, princess."

"I think I'm going to regret a lot of things," I countered, calling on a heftier brick to fly in his direction.

He shoved it aside before whirling into a gray cloud.

My lips parted, shocked by his disappearing act.

Which was exactly what he wanted—a distraction.

Shadowy ropes tied around my torso, yanking me backward into the nearby portal. "Oh Fae, no," I said, trying futilely to break the smoky bands, but they just reattached every time I sliced through one.

And then the doors closed.

I dove toward the buttons, but he was faster, his hand appearing to key in a foreign code that definitely didn't match the destination I had in mind.

"Oh dear," he murmured, materializing beside me. "It seems I need to confess to committing a crime. I hope you don't mind Midnight Fae, darling. Because you're about to meet a whole council of them."

AFLORA

I'D NEVER BEEN A PARTICULARLY VIOLENT person, but I really wanted to kill the smirking lunatic sitting across from me. He'd wrapped my wrists in some sort of impenetrable smoke before shoving me into a chair in what appeared to be a reception area of sorts.

Only there wasn't a receptionist.

And the room was anything but welcoming.

Snakelike vines climbed the walls, their beady red eyes glowing intently at the ends. I seemed to be the object of their focus, their rattling tails hissing to an ominous beat that unsettled my insides.

Every time I moved, they slithered faster. Just as they did now. The crazy Midnight Fae across from me tsked out a warning, suggesting I not irritate the guardian serpents, causing my jaw to clench. Not only wouldn't he tell me his name, but he also refused to explain why he'd bitten me.

I shuddered, the sensation of his fangs in my neck still very tangible and real. He'd left behind some sort of inky bond that I could feel more than see.

I smacked at it again, then flinched as the wall hissed louder in response.

"What are they?" I demanded.

"Magicked vines," my captor drawled. "Protects the royal grounds from intruders. Which, if I'm understanding their writhing correctly, they believe you're a threat. So I would stay put, princess, or they might just bite."

"Like you?" I snapped.

His lips curled. "Hmm, no, my bite inspires pleasure." His icy blue eyes glanced at the snake closest to my head. "Their bite, not so much."

I opened my mouth to offer a retort, when the ebony doors at the end of the hall swung open and a dark-haired male dressed in long, flowing robes stomped toward us. "What is the meaning of this, Shadow?"

Shadow? I eyed my companion. *Really?*

I supposed he did have a penchant for disappearing into thick clouds of smoke.

"What would you like me to say?" Shadow asked, his arms sprawled out across the back of the couch in the epitome of lazy nonchalance. "The Earth Fae Royal and I got a little carried away, my fangs slipped, and wouldn't you know? Her blood reacted to my bite."

My lips parted at his horrible recollection of what happened. "Carried away? Fangs slipped?" I repeated, jumping to my feet, only to be snatched back by the vines slithering across the wall.

I screamed, the smoke around my wrists tightening as a snake wrapped itself around my neck and squeezed to silence the sound.

The newcomer sighed and produced a wand. "*Release,*" he hissed, waving the violet stick through the air.

A sizzle of energy kissed my skin, the darkness of it in

direct contrast to my earth essence inside. I shivered, the wrongness leaving me unnerved even as the snakes and my smoky bonds disappeared.

My knees buckled on instinct, sending me crashing into something hard and masculine.

Shadow.

His chest met my nose, his arms wrapping around me as he caught me before I could hit the ground.

I nearly growled, but my modesty took precedence first.

After fixing my blouse and skirt, I shoved him away. "Don't touch me."

"That's not what you said an hour ago, princess."

A growl unlike any I'd ever released before burst from my mouth as I launched myself at him, desiring to do the utmost damage. Only, he caught me up in his arms again, chuckling the entire time.

"See what I mean, Father? She's a wildcat who can't keep her hands off me."

Father?

I shook my head. *Who cares?* "I'm going to kill you!"

"Try" was Shadow's arrogant reply.

Gah! I wanted to scream, to call on a tree to pound this dick into the ground, but my powers refused me here, my access to the source cut off through some means of dark magic. Otherwise, I would have used it to escape as soon as we arrived.

"You bit her," Shadow's father said.

A genius, he clearly was, because I still had the marks on my neck from the attack. And if I had my arms free, I'd have pointed to it for reference, just in case he needed to see it up close. But Shadow had me locked up against him, my breasts smashed to his chest as he held me captive in his far-too-muscular hold.

Shadow smiled down at me. "As I said, one thing led to another and—"

"Do you have any idea what you've done?" his father

demanded, cutting off his jackass of a son.

"Well, I thought it'd just be a taste, but yeah, I'm pretty aware of the mate-bond snapping into place. Why else would I have voluntarily stepped into this dreadful place if not to report the mistake?"

Mate-bond? "What mate-bond?" I wrestled in his arms once more, but he held me with the ease of a much stronger fae.

This was why I needed to take more physical defense classes. I'd grown used to relying on my element, which apparently didn't work in this dark realm.

"Our mate-bond," Shadow murmured. "We're connected now, princess. Forever."

"Stop calling me that."

"It's what you are, right? An Earth Fae Princess?" He cocked his head to the side. "Or are you a queen as the only Earth Fae heir?"

"*Enough*," his father inserted, his cloak billowing around him with power. Blue eyes—the same color as his son's—narrowed at Shadow. "You realize you could be excommunicated for this."

Shadow shrugged. "Saves me from another year at the Academy."

A low, angry sound rumbled from his father's chest. "And what about the girl? Interspecies mating is illegal. They might demand her death, or worse, *your* death."

Wait, how's his death worse than mine? "I don't even want to be here," I said, furious. "And you can't kill me. I'm the sole heir to earth. If I die, the element dies with me." Not exactly true. Someone, maybe Sol, would probably take over my access to the source. But hopefully, they didn't know that.

His father didn't even look at me, his smoldering gaze on his son. "Take her to the dungeon and lock yourselves inside. You know the way. I'll come for you if and when the Council needs a comment."

"Excuse me, but I'd like to give a *comment* right now," I

demanded. "Your son bit me against my will, then kidnapped me and brought me into this realm. I shouldn't be here. Nor can you keep me here. The Elemental Fae Council will not stand for this."

Well, they might.

Being bitten by a Midnight Fae definitely broke several of the interspecies laws governing fae relations. But it was against my will. Queen Claire would side with me. She knew me well enough to know I would never do something like this.

"I'm the sole Earth Fae heir," I added. "My people rely on my connection to the source to thrive. Every moment you keep me here is—"

"Enough," Shadow's father bit out, his expression resembling stone. "The Midnight Fae Council operates very differently from your own. If you have something of importance to say, your intended will deliver the information on your behalf, as females are not permitted within the Council Chamber."

My eyebrows hit my hairline. What kind of backward-thinking realm had I been swept off to? *Nope, better question...* "Who the hell is my intended?"

Shadow chuckled. "Me, darling."

"*What?*" I sputtered. "He assaulted me and you want to let him speak on my behalf?" Un-freakin'-believable. "This is utter wallopberries."

"Utter what?" Shadow asked.

"Let go of me," I replied instead. He didn't deserve an answer to that query or any other.

"Can't do that, princess. I've been ordered to take you downstairs. Council rules." He gave an unapologetic shrug that had me itching to punch him.

"Now, Shadow," his father said, the command in his tone sending a shiver down my spine.

What in the pixie dust have I gotten myself into?

Shadow lifted me off the ground as if I weighed nothing at all—which, compared to him, I probably did.

He had at least a foot on me, the bastard.

"Put me down."

"And you questioned my nickname," he muttered in reply. "Issuing demands left and right just like a goddamn princess."

"Because you insist on manhandling me," I snapped, wishing more than ever that I could access my gifts. I'd wrap a vine of my own around his neck and see what he thought of it. Then I'd take a tree root and smash his skull.

The beautiful image behind my eyes dispersed as he kicked open an iron door and began descending the steps.

Every part of me iced over at the very real threat of going underground.

"Shadow," I whispered. "Please."

He frowned at me. "Please what? It's not like I'm going to hurt you. Yet, anyway." He shook his head. "Seriously, I expected a little more fire, princess. Instead, you're as weak as a youngling."

My jaw clenched even as my heart began to pound.

Each step brought us deeper underground. My lungs began to seize from my inability to pull in a breath.

Elemental Fae didn't belong here.

Elemental Fae required sunshine.

Elemental Fae *died* underground.

It took weeks, sometimes months, but just the very threat of being taken somewhere so dark and murky had panic freezing every limb.

Shadow said something, but I couldn't hear him over the harsh beating in my ears.

My back hit a soft cushion that I barely felt.

Stone and vines and unspeakable things danced through my vision. A dark cloud. New voices.

Fight, some part of me urged. *This is all in your mind.*

Yeah, pretty sure the gargoyle statue glowering down at me was pretty damn real.

Oh, I'd read about those. They shot lasers from their eyes. Good. Fun. Why was one in my cell?

Shadow appeared to be talking to it.

Right, because they were likely old friends.

Except they seemed to be arguing.

Maybe I'd get to watch the stone creature flay my "intended" alive. Mmm, I'd enjoy that very much. Warmth began to stir inside me at the thought, my initial terror subsiding beneath a much more violent wave.

As long as he didn't keep me down here for long, I'd be fine.

Which meant I needed to pull myself together and find a way out. Not an easy feat considering he'd locked the door.

What kind of idiot willingly puts himself in a dungeon?

"A smart one," Shadow replied.

My brow furrowed. "Did I ask that out loud?"

"No, but you practically shouted it at me." He winced and collapsed onto a pile of pillows on the obsidian floor.

"That doesn't make any sense."

He tapped his head. "Use your mind, princess."

Yeah, because you're so great at using yours, I thought sourly.

He snorted as if he heard that.

Then I realized what he meant.

"Ohhhhh, no. You are so not in my head." I'd have a colossal headache otherwise.

"No, I'm in your blood, Princess Flower," he replied, sounding exasperated. "Seriously, do you not study the mating of other cultures where you're from? Because I had to take an entire semester on your weak kind last year, and while it's proving to be useful now, it bored me near to death."

"We are not weak," I countered. "And for your information, yes, I took one class on fae politics. You want to talk about boring, *that* course takes the lily cookie."

"Lily cookie?" he repeated, arching a brow. "What the fuck is a lily cookie?"

"I thought you studied my kind, Shadow. Perhaps you missed that chapter in your book."

He snorted. "Whatever." He stretched out his long legs, crossing them at the ankles as he relaxed further into his makeshift bed. "We're going to be here a while, princess. Best get some rest before the Council delivers their verdict."

Sleep. Yeah, that was going to happen.

Even with him giving me the bed—a gesture I refused to evaluate—I would never be able to sleep down here. Not with him lurking so close. Or that stone gargoyle hanging out in the corner.

I met the creature's red eyes and flinched.

As a product of the earth, I should be able to command him.

But the source refused my call just as it had since I arrived in this hell.

"What if I have to use the restroom?" I asked, looking for a way to leave this cell.

Shadow pointed at a bucket in the corner. "Enjoy."

I gasped. "That's unacceptable."

"What's unacceptable is you still talking. I said it's time to sleep."

"Yeah, because I take orders from you. Oh, wait…" I rolled my eyes and stood up, pacing across the rocks in my heels.

Why had I dressed up for Glacier, again? Because I wanted to impress him. And he stood me up.

Which meant he wouldn't be looking for me later, and when he tried to call to apologize, he'd just assume I was ignoring him.

Pixie sticks.

Maybe Sol would feel my missing energy.

Yes. Yes, he would. He'd alert his mate, Claire, and they'd search for me. But would they know to look here?

I blew a raspberry with my lips.

"Wow, do not make that sound again," Shadow said, giving a theatric shudder. "Talk about an irritating noise."

"Similar to your voice," I replied sweetly. "Maybe we

are *intended* to be together."

He smirked. "You have no idea, baby."

"Seriously, cut it out with the nicknames."

He blew me a kiss. "You love it, princess."

That's it. I took advantage of his prone position, jumping on him and straddling him, and sent my fist directly into his too-perfect nose.

A sensation of victory warmed my veins at the sight of his blood, only to have it washed out of me by a cold wave as I suddenly found myself beneath him on the floor.

"Not a smart move, darling," he murmured, my wrists locked over my head beneath one of his hands.

How the heck did he do that?

"Magic," he breathed, replying yet again to the thought in my head.

"Stop that."

"Make me," he countered, dropping his head to my neck.

"Shadow."

"Aflora." His hips settled into mine, his lips caressing the bite mark on my skin.

"What are you doing?"

"Enjoying myself," he said softly, his tongue tracing my throat. "You remind me of the sun. Warm, yet brutal."

I squirmed beneath him, which only caused him to lie more heavily upon me. "Don't you dare bite me again, Shadow."

"Mmm, but it was so fun the first time." His incisors skimmed my pulse. "And you moaned so beautifully."

"Because you enchanted me!"

"Only partly," he replied, not sounding the least bit contrite and far too intrigued. "I didn't expect to enjoy it," he added in a whisper. "But I did."

"Shadow," I warned.

He sighed. "Relax, pet."

"How can I relax with you on top of me?"

"You started it," he returned, nipping my chin on his

way back up. "You tried to break my nose with a poor excuse for a punch."

"Poor excuse for a…?" My eyes widened. "You're such a dick!"

"Tell me how you really feel, darling," he taunted, cocking his head to the side. "I'm listening."

"I want to kill you."

"Yes, and…?"

"Gah, would you just get off me, please?"

"Please?" he repeated, snorting. "My, but you are a polite little girl, aren't you?"

"I am not little."

"You act like an innocent child."

My blood boiled at the unveiled insult. "You know nothing about me."

"Likewise."

"Pixie dust, you are impossible. Get. Off. Me."

"Pixie dust?" He actually appeared confused. "Wait, is that your version of a curse?" When I didn't reply, he started to laugh. "Oh, sweet girl, the things I'm going to teach you."

"Not if I kill you," I muttered.

A pair of dimples flashed as he studied me intently. "I truly hope you try. Punishing females is a favorite pastime of mine."

"As is raping them, apparently," I tossed back.

His eyebrows shot up at that accusation. "Rape? I've barely touched you."

"You bit me against my will!"

"You were quite willing, Aflora. Trust me."

"Because you freakin' cast a spell over me or whatever it is you did."

"Freakin'?" He shook his head and tsked. "*Fucking*, darling. The word you're looking for is *fucking*."

"Dear gods, just get off me already!"

"No." He had the audacity to bend and brush a kiss over my lips. I immediately tried to bite him, which earned me an amused sound. "You need to rest. There'll be trials ahead."

Yeah, whatever that meant. "I need to go home," I corrected.

"You are home, Aflora. You just haven't realized it yet." With that proclamation, he began to hum the most beautiful melody.

"What are you doing?"

He didn't reply, his strange song continuing and surrounding me in an odd sea of bliss.

Another spell, my mind recognized.

But my lips refused to issue a retort, my kidnapper captivating me with his song.

Stop, I pleaded in my mind. *Please stop.*

"I'm only trying to calm you," he whispered in response.

I shook my head, trying to clear it and force him out. *This is wrong. Everything you've done is so wrong!*

A deep sigh.

The hint of mint on his breath as he pressed his forehead to mine. "I know," he agreed. "Trust me, I know."

What?

Only, he didn't elaborate.

Instead, he hummed even louder, causing my eyes to roll back in my head.

Soon darkness took over, lulling me into a restless sleep filled with nightmarish images that depicted my new reality. Including the cruelly handsome fae who held me tight, his lips whisper-soft against my ear as he said, "I'm sorry, Aflora."

That was when I knew I truly dreamed.

Because from what I knew of Shadow, he wasn't the kind of male who ever apologized.

KOLS

"ANY IDEA WHAT THIS IS ABOUT?" Tray asked as we stepped into the portal.

I entered the Council Chamber code and shook my head. "No idea, but Dad said it's urgent."

"Clearly," my twin replied, adjusting his tie. We wore matching suits, but that was where our similarities ended. He represented the darkness of our kind in his hair and eyes, similar to our mother. My features, however, favored the golds and bronze tones of our father's lineage. "You think it's related to Aswad?"

I lifted a shoulder. "Could be anything, but probably." Whatever this was, I just wanted to get it over with so I could enjoy my final week of freedom before the Academy started up again.

Only six hundred and nineteen days to go, I thought, rolling my neck to loosen my stiff muscles. Then fate would take over, and I'd officially have to step in line with Emelyn Jyn at my side. *Can't fucking wait*, I thought, fighting an internal groan.

Royal politics came with certain privileges. Arranged marriage was not one of them.

The doors opened to reveal the obsidian interior of Council Headquarters.

I glanced sideways. "Ready?"

"Am I ever?" Tray countered.

With a snort, I led the way inside. Several Councilmen nodded at us as we moved into the room toward our father at the head of the table. He always left the two chairs to his right available for us, and we took them as expected.

Emelyn's father, Lima, sat in the position of Second Elite Blood on my dad's other side. In less than two years' time, he would serve beneath me in the same capacity unless I chose to replace him.

The stoic male gave me a nod of acknowledgment, as he always did. He expected my betrothal to his daughter to be enough to maintain a partnership. Little did he realize I loathed Emelyn. Being related to the female devil incarnate did not win him any points in my book. But I returned the gesture. I was kind like that.

Then I nodded at the other Councilmen in the room who had arrived with their Seconds. My father and Aswad were the only members with heirs of age and status to attend, yet Shade seemed to be playing hooky again. He couldn't make it any clearer that he had no interest in taking over the Death Magic mantle from his father. *Prat.*

Silence fell as Tadmir entered, his white hair flowing down his back. "Apologies." The Malefic Councilman dropped into his chair beside Raz, his second-in-command. "I wasn't in the realm when the notice arrived."

My father dipped his chin in acceptance of the apology, then focused on the male sitting at the opposite head of the rectangular-shaped table. "Well, get on with it, then. Why are we here, Councilman Aswad?"

Those two final words dripped with disdain, thickening the air with unveiled animosity.

My twin stiffened beside me, just like half the damn board.

The Elite Bloods and Death Bloods had been at odds for centuries, never seeing eye to eye with how the Midnight Fae Council ran itself. Unfortunately for Aswad and his dark line of necromancers, my family had no intention of stepping down. I accepted the ascension rites on my eighteenth birthday, hence the inky black vines writhing across my skin. They fueled my veins with more power every day, waiting to unleash on my twenty-fifth year.

Ergo, the ticking time clock on my life.

And the dwindling minutes on my priceless freedom.

"Well?" my father prompted, his patience clearly at an end.

The Death Blood actually appeared paler than usual as he cleared his throat. "Shadow has taken a mate not of the Council's choosing."

I could've heard a pin drop after that announcement.

My eyebrows actually hit my hairline.

What?!

"And there's more," the Death Blood Councilman continued. "She is not a Midnight Fae but an Elemental Fae."

Phoenix fires, I thought, my jaw on the fucking ground. Of all the things for this meeting to be about, I never in a million years would have guessed that.

Tray seemed just as startled beside me.

Meanwhile, the rest of the Council went up in literal flames as magic lashed across the obsidian stone table.

Aswad deflected the incoming blow with his wand, sending Tadmir's burst into the high ceiling above, where my father trapped it beneath a web of energy that sizzled across my skin. "*Stop*," he demanded, his single word laying down the law without fail.

23

Malik of Elite Blood had led the Midnight Fae Council for over a thousand years.

Ignoring him earned the harshest of penalties.

I knew firsthand what he could do, had sat through countless trials where he stripped other Midnight Fae of their lives for infractions far less potent than the one Shade had just committed.

The bastard had been promised to Tadmir's oldest daughter, Cordelia.

To take another mate against the Council's wishes not only broke the laws of our kind but it also issued a massive insult against the Malefic bloodline.

"Excommunication," Tadmir hissed.

"How bonded?" Svart asked instead, his Warrior Blood energy swarming him in an inky cloak of impenetrable magic. His kind excelled at defensive arts. The complete opposite to the Malefic Blood, who favored offensive talents.

"First level," Aswad said, taking his seat with a sigh. "And we don't even know if it'll hold. She's not a Midnight Fae."

"Which doesn't make the infraction any better," Lima muttered. My betrothed's father was clearly not amused, his black irises narrowing at the Death Blood across from him. "What did he have to say for himself?"

"Nothing of importance," Aswad replied.

"Meaning he's not even apologetic," my father translated.

I nearly snorted. Shadow, a.k.a. Shade, was never apologetic about anything. The arrogant dick fancied himself untouchable, even on Academy grounds. His taking a mate against Council wishes didn't surprise me in the slightest.

But I couldn't pretend it didn't leave me a little jealous. I'd considered similar acts more than once throughout my twenty-four years.

Anything to avoid marrying Emelyn Jyn. Just thinking

of her gave me hives.

"That's what I thought," my father said when Aswad didn't voice a comment to the contrary. "Then his punishment is easy—kill the partially bonded mate and force him to uphold the binding contract with Tadmir's Malefic bloodline. Shadow will suffer an eternity of an unfulfilled connection yet produce the requisite heirs." He spread out his hands. "Now, that wasn't so hard. This emergency meeting is—"

"She's the last Earth Fae Royal," Aswad interjected. "To kill her would be perceived as an act of war against the Elemental Fae. It would also sever them from the earth source."

Tray whistled low beside me, his reaction one I rivaled in my thoughts with an added, *Oh, fuck.*

"Aflora?" I asked, unable to remain quiet.

All eyes turned to me with questions in them.

Yeah, I knew of the Earth Fae Royal. I'd never met her, but I saw her at the Water King's coronation a few months ago. I explained that to the Council and added, "One of Queen Claire's mates is an Earth Fae. I doubt he'll take lightly to us exterminating the sole Earth Fae heir."

A note of respect glimmered in Aswad's gaze as he considered me, but it disappeared before my father turned to face him.

Was he surprised that I knew the politics of other realms? I'd been training for my father's position since the day I spoke my first word. Understanding all the fae, regardless of the type, was critical to my future. So yeah, I knew pretty much everything about the Elemental Fae. It also helped that two of the kings of that realm were acquaintances of mine.

"This complicates matters," my father muttered.

"Yes," Aswad agreed. "It does."

Silence befell the room while Tadmir stewed in his chair, his fury palpable.

Councilman Svart and Councilman Chern looked on in

contemplative silence.

Lima stroked the dark hair dusting his chin, considering.

I shared a glance with Tray, who seemed as perplexed as everyone else.

"Do we even know if the bond will hold?" I wondered out loud. "Elemental Fae mate differently than we do. What if the mating bond fades?"

Everyone looked at me again, and this time my father's expression held a hint of pride. I'd begun speaking up more often lately, taking charge where I could, just to prove my worth. And each move I made seemed to appease him more and more.

"Has anything like this ever occurred in our history?" I asked him.

"No, because it's forbidden to mix fae lines," he replied.

Right, which meant Aflora and Shade could never physically mate to produce an heir—the various Fae Councils would require the immediate death of their child. Abominations were not tolerated. Intermingling between species created beings of too much power, and too much power led to insanity.

Case in point, the most recent incident in the Elemental Fae realm where a hybrid Midnight-Elemental Fae tried to absorb too much power, costing several fae their lives.

"So we don't know what will even happen to their bond, or to her." Midnight Fae were supposed to bite humans, not other fae. Rumors suggested our powers would mix if we drank from another fae, which was why the Council forbade the act. "As I said, it could fade."

"Or it might morph her into an abomination," Chern spoke up, his Sangré bloodline known for their infinite wisdom. "But I agree with the future king that we won't know until the transition has taken its course."

"Which could take months," Tadmir put in sourly.

"How old is she?" my father asked. "Twenty-two?

Twenty-three?"

"She just turned twenty-two," Aswad replied. "I had my assistant pull all the information she could while I waited for the meeting to begin." He waved his wand through the air, causing papers to appear before all the Councilmen. "This would be her final year at Elemental Fae Academy, marking her as a third year at our own, but given her impressive test scores, she could probably join the fourth-year class."

Tray and I shared a look.

He couldn't be suggesting—

"You want her to attend Midnight Fae Academy?" My father sounded as dubious as I felt. "Have you lost your damn mind?"

"Actually, it's an interesting suggestion," Chern interjected in that thoughtful way of his, his gray irises surrounding his pupils blinking in and out of focus.

His calm demeanor always appealed to me. I leaned forward, curious to hear what other wisdom he would bestow upon us.

"The Elemental Fae will be just as concerned by their potential mating as we are," he continued. "However, extermination in this situation is impossible with her being the lone Royal Earth Fae. Sending her back could potentially upset the balance. Keeping her here, well, we have wards in place to monitor her."

"And Shadow?" Tadmir interjected, his white hair flickering with blue flames at the ends. "Does he just return to the Academy as if nothing has happened?"

"I daresay he also requires monitoring," Chern replied. "He's initiated the mating with a powerful Earth Fae. That may impact his powers as well."

Silence met his reply.

If what he predicted was true, then Shade's life might be in jeopardy. All Fae Councils took the balance very seriously. Any disturbance to it typically resulted in death.

"What do you recommend?" my father asked, his focus

on the Sangré Councilman. "Your line is known for strategy and analytics. How do you see this playing out?"

Chern considered for a long moment, his thumb and forefinger stroking his silver goatee. It was the only sign of hair on him, his familial line preferring to tattoo their bald heads with vibrant colors. The more intricate the design, the more intelligent the Sangré Blood was considered to be. In Chern's case, he wore the most complex pattern of all as the leader of his line.

"Mating the Earth Fae will awaken her access to dark magic, and the Elemental Fae Council doesn't have the means to control her. We do. The Academy professors can train her on the various lines while we supervise her growth and work on a contingency plan for her strengthening powers. It's an appropriate interim solution while we work with the Elementals on a complete solution. They will be just as keen on finding a resolution as we are."

He tapped his fingers on the table, his focus shifting to Aswad.

"As for Shadow, he will require the same monitoring. I suggest we observe the damage he's caused before assigning his punishment."

Meaning Shade would temporarily get away with breaking some of our oldest customs. Not to mention the slight against Tadmir's familial line. The Malefic Councilman's expression confirmed how he felt about the suggestion. Disapproval radiated from him in waves, but he smartly kept quiet.

Shade would be punished in due time.

Just as soon as we assessed the damage.

It made sense, but I wanted to know *how* this would work. "Who is going to observe Aflora's growth?" I wondered out loud.

Then the implication struck me across the face.

Chern's knowing glimmer as he met my gaze confirmed it.

"Me," I said. "I'll be the one monitoring her."

"You are the most capable, yes," Chern agreed. "Your connection to the source will grant you the insight into power fluctuations. You're also the only one with the ability to shut her down, should the need arise."

The only one with the means to kill her, I translated. Being the future king came with harsh responsibilities. This was one of them.

I nodded to confirm my understanding and acceptance of the burden.

My father considered me for a long moment, then nodded as well. "If this is the path we choose, then I move for this to be considered one of his ascension trials."

Murmurs of agreement echoed around the table.

I had seven that would need to be completed before I could fully ascend.

Three were already done.

This would be item number four.

Babysitting an Earth Fae Royal.

Well, there were worse burdens. I'd seen Aflora before. She was certainly pretty to look at. I wouldn't mind having a reason to watch her. Maybe she would make my final year more intriguing.

Or harder.

That remained to be seen.

I just hoped she stayed in line because if she became a threat, I'd exterminate her without blinking an eye.

It was my duty, after all.

My future.

And I intended to fulfill it appropriately.

AFLORA

TALK ABOUT A WICKED DREAM, I thought, stretching against something warm and solid.

I frowned.

Did I fall asleep at Glacier's place again? I wondered.

Wait...

My eyes sprang open to find an icy gaze watching me intently.

I attempted to scramble backward, but a set of iron bars held me captive while my front was entirely caged in by a lounging predator in jeans and a shirt. "Shadow," I whispered, recalling the reality I'd hoped was a really bad dream.

"Shade," he replied.

"What?"

"It's my name, darling flower. As we're betrothed now, I imagine you should use my preferred appellation."

Appellation? I repeated to myself. *Seriously?* His vocabulary matched the pompous arching of his dark brow.

"Are you ready to leave yet?" he asked. "Because we're well into the midnight hours and I have things I want to do today."

"What?"

He sighed. "Is that your chosen word of the day? Because I'm already bored. What a dull mate you'll turn out to be at this rate." He rolled along the concrete floor, popping easily to his feet and holding out a hand. "Jacket, please. You've been drooling all over it for the last hour."

I nearly repeated my "chosen word of the day" because I felt like needling him, but the realization that I was snuggling into his coat captured my attention. Black leather surrounded my entire upper body, the soft part of it under my head.

How…? I glanced up at him. Had he given me this while I slept?

His expression told me not to bother asking, that he would probably insult me if I tried. So I shoved away from the makeshift bed on the ground and stood. If he wanted his precious jacket back, he could pick it up himself.

He did.

After putting it around his shoulders in a quick shift of his strong arms, he rolled his neck. "Prince Kolstov is waiting for us upstairs." With that, he opened the door and left.

I glanced at the stone gargoyle, waiting for him to react. When he didn't, I tentatively followed and practically had to run to catch up to Shade on the stairs. It seemed he wasn't wasting any time.

"Does this mean I'm free to go home?" I asked as we reached the top floor.

"No."

He didn't elaborate.

Just pushed through the door and led me back to the

obsidian reception area we'd originally waited in.

A male in a suit with a long black cloak stood waiting for us in the center of the room. His golden irises smoldered with power as he glowered at Shade. "You took your fucking time."

"My mother taught me never to interrupt a woman in the middle of a beauty nap," my captor drawled. "Besides, I enjoyed watching her sleep. She is quite fetching." He winked at me, causing me to glare at him almost as harshly as the other man was.

"You're a willow stump," I told Shade, folding my arms. "I hope I never have to see you again."

"A willow stump," he repeated, considering. "Most women refer to my cock as more of a tree trunk than a stump, but we can elaborate on the nuances of my girth later. Prince Kolstov is in charge of you for now." He gave a little bow, backing away. "Do enjoy your time together, and I'll see you both next week."

He disappeared into a swarm of shadows before either of us could reply.

"Next week?" I repeated. "No, no. I don't want to see him again. I'm going home."

"Afraid not, sweetheart," Prince Kolstov replied. "You're going to Midnight Fae Academy. With me."

What?! "Like hell I am." I made to move around him, but he stepped into my way, my head barely clearing his shoulder.

Glowering up at him, I took in his familiar features. Strong cheekbones. Chiseled jaw. Neatly trimmed facial hair that appeared to be darker than the bronze locks on his head. Well, not exactly bronze. More like brown with streaks of red that seemed to flare beneath the lighting. Handsome, really.

No, downright hot.

But that didn't mean—

Wait...

"I know you," I said, my eyes widening. "You were at

Cyrus's coronation."

I'd asked Claire who the handsome foreign fae was after catching a glimpse of him in the crowd. If I remembered right, he knew Cyrus and Exos. Which meant he could get a message to the Elemental Fae Council for me.

"Yes, I was," he confirmed.

My shoulders instantly relaxed. "Oh, good. Then this is all just a misunderstanding. You know I can't stay here."

"What I know is, you can't *leave* here," he corrected. "Not until we see how Shade's bite affects you."

"You mean the bite that was against my will? The one he forced on me before taking me captive?"

A muscle in his jaw ticked, the only indication my words meant something to him. "Regardless of how it happened, you're here now and we can't change the past. All we can do is prepare for the future. So, if you'll follow me, I'll take you to Midnight Fae Academy and your new accommodations."

He turned as if he expected me to magically agree to his command.

I placed my hands on my hips. "Yeah, no. I refuse."

Kolstov glanced at me over his shoulder, those golden irises flaring with power. "Refusal isn't an option." He turned a little and produced a wand from his cloak. "I'm trying to do this the kind way, Aflora. If you prefer the harder route, then we can dance. But I assure you, you'll lose."

I narrowed my eyes. "Queen Claire will not approve of this treatment."

"Queen Claire has no jurisdiction here or over me." He faced me once more. "Which road are we taking, sweetheart? Because my patience is already at wits' end due to Shade taking his fucking time downstairs."

Given that my powers still didn't work here, my options were limited. Either I tested the extent of what that wand in his hand could do or I pretended to play along.

Maybe my powers will regenerate outside these walls, I thought, considering him and his casual stance. *Worth a shot because staying here isn't going to fix anything.*

"All right. Fine. Take me to the Academy."

Amusement sparked in his gaze. "Dancing it is," he mused and put his wand away. His response suggested he expected me to act out despite my words. He was probably right. "Come along, pet."

I glowered at his back after he turned, not appreciating the "endearment" one bit.

Pet, I thought at him. *Yeah, I'm a pet all right. With teeth.*

He led me into an elevator of sorts, then keyed a code in plain sight, suggesting he didn't mind me knowing it. Or maybe he was just that stupid. I memorized the alphanumeric mix, just in case.

The walls shifted around us, crickets sounding in the distance. I focused on the shifting scenery, searching for anything familiar, when we suddenly materialized outside a set of iron gates that were nearly three times my height.

Kolstov murmured a foreign command that caused the doors to open, then gestured for me to cross the creepy threshold. Two stone gargoyles stood watch, their red gazes analyzing my every move.

I swallowed.

They're technically made of earth, so if I just—

"Even think of harming me, and they will cut you down," Kolstov warned. "And while they may be beings of your element, they're not yours to command, but mine."

I considered testing that theory, but the writhing snake-vines slithering along the iron posts had me retracting the idea. On top of that, I still couldn't feel my element. Closing my eyes, I searched the fractured connection, frowning when I found frayed ends flickering with lost power.

A hiss from the gate had me jumping backward.

Kolstov tsked. "Careful with your thoughts,

sweetheart. They'll be on you in a second, and you can bet your ass I'll let them bite a few times before I call them off. Just to teach you a lesson."

Meaning he could control these vile creatures.

"Prince Kolstov," I mused out loud. "You're next in line for the Midnight Fae throne." Hence his ability to tame the beasts. I'd read enough about international fae politics to know the important names throughout the realms. It was why I'd been surprised by his presence at Cyrus's coronation.

And maybe I'd been a little interested because of his looks.

Not so into those traits now.

"Just as you're Princess Aflora, the sole Earth Royal," he returned, pressing his palm to my lower back to give me a nudge. "On you go."

I stumbled forward, my heels not made for the pebbled pathway. "If you know who I am, you know how wrong this is. The Earth Fae need me and my access to the source."

"Yes. We're working on that." Another push to the base of my spine compelled me to walk alongside him. "Your bindings are temporary until Councilman Chern can develop a better harness for your natural gifts."

Bindings? That explained why I still couldn't access my element. "It's dangerous to keep me severed from the source. I'm the conduit that allows the Earth Fae to thrive."

"We're aware," he said, directing me to the left.

Gothic architecture met my vision. The entire campus resembled a castle of horror set against a moonlit landscape. Large trees void of any life or leaves decorated the ground with black branches, their roots thicker than both Kolstov and I combined. Bats dangled from the limbs, along with other foreign winged animals of varying sizes.

A phoenix landed on top of one of the obsidian towers

in the distance, its fiery wings fluttering in the breeze.

"Given your royal status, you will be housed with the Elite Bloods. Specifically, in my family's wing. Our suite has four bedrooms, a living area, a kitchen, a study room, and several bathrooms. I think you'll find it to be up to your standards."

"Elite Bloods?" I repeated, swallowing. *I have to live with this guy?*

He stopped to gape down at me. "You haven't studied the Midnight Fae lines?"

"N-no."

His expression told me that was not an appropriate response. "You're *the* Earth Fae Royal, and you know nothing about our political structure. How is that possible? I can tell you everything of importance regarding the Elemental Fae Council."

"Interspecies politics is on my course agenda this year."

"*Was*," he corrected. "Your new schedule will be assigned this week. I'll see what I can do about having Midnight Fae politics added to it." He shook his head and continued walking. "Absolutely ridiculous."

"Oh, I'm sorry. I wasn't expecting to be kidnapped and forced into attending school in this realm. My bad for not taking a course about vampires."

He halted once more, turning slowly. "Careful, sweetheart. That tone could earn you a lot of hurt on these grounds, especially when in reference to our existence and what we are—Midnight Fae."

"Bloodsuckers. Yeah, I'm aware."

Kolstov stepped forward, invading my personal bubble. "You know all about that, don't you, love? What with Shade having already snacked upon your neck?" He hummed, the sound low and menacing. "Call me a bloodsucker again and I'll give you a thorough demonstration of what a *Midnight Fae* can do."

"As you said, I already 'know all about that.'"

"Oh, sweetheart, no. A bite is nothing compared to the

power I can unleash upon you." He reached up to tuck a strand of my hair behind my ear, then cupped my cheek to allow me to feel the energy throbbing beneath his skin. "I could destroy you in seconds, baby."

"Only because you've handicapped me," I seethed. "Take off my bindings and let's see what happens."

His resulting smile oozed condescension. "As entertaining as it would be to put you in your place, I have other plans tonight that are far more important than indulging a little Earth Fae." His palm landed on my ass this time, pushing me forward.

I elbowed him in the ribs. "Do not touch me there. In fact, do not touch me at all."

He smirked and produced his wand. "Fine." With a flick of his wrist, he created a strand of magic that wound around my waist. He gave it a little tug and I jolted forward.

"Oh, come on!" I snapped. "I can walk on my own without all the theatrics."

"I know, but this is more fun." Another yank had me nearly falling on my face, but his magic righted me before I could fully trip.

A growl caught in my throat. "Stop."

He chuckled. "Make me. Oh, right…"

I ground my teeth so hard my jaw popped.

As soon as this rope disintegrated, I would introduce my fist to his arrogant jaw.

We walked the rest of the way in silence, my fury boiling hotter with every step. At least there wasn't anyone around to witness this humiliation. I nearly asked why the Academy was empty but decided against speaking again. He didn't deserve my words, my questions, or my compliance.

Instead, I studied the campus around me, searching for escape points.

There had to be a portal somewhere, because the gargoyle-guarded entrance was out of the question.

Of course, I had no way of knowing if my codes would

whisk me home or to another part of this realm or to nowhere at all.

Trial and error, I decided. I just needed an exit.

"These are the Elite Blood quarters," Kolstov announced, his amusement seeming to have faded into a serious tone. He escorted me up the marble stairs to a set of grand doors. "To enter, you need to know the right spell. It also requires a wand." He glanced at me. "I'll ask Zeph to get you set up with one this week before classes begin."

Zeph? And they intended to give me a wand? *Does that mean they expect me to learn dark magic?* The questions all lined up behind my lips, but my teeth held them at bay.

This monster had already proven to be unhelpful. Why bother opening up to him now?

He arched a brow. "Silent treatment?"

"I'm cooperating," I bit back at him.

His lips twitched. "Indeed you are." With a muttered word, the magical lasso around my waist disappeared, and I launched myself at him. My palm connected with his cheek while my opposite hand formed a fist that he caught deftly before spinning me around and trapping me in his arms.

"I'm adding warrior training to your curriculum," he said, his lips at my ear. "Your form is atrocious."

"Sprinkle dust!" I shouted at him, squirming against his too-hard body.

"Sprinkle dust?" he repeated, his humor palpable. "Who taught you how to curse? A dessert pixie?"

Gah! "Release me."

"No." He held me captive with one arm and pulled out his wand with his free hand. "Listen and learn, as I won't be repeating myself." Hypnotic words fell from his lips, the language foreign to me. "*Al'damu almalakia.*"

The tip of his charcoal-colored wand created an infinity pattern, causing the doors to creak and open beneath his command.

He kissed my temple, his arm releasing me. "After you, gorgeous."

I practically sprinted through the threshold, just to escape him, but my face burned from where his mouth had brushed my skin. As though he'd branded me with his power via that simple act alone.

He fixed his cloak and hid his magical tool once more, then snapped his fingers.

Flames sprang to life all around us, lighting the interior of a grand hallway with a master staircase to the left. He gestured toward them. "Two flights. We're on the top floor."

Not wanting to give him a chance to touch me with his hands or his power, I darted up the steps to the third floor and waited for him to join me.

"Someone's eager," he teased when he reached the top.

I didn't deign to offer him a reply, just waited for further instruction.

He nodded with his chin toward the end of the hall. "Three forty-seven is our suite."

Our suite. I shivered with the statement. *This is temporary. I'm not staying here.*

Only, the entire hallway was lined with more of those rattling monstrosities, all of which were watching my every move as though waiting for me to step one toe out of line.

I never did like snakes.

And these appeared to be far more deadly than the reptiles of my realm.

They wriggled along, gliding over the wooden panels I thought might be doors except for the fact that they were all missing knobs. Including our own at the end of the hall. However, there was a knocker with a tiny gargoyle lounging upon it, his blood-red eyes narrowing at me.

I paused so suddenly that Kolstov ran into my back, his hands finding my hips in the process. It aligned us perfectly, sending a shudder down my spine.

No. I'm not attracted to this jerk. Do not get any ideas.

"Sir Kristoff, this is Aflora. Scan her as appropriate, then allow us both entry. She will be staying in the suite for the foreseeable future, so you are to grant her access as you do the others on our list."

The red eyes flared to life, little black pupils moving over me in lazy regard as the gargoyle's lips curled to the side.

"Hmm," the being hummed in a low, masculine tone that sent a chill down my spine. He pushed out of the door, his little hands holding on to the ledge of the knocker while his bottom half remained inside the wood. Almost as if he were hanging out a window. "Something's not right with this one. Not right at all."

Right back at you, I thought, mortified by his lifelike form that had been made of rock just seconds ago. *Talking-goblin stone thing.*

"Perhaps, but you bow to my commands. Now scan her and allow her entry." Kolstov's tone brooked no argument.

"Yes, yes," the thing hissed. "As you wish, Master."

A blinding light beamed from the gargoyle's eyes. I would have jumped backward if Kolstov wasn't still holding me. The damn stroke of the creature's gaze burned over me, leaving an inky sensation in its wake as if it had marked me with its magic.

"You may enter." The eyes rolled back into a red gleam, the knocker turning to marble once more.

Kolstov used his hands on my hips to walk me forward *through* the door. As in, it didn't open. We moved through the wood.

A shimmer of energy passed over my skin along the way, causing all the hair along my arms to rise.

This isn't natural.

"Welcome home," Kolstov said as an elegant living area appeared before us. "I hope you like it, because I suspect you'll be staying for the year."

KOLS

"A YEAR?" The gorgeous Earth Fae spun in my arms. "That's a cruel joke, right? Tell me you're kidding."

"I thought most females fancied the truth over lies, but if it's a lie you prefer, I'll happily give you one."

She shoved away from me, her petite form proving to be stronger than one would expect. I could subdue her in less than a second but opted to give her the space she required. It was the least I could do considering her circumstances.

While, outwardly, I might have appeared unapologetic, inwardly, I felt for the poor girl.

"You mean the bite that was against my will? The one he forced on me before taking me captive?"

Her admission was on repeat inside my mind. I hadn't expected her to say that. Most women fell at Shade's feet, all of them adoring his bad-boy persona. Yet it appeared this one hadn't been a willing subject in his attentions at all. Unless she'd lied to me, but I doubted it. She'd glowered at Shade with a similar contempt as the glare in her gaze now.

Not the look of a woman smitten over her betrothed.

Nor one that seemed to care for me all that much.

Well, I deserved that. I hadn't exactly been kind to her.

"Are you hungry?" I asked her, walking through the living room and to the open area of the kitchen toward the back. Windows lined the walls, overlooking the courtyard out back. Flickers of lights drew my attention to the fire gnats buzzing about the forest below. I'd have to warn Aflora to stay away from those. Dangerous little buggers.

Aflora didn't reply to me, her feet apparently glued to the runner in the foyer. She glanced up at the cathedral ceilings, took in the skylights showcasing a star-filled night, and then looked at the ample seating room. Three couches, two recliners, and a massive movie screen. Perfect for entertaining, which Tray and I did often during the school year.

Well, I did.

Tray tended to hide in his room with Ella.

Pulling open the refrigerator, I found it empty. *Idiot.* We hadn't been here all summer, and I just learned two hours ago that I needed to bring Aflora here.

Using my wand, I muttered a few incantations to create tea mugs. That would have to do until I could arrange for an Academy food delivery.

Or Zeph could handle it.

I set the mugs on the black bar counter that hung over into the living area, and slid my phone from my pocket.

Where are you? I typed, hitting Send.

Packing, was the immediate reply. *Your Highness,* came a second later.

I rolled my eyes. *Don't be a dick.*

Just doing my job, Zeph replied.

Of being a dick?

I'll be there soon. Surely you can find something to do with her until I get there. She's a female fae, right? You like those.

I snorted. *Who set your boxers on fire?*

You did.

My eyebrows shot up. *Not in a few months, if I recall right. Fuck off, Kolstov.*

Not what you said to me the last time we met up, I sent back.

No reply.

Not that I expected one.

With a smirk, I slid the phone back into my pocket and looked up to find Aflora watching me from the other side of the bar.

"Girlfriend?" she guessed.

"I don't do girlfriends," I replied, leaning over to rest my elbows on the counter. "So don't get any ideas."

She scoffed. "Don't worry. You're not my type."

Liar, I thought. I recognized the attraction in her eyes earlier, and I could taste the lust in the air when I had her in my arms. She might not want to admit it, but the Earth Fae Royal definitely found me appealing. And the feeling was very mutual.

"I conjured you some tea," I said, nodding to the mugs. "Once Zeph arrives, we'll figure out how to find food."

She didn't touch the mug or reply, instead choosing to gaze out the windows. As I hadn't turned on any of the lights, she could see everything with clarity, including the gnats glowing below. But it was the Academy beyond that she seemed to be studying—the endless sea of gothic architecture.

"It's several blocks wide," I said. "The living quarters are spread throughout. In case you were curious, Shade resides on the opposite side of campus, which is about a fifteen-minute walk."

"I wasn't curious."

Maybe not, but I caught the glimmer of approval in her expression.

Yeah, she definitely doesn't like him.

"Zeph will give you a proper tour tomorrow, and once you have your schedule, I'll help you map out your courses." I picked up the mug closest to me and took a sip of the warm, minty liquid.

Perfection.

If she chose not to touch hers, then I'd help myself to it next.

After another swallow, I dove into an explanation of her future. "You'll have four days of classes, then two days off, then three days on again, followed by three days off. The cycle repeats after that. So twelve days total. There will be a longer break in the middle of the year for the Solstice, but otherwise, the schedule keeps."

"And what will I be learning?"

"You'll have a mixture of dark arts courses, physical training, and likely a political course." Because apparently she knew nothing about the five Midnight Fae bloodlines. Well, technically six. But only five were still in existence today.

"I'm an Elemental Fae, not a Midnight Fae."

"An Elemental Fae who was bitten by a Midnight Fae, thereby introducing you to the dark arts. It's in your blood now." Or that was what Chern had hypothesized. Given what I'd observed so far, he was likely very wrong. Without her access to the elements, Aflora seemed as harmless as a human.

Hopefully, she remained that way. Then this could all blow over. She'd return to her realm, Shade would be punished for his transgressions, and all would be right with the world again.

I met her wide gaze as I took another pull from my drink and noted her ashen cheeks. My brow furrowed. "What?"

"I... It's..." She swallowed. "His bite infected my blood?" Her small hand went to her throat as she took a step backward, her expression falling. "A... abomin... I'm a..." She collapsed onto the sofa, and her head fell to her hands.

I frowned at her. "You hadn't pieced that together already?"

No reply.

Only a hitch of her shoulders as she fought off what sounded like a sob.

Fuck.

Crying women were not my thing. I didn't know how to handle them or how to calm them. Did I walk over there and pat her head? Offer condolences? Lie to her about the inevitable?

I palmed the back of my neck. "I, uh, I'm sor—"

"I'm going to kill him!" Aflora snapped. Her tear-filled eyes captured my gaze, her cheeks red with emotion.

But it wasn't sadness or self-pity.

Aflora was *livid.*

And those weren't tears.

No. Her bright blue irises were aflame with power.

Oh, shit...

"Where is he?" she demanded, jumping to her feet. "Where is that willow stump who did this to me? If I'm going down, he's going down with me." She stomped into the kitchen, energy swarming around her in a hypnotic wave that called to my royal blood.

Ideal mate, a part of me recognized. *She's an ideal mate.*

"Tell me where he is!" she shouted in my face.

Okay. This wasn't going to work.

I set my mug down and crowded her against the bar by placing my hands on the marble on either side of her hips. "Calm down."

"Calm down?" she repeated with a semi-hysterical snort. "Are you kidding me? That pixie stick made me an abomination!"

My lips twitched at her adorable curse.

Which was apparently the wrong reaction because more of that delicious red fury coated her cheeks.

"Are you *laughing* at me? Do you find humor in him

45

essentially raping me with his fangs and turning my world upside down?" She jabbed a finger at my chest. "You're no better than he is, and here I thought you might have a little moral high ground as a fellow royal. Apparently not."

I caught her wrist before she could stab me again and brought the offending digit up to my mouth for a reprimanding bite. Not sharp enough to break the skin—*that* was exactly what got her into this mess—but enough to assert my dominance. "I took humor with your nickname designation. *Pixie stick* has a nice ring to it. I think I'll borrow it for Shade going forward."

Some of her ire cooled, but that liquid fire in her gaze continued to burn. She reminded me of a furious Valkyrie with her waves of blue-black hair, creamy skin, and glowing eyes. All she needed were some wings.

Clearing my throat, I released her hand and reaffixed my grip to the counter beside her. "The past is already done. What you need to focus on is moving forward. Shade won't be here for another week. If it's any consolation, I imagine his father has some punishments in mind for him in the interim."

She nibbled her lower lip, drawing my focus to her alluring mouth.

Aflora really was a beautiful fae. A queen with regal bone structure and a gorgeously formed figure. *Fantastic tits*, I thought, taking in her skewed blouse. *Long, athletic legs*. If she were human, I'd seduce her in a heartbeat. Bend her over this counter, tuck up that little skirt, and fuck her raw.

Alas, her Elemental Fae blood made that problematic.

Still, it could be done.

"You're looking at me like I'm food," she whispered, her fingers curling into fists at her sides. "Please don't bite me."

"Mmm." I leaned into her, my mouth skimming the shell of her ear and eliciting a shiver from her in response. "Don't worry, sweetheart. When I bite you, I won't break the skin." I brushed my lips against her temple for the second time tonight, then forced myself to pull away. "Let's get your quarters sorted. It'll provide us both a much-needed distraction."

Because if I wasn't careful, I'd devise a different way to pass the time while we waited for Zeph. Which would only prove the Guardian right about my proclivities and earn me a world of chastisement.

And Zephyrus was the last one I wanted a lecture from right now.

I led Aflora through the living area again. She had fallen silent once more, her hands twisting in front of her. As horrifying as this had to be for her, she appeared to be handling it well. Which told me she had an escape plan in mind. It was what I would do in her position. Unfortunately, she didn't stand a chance.

Something told me the only way for that point to be driven home was to allow her to try and fail.

Allowing the starlight from the windows above to guide us, I turned into a hallway lined with doors. Stopping at the first one, I opened it to reveal a large space filled with more seating, pillows, books, and an array of bottles filled with potions. "This is the loft area where Ella and Tray lounge the most. They like to study here."

"Ella and Tray?" Aflora repeated in a low murmur.

Right. She hadn't studied Midnight Fae politics yet. Annoyance simmered in my blood, but I held it back and offered her a brief explanation.

"Trayton Nacht, also known as Tray, is my twin brother. Isabella Cinder, a Halfling, is his chosen mate." I shut the door. "You'll meet them next week."

"Oh" was all she said.

I gestured to another threshold. "Tray and Ella's room." Then I pointed across the hall. "That's a guest area and option number one for you." Several more steps brought us to another door. I motioned to it, saying, "Option number two." And finally, at the end of the hallway, I said, "This is my room."

I twisted the knob because I needed to find her some temporary clothes. Making them with my wand would likely result in something too scandalous for her to actually wear. While appealing, I couldn't risk the temptation. "I'll grab you something to wear, if you want to stay here." I pointed to the spot just inside the door, then ventured into my Academy sanctuary in search of my walk-in closet, which existed on the other side of my spacious bathroom. The familiar, warm brown tones caused my lips to curl, the scent of mint and spice still lingering from my last visit.

Mine, I thought. *At least for another year.*

Sifting through my wardrobe of Academy-sanctioned outfits, suits, and casual items, I found a plain black shirt and a pair of flannel pajama bottoms. Then I grabbed some boxers just in case the pants didn't fit.

Aflora stood in the entry, stiff as a board.

"Never been in a man's room before?" I teased.

Her lips curled down. "I'm not an innocent, Kolstov. I have a boyfriend. It's *your* bedroom I don't want to enter."

Amusement touched my chest. "Keep telling yourself that, sweetheart. Maybe you'll convince us both."

She snorted. "Are all Midnight Fae as arrogant as you and Shadow?"

"I prefer *sexy* and *confident*, at least in the description of myself," I said, winking at her. "Now which will it be, option one or option two?"

Her blue eyes rolled. "As if I care."

"Well, option one is across the hall from Ella and Tray, so you'll probably hear them fucking on occasion. Option two is between both our rooms, which means you'll get to hear me entertaining as well as Tray and Ella fucking. Therefore, perhaps you'd prefer the second option so you can think of me when you're alone at night? Picture yourself between my sheets instead of whomever I've chosen to indulge that evening?"

Aflora's full lips parted on a gasp. "What a crude thing to say."

"Better get used to it," I replied, crowding her against the wall. "This is my territory, and I won't be changing my habits just to suit your *prudish* ways."

Her nostrils flared. "I'm *not* a prude."

"Prove it," I dared, walking a dangerous line.

A muscle ticked in her cheek as she clenched her teeth. "I don't need to prove anything to you," she finally said after a beat, turning on her heel. To my utter shock, she marched off to option two as if to make her point. "I'll sleep here."

She opened the door.

And proceeded to slam it behind her.

The shift of her lock echoed in the hallway.

"Well, she has spirit," a deep voice drawled from the opening of the corridor.

My heart skipped a beat as my one weakness stepped beneath one of the skylights, his striking features glistening beneath the stars.

"Hello, Zephyrus," I greeted, my confidence seeping from my veins.

"Prince Kolstov," he returned, formal and direct. "I'll take the other guest room. Then you and I are going to have a long talk."

Two hits in one sentence.

Not only was he denying a night in my bed—which we both knew I'd be more than happy to accommodate—but he also wanted to have a discussion.

Discussions with Guardian Zephyrus never went in my favor.

I should have volunteered myself for the role of introducing Aflora to the Academy rather than allow my father to delegate the task to Zeph. The selfish part of me had rejoiced, while the practical side knew better.

Unfortunately, my selfish half had won.

And now I would pay the price for it.

AFLORA

FINALLY, SOMETHING NORMAL.

No snakes or gargoyles or fiery bugs or anything unseemly. Just a standard bedroom equipped with a double bed, a dresser, a small attached bath, and a closet.

Easy.

Elegantly furnished.

And boasting a window overlooking the Academy grounds. The entire property reminded me of a human cathedral with all the stained-glass windows and obsidian stone. Most of the buildings appeared to be the same height as this one, with random spires interspersed between. Framed by the stars and moonlight, it really did have a vampiric appeal.

Appropriate, considering the Midnight Fae's penchant for blood.

I touched my neck and walked into the bathroom in

search of a mirror. Apart from my untamed hair, I still looked the same. The mark on my throat resembled more of a hickey than a bite. At least my fae healing abilities still worked. Unlike my access to the source.

Grasping the cold marble sink, I leaned in to study every crevice of my face.

What binding power did they put on me? I wondered. *And how do I break it?*

I ran my hands over my blouse and skirt, down my legs, and to my shoes, searching for anything that felt wrong or foreign. Nothing.

I stripped out of my clothes, just in case.

Still nothing.

Grabbing the sink, I scowled at my reflection. It had to be some sort of magical net that I couldn't sense. So how did I defeat it?

Padding into the bedroom on bare feet, I went to the window to search for a tree or any kind of life outside. If I could find a piece of earth and latch onto it, I might be able to call to my source and break through—

A knock interrupted my concentration, and the door opened a second later.

I spun around with a glower, irritated by the interruption.

"Aflora, Zeph is…" Kolstov trailed off, his eyes wandering over me.

I frowned at him. *What is his prob…? Oh. Oh!* My arm flew up to cover my breasts, my opposite hand falling to my lower half. "Get out!"

His palms rose in surrender as he took a step backward.

Then he bent and tossed something inside. "Clothes to, uh, wear." He seemed to shake himself before closing the door.

I scowled at the wood. *Pompous, intrusive wad of—*
Wait.

How did he open that door? I'd locked it.

Marching over, I found it distinctly unlatched.

Not okay.

Plucking the shirt off the floor, I pulled it over my head before donning the boxer shorts—an item I really hoped was clean—then threw open the door and stomped outside.

Only to freeze with one foot in the hallway.

The scene at the end of the corridor held me captive, my jaw hitting the floor.

A male had Kolstov pinned up against the wall with a palm around his throat, the other on his hip. They were locked in some sort of heated stare. And from the looks of it, the newcomer with the sharp cheekbones was definitely winning.

"Let. Go." Kolstov's command was a rasp against the air. He had the other man's lapels clenched tightly in his fists, his golden irises swirling with fire.

"You first," the male replied, his voice rich and dark and holding an edge of domination that had my knees wobbling.

Well now, who is this guy? Zeph?

He appeared slightly older. Definitely stronger. Same height as Kolstov, but with an aura of superiority that I found surprising. Who could be more powerful than a Midnight Fae Prince? Maybe the king, but this guy wasn't him. Too young for that. And he looked nothing like Kolstov, either.

"*Fuck you, Zephyrus,*" Kolstov hissed.

"That's Headmaster Zephyrus to you, *Prince Kolstov.*"

My eyebrows lifted.

Wow, so these two clearly had some sort of history. I couldn't tell if they wanted to kill each other or rip each other's clothes off.

I sort of wanted to watch just to see how it all turned out.

But I also wanted to know how Kolstov unlocked my door.

I opened my mouth to ask, when flames erupted

between the two men, causing me to jump backward. There weren't any wands present, no words spoken, just fire dancing in the air as if summoned from one of their minds.

It quickly became obvious *who* created it when Zephyrus tossed Kolstov to the ground while muttering, "Foul play."

"Just using my gifts to my advantage like my mentor taught me," Kolstov tossed back at him, his hand on his throat.

Zephyrus snorted. "If that were true, you'd have relied on your physical strength and not your Elite Blood." He brushed the flames from his sleeves with a flick of his wrist, the energy dissipating into a gray cloud, leaving his blazer untouched.

Kolstov rolled his neck and shook the flickers from his own clothes, creating a tendril of steam that disappeared with the others.

The smoke cleared, leaving them both unharmed without a shred of evidence on them. Almost as if I'd imagined the whole thing.

Huh. That's interesting.

Cold green eyes met mine, narrowing. "Is this my project?"

"Yes," Kolstov replied. "Aflora, meet Zeph. Zeph, this is Aflora."

Zephyrus's gaze passed over me in clear disinterest. "How fun." His sarcasm wasn't lost on me. "I'm Headmaster Zephyrus, your new Guardian. Try to leave this suite without me and you'll regret it." With that proclamation, he turned on his heel and headed toward the living area, leaving me alone with Kolstov.

"Charming," I grumbled.

Kolstov palmed the back of his neck and blew out a breath, shaking his head. Then he followed the *headmaster* out of the corridor.

Great. A game of Chase the Pixie.

I supposed if I wanted any answers—not to mention *food*—I had to join them.

Huffing, I stomped down the hallway in their direction and found them standing off again in the living area. Only without touching this time. Tension poured off them in waves. Neither of them speaking.

I cleared my throat. "So, uh, my lock is broken."

No reply.

"You can't just barge into my room without—"

"Your room?" he questioned, breaking his staring contest with the headmaster to glance my way. "This is *my* suite. The locks don't apply to me."

My jaw tightened. "They do in my *guest* room."

He snorted. "No, sweetheart. They don't."

Fire licked through my veins at his declaration.

First, Shadow bit me against my will.

Then, the Council forced me to attend Midnight Fae Academy for reasons no one bothered clarifying.

And now, Prince Kolstov claimed I would have no privacy here in his quarters—a place I didn't even want to stay.

Not. Acceptable.

"Kolstov has a problem with being locked out," Zephyrus put in, completely oblivious to the turmoil brewing beneath my skin. "Don't worry. You'll get used to it."

"Are you going to be an ass to me all year?" Kolstov demanded, his focus on the headmaster.

"Likely," Zephyrus replied.

The thumping in my ears drowned out the continuation of his statement, my focus on the little tendril of power peeking at me from beneath the thick, inky waves inside me.

Oh, hello, I thought at it. *Come here.*

Closing my eyes, I followed the flare of light through the dark web in my mind.

This is where they've trapped me, I realized, the map clearing behind my eyes. *They've cast a binding spell over me.*

It must have happened while I was asleep.

Did Shade do it? Kolstov? Another fae?

It didn't matter.

What I needed to do was unravel it.

Zephyrus and Kolstov continued to bicker in the living area, neither of them seeming to remember my presence. Normally, I would consider that rude. In this case, their impudence worked in my favor.

Energy swirled inside me as I navigated each thread, carefully plucking them apart with my invisible scissors, longing to free that spark at the bottom.

The design wasn't too intricate, suggesting it'd been done in a hurry. The fact that I could suddenly see the binds implied Shade had indeed contaminated my blood and that perhaps my power was growing in darkness as a result. Or maybe I just hadn't looked in the right place.

Regardless, I could see it now.

And I seemed to be able to undo it.

Kolstov raised his voice.

Zephyrus remained calm.

The two of them were engaged in some argument about Kolstov throwing Zephyrus to the wolves three months ago. I only half listened, my attention on the growing light inside me.

There you are, I breathed, smiling at the earth source. *Come to me now. Help me.*

Power hummed through my being, revitalizing me in the strength of my core essence.

Yes, yes.

I felt alive.

Exuberant.

Whole.

I sighed, the plant life around the Academy prickling at my instincts. The trees weren't dead at all, just a different species. *A burning thwomp*, the roots told me, giving me a proper name to work from.

Nice to meet you, I murmured, rolling my neck and memorizing the heart of the species in my mind. *You'll do very well.*

With a twirl of power, I began to reconstruct the base of the charred tree, rooting it in the guest room.

Kolstov didn't want to give me a lock? Then I'd make one.

And I'd rip his suite apart in the process.

"Do you feel that?" Zephyrus asked, interrupting whatever Kolstov had just been saying.

Must work faster, I thought, directing my nurturing waves from the gap in the web to the new creation.

"What are you doing?" Kolstov demanded.

I ignored him.

His palm was suddenly on my neck, his hard body pressed along mine. "Aflora."

I didn't open my eyes.

I just continued to unweave and weave, unweave and weave. *Grow, little tree. Grow.*

The earthy force pulsed inside me, breaking through the final binds and flourishing to life. I sighed in content, my powers finally free.

Flowery scents perfumed the air, vines of my own making climbing over the walls to protect me from the snakes outside. Because I could feel them slithering in agitation, their intent to break down the threshold palpable.

Oh, but the gargoyle held them at bay.

Why?

Ah, because I'm part of this suite now. It protects everyone inside. The knowledge slammed into my mind from an unknown source, but I felt the veracity of it deep inside my bones.

"Aflora!" Kolstov yelled.

My lips curled, power rippling through me in energizing waves. *What was it he said to me earlier? Oh, right.* "I'm ready to dance now, Midnight Prince," I told him, shoving him away with a pulse of energy that put him on his ass.

He coughed, then cursed as roots grew from the ground, trapping him.

I smiled. "Those burning thwomps sure are sturdy." The one in my guest room was almost complete, the branches reaching the ceiling above. Content with the design, I told it to grow outward. I'd left the door open, giving it the opportunity to inch thick black roots down the hallway toward us.

An explosion sent me sideways into the wall, my focus temporarily disrupted as Kolstov launched to his feet. He'd lost his cape and jacket, his shirtsleeves rolled to his elbows. It all happened so quickly that I didn't know how or when he'd made the wardrobe change, but I caught the writhing lines twisting along his skin.

The dark source, I realized.

It thrived inside him.

And he was about to use it against me.

I ducked the oncoming blow, a shield of petals building along my skin in an instant.

"This is ridiculous, Aflora," Kolstov snapped. "Stop."

I tripped him with one of the roots, then stirred a myriad of pollen mites into the air around him, eliciting a sneeze.

Zephyrus stood off to the side, completely unfazed. As he didn't seem to want to join the battle, I left him alone—for now—and concentrated on my fellow Royal Fae.

Zings of electricity shot from his fingertips, all aimed my way. I deflected them with flowers, frowning as he turned the gorgeous creations into ash.

"No respect," I muttered, stirring an array of blossom motes to blind his vision. My tree from the bedroom had finally reached me, grounding me in life as I directed the thick black ropes toward my attacker.

If I could incapacitate him and Zephyrus, I could find a portal and escape.

Maybe.

I honestly hadn't thought that far ahead. I just wanted out of this damn suite.

The snakes, however, would prove to be a problem.

Hence the petal shield.

A root wrapped around Kolstov's ankle, tightening, only to be engulfed in red and yellow flames.

I screamed as the fiery embers reached my heart, my tree crying out in pain. "Stop!"

"You first," Kolstov ground out, his destructive essence screeching across the floor and destroying my creation with horrifying ease.

I fell to my knees, agonized over the destruction of life, his vile powers eating at the goodness of mine.

Hatred unlike any I'd ever experienced bloomed inside me, all directed at this monster of a royal. Energy blazed from his golden eyes, overtaking mine in murderous lashes that obliterated my vines and all traces of the earth I'd brought into his suite.

Including my beloved tree.

He hadn't stopped at the roots, taking the entire thwomp and incinerating it into ash in a matter of seconds.

My chest ached at the loss.

So wrong.

How could you?

Why?

The thwomps outside wept with me, their branches rattling angrily in protest.

"That was fascinating," Zephyrus murmured.

"That's not the word I'd use for it," Kolstov retorted, his booted feet appearing in my vision. "What the actual fuck, Aflora?"

I glowered up at him. "You're a monster." My voice was hoarse, the black magic coating my earth source leaving me breathless.

He scoffed at that. "You just unleashed a *monster* into my suite, nearly killing all of us in the process. Have you lost your fucking mind?"

"It wasn't going to kill us," I returned, livid. "*You* are the murderer here."

His eyebrows lifted. "Really?" He bent down, grabbed me by the neck, and hauled me to my feet. "Let's see about that." He dragged me through the living area to the back windows. "Watch."

"No."

When I tried to struggle, he wrapped his arms around me from behind, capturing me with my back to his chest. His lips were at my ear. "Fucking watch or I'll drag you back to the Council and throw you in the dungeon for the week."

I bristled at the threat and considered conjuring more pollen dust to suffocate him with, but our heads were too close together. I'd probably end up inhaling the potent mix, too.

An outburst in the distance caught my eye, causing me to gasp. "What was that?"

"Keep watching."

I had no idea *what* he wanted me to see. It was pitch-black outside, which seemed to be their version of the day. From what I recalled, Midnight Fae held opposite hours to Elemental Fae, choosing to sleep when the sun rose and to work during the night. Not a schedule I wanted to—

An inferno billowed into the sky, followed by two more from different positions on the Academy grounds.

Narrowing my gaze, I focused on the source and gasped when I *felt* the burning thwomp closest to our building expel its burning embers into the sky.

Oh.

That was why they possessed charcoaled stems and didn't have leaves.

They literally *burned.*

"Now imagine what would have happened had your little creation gone through its hourly process inside my suite?" Kolstov released me, taking a step back.

I swallowed and pinched my lips to the side. "Well,

how was I supposed to know that?" I asked, facing him.

Zephyrus stood off to the side, arms crossed, his chiseled features devoid of emotion.

"How about you not play with things you don't understand?" Kolstov suggested. "That's why you're here—*to learn.*"

"No, I'm being held here because a Midnight Fae bit me against my will and you think his powers are going to mix with mine. Well, I feel fine now that I'm grounded again in my earth essence. So how about you let me leave and we call it a night?"

"You feel fine," he repeated, his skepticism evident. "Yeah. Because it's perfectly normal for an Earth Fae to be able to unravel a dark arts spell. One my father put on you, by the way. And it was a binding spell that other Midnight Fae wouldn't be able to dismantle in a week, let alone minutes. So yeah, I think it's safe to say Chern's suspicions about your future are already coming true."

My mouth worked without sound, his words effectively freezing me in place.

Was he right? I hadn't noticed the web before, but once it came to me, I worked through it rather quickly. And I'd wondered if the reason I could suddenly see it meant something about my growing power. It seemed it did.

Which meant… "I really am morphing into an abomination." Something I already acknowledged once, but now… now I had proof.

"It would seem so, yes," Kolstov agreed. "However, it might—"

"How is this possible?" I asked, cutting him off. "All that willow stump did was bite me. We didn't exchange powers. If anything, he should be inheriting mine, not the other way around."

"A bite creates the mating bond in our world," Kolstov replied, irritation lacing his tone. "Something you should know about Midnight Fae culture. Except, that's right, you haven't studied us at all. What a fantastic royal you are turning out to be."

His barb failed to penetrate my already whirling emotions because we were beyond my studies and what I knew. What I cared about now was the future and how to use it to my advantage.

"Elemental Fae don't bond through blood. We bond with the source. So it's one-sided. I don't even feel him, and if we were truly mated, I would." *Or I hope that's the case*, I added to myself.

"It's still forming," Kolstov gritted out. "Midnight Fae mating is initiated with the first bite, sealed with the second, and promised for eternity with the third. Shade only initiated it, which means your powers and blood are mingling now, forming a new life together. Hence, you suddenly have access to dark magic. What we don't know is how deep it will go."

"Which is why the Council decided to keep her here," Zephyrus interjected. "To observe her progress. And you're the one charged with managing her."

A muscle ticked in Kolstov's jaw. "Is this the part where you call me a babysitter?"

"No. *Executioner* seems like a better term." Zephyrus pushed off the wall, his eyes narrowing. "You are the one who will have to kill her if she proves to be an abomination, yes?"

My heart stopped.

No.

Except the look on Kolstov's face said, *Yes.*

I started shaking my head in denial, refusing to believe that could possibly be a recourse, yet all the while knowing it had to be an option. Because abominations couldn't exist. Too much power led to insanity.

And I'd witnessed firsthand what happened when someone achieved too much power.

A shiver traversed my spine at the memory of Elana trying to destroy all of Earth Fae kind with her dark magic. She'd tried to suck our souls from our bodies, to absorb our abilities.

My connection to the earth source nearly fractured because of her.

I'll never be like that, I thought to myself.

But what if that was my fate? What if this connection Shade had forced upon me drove me insane?

I'd nearly unleashed a burning thwomp on this suite. What else could I do?

It didn't matter that I hadn't known. I should have known. Should have dug deeper into the being's core to determine its purpose before picking it for my plight.

My knees buckled and I hit the ground, my eyes on the floor.

How had everything gone so horribly wrong? What could I do to stop it? Learn dark magic? Control it? Would that even help?

"We're going to need a new binding spell," Kolstov muttered. "A more powerful one."

I remained silent because he was right.

Returning to the Elemental Fae realm was impossible in my current state. Bringing dark magic there would upset the balance.

I had no choice but to remain here while my future revealed itself.

All because a Midnight Fae took advantage of me in the Human Realm.

My eyes narrowed.

Kolstov might have pissed me off with his high-handedness, but it was Shade who earned my ultimate wrath.

That male would pay when I saw him again. I'd wrap him up in vines and squeeze until his gorgeous head popped off. Then I'd burn him for good measure.

"He warned me you would be beautiful, Aflora," he'd said.

He who? I pondered now. *And why did you do this to me?*

Death and I were already well acquainted, as I'd been placed at the lethal doorstep a few times before. Once as a child. And again just last year. Yet my life had won both times before.

I wasn't one to just give up and accept fate. I fought it every step of the way. And this wouldn't be any different.

A new task list brewed in my thoughts, providing me with renewed purpose.

Play along.
Learn how to control the darkness.
Behave.
Demand answers.
Kill Shade.

Yes. Yes, this would work.

And then, when I finished, I'd escape.

AFLORA

I PUSHED THE BLOODY SAUCE across my plate with a frown. The giant hunk of brown crap sitting in the middle didn't appeal to me, nor did the strange, long white worms surrounding it.

When Kolstov claimed to be heading out to pick up some food, I thought he meant *edible* food. This was not edible. Yet Zephyrus and Kolstov seemed pretty satisfied with it, their plates already half-empty.

My lips twisted. *I can't eat this.*

Fortunately, they hadn't cut off my elemental power yet, which meant I could grow—

"It's spaghetti," Kolstov said, interrupting my thoughts. "Fresh from Italy. Why aren't you eating it?"

"Human food." My nose scrunched. "Why are you eating human food?"

Kolstov shared a look with Zephyrus. "I told you. She

knows nothing about Midnight Fae."

I ground my teeth together, tired of this rhetoric.

But he wasn't done.

"When did you start learning about other fae realms, Zeph?"

The headmaster finished swallowing before saying, "As a child."

"Me, too. I remember Dorthia quizzing me about the Fae Royal names when I was, like, six or seven." Kolstov pinned me with a gaze. "Midnight Fae frequently enter the Human Realm because we need their blood to survive. As a result, our palates have evolved with theirs, making mortal food very common in this kingdom. Consider that your introductory lesson. Now open your mouth and eat what I've given you."

I considered his words and decided to go for an honest response. "Six or seven years old," I repeated, tasting the words. "Hmm. When I was around that age, my parents left me with a single mother and her two children, stating they would return. Except they didn't. Their links with the source disappeared, leaving me as the sole heir. Then, a little while after that, a psychotic fae tried to kill me and absorb my earth magic."

I paused for effect.

"So yeah," I drawled. "I've been a little busy trying to survive for the last fourteen or so years. Forgive me for not adding fae politics to my *pampered* agenda." I shoved away from the table, done with him and his pompous criticisms.

None of this was my fault.

And I was very tired of his condescending attitude.

He caught my wrist as I rounded the small dining table, his golden irises flaring. "You need to eat."

"I don't drink blood, but thank you anyway."

His brow furrowed. "I wasn't offering my neck."

I rolled my eyes. "No, just the bloody worm soup. I'm good. I'll make myself something from the earth."

Assuming I could conjure up an edible plant in this realm. All the plant sources I felt around me were far from friendly.

Case in point, the burning thwomp.

Definitely not going to try to eat that.

"It's spaghetti," Kolstov repeated, tugging me back toward my chair with his too-strong arms. "Noodles, not worms. Tomato sauce, not blood. And a meatball." He finished his explanation with a shove that had me landing square in my seat again. "Take a bite. Aside from the heavy garlic, I think you'll like it."

"A meatball?" I repeated, my stomach churning. "Like, from an animal?"

"Probably a mix of pig and cow, yeah."

I gagged. *"You're eating an animal?!"*

He shared another of those looks with Zephyrus, then reached across the table to pluck the giant ball of crap off my plate and tossed it onto his own. "Now you just have noodles and tomato sauce. Bon appétit."

Zephyrus snorted, sliced a knife through the glob on Kolstov's plate, and took half the meat pile for himself.

I shuddered. *So gross.*

Elemental Fae didn't eat Human Realm animals. Their diets weren't adequate enough for our tastes. I preferred a nice slab of medium-rare orc, or even a grizzly pink potpie.

My stomach growled at the thought.

Zephyrus's gaze narrowed, those sharp green eyes seeming to peer right through me.

He patted his shirt, producing a wand from a pocket I couldn't see, then waved it around with a few muttered words. A plate appeared a moment later with a shroom loaf on top of a bed of purple leaves. He swapped it for my dish without a word and dumped the bloody worms onto his own plate.

Kolstov smirked.

Zephyrus remained silent.

And I eyed the magical creation with strong skepticism.

"What did you put in it?"

"Take a bite and find out, princess," he replied with a wink.

I huffed. *Well, it's better than what they're eating*, I decided, taking my knife and fork to cut a sliver from the magically produced food.

Zephyrus ignored me, his focus on his own plate. Meanwhile, Kolstov's brow furrowed as I brought the browned fluff to my lips and took a bite.

"What is it?" he asked, sounding appalled.

"Shroom loaf," Zephyrus informed him. "Popular in their realm."

"How the hell do you know that?" he demanded.

"You're not the only one who took cultural courses, *Your Highness*." Zephyrus gave him a look that resulted in a scowl from the Midnight Prince.

Such a strange dynamic.

Zephyrus struck me as older, not because of his title, but because of the experience underlining his features. Definitely not of Academy age, yet not too much older.

Headmaster.

Something told me that term didn't mean the same in this world as it meant in others.

He wasn't in charge of the Academy because he didn't have the right air of authority for that. Too laid-back in his treatment of Kolstov. Not proper enough in my presence either.

But he could definitely pass for a professor.

"Do you teach?" I asked him while cutting off a large bite. It wasn't the most amazing shroom loaf of my experience, but I liked the smoky flavor. It provided an exotic touch, as if Zephyrus had singed the ends himself with his Midnight Fae energy.

"That is what a headmaster does, yes." He tapped his fork on the plate, staring at his food, and sighed. "Do you know anything about how Midnight Fae Academy is run? How our Houses of Magic work? The bloodlines that drive our course studies?"

My cheeks heated. "As I told Prince Kolstov, I haven't taken a course on your political structure yet. It was on my calendar for this year, in addition to devoting my time to helping my fellow Earth Fae rebuild. Which I apparently won't be doing now."

Over half of my kind had perished in the last few decades due to a wicked abomination sucking the energy from our souls in an attempt to gain access to additional elemental sources. It left the Earth Fae in shambles. Something I expected to help nurture and fix over the next fifty or so years.

Then Shade bit me and turned my plans to dust.

"I'm aware of what happened in the Elemental Fae kingdom," Kolstov murmured. "I supplied textbooks to Exos and Cyrus for—"

"Master Kolstov," a gravelly voice interrupted as the gargoyle swooped in over our heads.

My eyes widened at the breadth of his stone wings. For such a tiny body, I expected a few inches at most. But no, the width was as long as my arm.

Wow, where does he hide those while in the door?

"Yes, Sir Kristoff?" Kolstov prompted, arching a brow.

"A Sangré Blood is at the door for you, sir," the gargoyle replied, bowing low before whirling around to return to the foyer.

"Ah, Chern must have sent us a party gift." He dabbed his lips with a napkin, then excused himself. "Be back in a few minutes."

"Party gift?" I repeated, glancing at Zephyrus. "And what's a *Sangré Blood*?"

"One of the Midnight Fae bloodlines." He sipped from a glass of red liquid that was either wine or fresh from a human's veins. I didn't ask. Considering my glass contained water, I suspected it was the latter. "There are five active houses of our kind: Death, Elite, Sangré, Warrior, and Malefic. I'm a Warrior Blood. Kolstov is an

Elite Blood. Shade, your betrothed, is a Death Blood."

"*Betrothed*," I muttered, hating that word. "Soon-to-be-dead betrothed."

If Zephyrus heard me, he didn't acknowledge my comment. "Each line has an affinity for different types of dark magic. It's similar to your elemental assignments, except ours is defined in the blood more than in our souls. As your bond with Shade settles, you'll likely join his line. But your Royal Fae essence may contradict it."

"That's why the Council wants her to take courses under all the houses," Kolstov said as he returned. Rather than reclaim his seat, he moved to stand behind mine. "Lift your hair for me, gorgeous."

The request sent a chill down my spine, my hands locking around my knife and fork. "Why?"

He combed his fingers through my dark strands and bent to press his lips to my ear. "Because I need access to your throat."

I jolted, the silverware crashing against my plate as I covered the pulse points beneath my neck. If he thought to bite me, then he had another think coming. "No!"

His hands landed on my shoulders before I could even jump out of my chair. "Chill, Aflora. I just want to put a necklace on you."

"A necklace?" I repeated, trying to glance back at him. His hold kept me in place.

"It's necessary."

"That doesn't tell me—"

"The Council needs to temper your elemental abilities to ensure the safety of the students," Zephyrus explained in a bored tone. "The choker will keep you under control." He glanced up at Kolstov. "Now, was that so difficult an explanation?"

Temper my abilities?

Leather wrapped around my neck before I could voice the question out loud, Kolstov already moving my hair out of the way.

I tried to shift out of his grip, to stop him from sealing the brace around my throat, but it snapped into place with a zing that pierced my soul.

My hands flew up to tug at the choker, to find the clasp and unfasten it. Only, it was solid all the way around, sealed by magic.

"Remove it," I demanded, my spirit whimpering inside at having been cut off from my source yet again. "Remove it now."

Kolstov settled into the chair at the head of the table, his sigh long and loud. "It's necessary, Aflora. We can't risk you disturbing the balance or creating another burning thwomp where you shouldn't." He looked pointedly at the ashes still littering his living room floor. "This will also help us observe your dark-magic growth. Zeph is going to take you shopping tomorrow for a wand and other essentials."

"Yes, because apparently it's my job to play babysitter," the headmaster retorted. "If the Council is so concerned for her safety, perhaps forcing her to attend the Academy wasn't the brightest move."

Tears stung my eyes.

Protection was the least of my concerns considering they'd just wrapped a shackle around my neck to control my abilities.

It suffocated my ability to think, to continue listening to their maddening conversation. All I wanted—no, *needed*—was to rip this offending collar from my throat.

But it wouldn't budge no matter which way I pulled or yanked.

"Why are you even still here?" Zephyrus's harsh tone drew me from my turmoil, lifting my focus back to the two bickering males.

Kolstov's cheeks were a dark shade of red, his lips flattened. "To help with the transition."

"Bullshit. Your father sent me to handle it so you could go enjoy your final week of debauchery before classes begin again. If you're not planning to do that, then I'll go back to my life and you can manage her *transition*."

Kolstov slammed his fist onto the table. "I didn't ask for you to be here."

"Well, you didn't suggest otherwise either, did you?"

Silence.

"Yeah, that's what I thought. Just like the headmaster position. You claim to have balls, Prince Kolstov. And while I know they exist, they sure do seem to shrivel up into nothing where your father's edicts are concerned." With that crude statement, Zephyrus shoved himself away from the table so hard his chair toppled onto the ground.

He didn't bother righting it.

Just turned on his heel to leave.

"Ten hours, Aflora," he tossed over his shoulder. "Be ready to go."

Kolstov watched him go with burning gold irises. When the door slammed in the distance—presumably to the guest room—the Midnight Prince snapped his fingers.

An apparition appeared beside him, the ghostly female boasting a maternal glow as she stared down at him.

"Clean it up," he demanded as he stood.

"Of course, sir," the apparition breathed, her words ghosting through the air and leaving a chill in their wake.

Rather than follow Zephyrus, he headed toward the front entry, exiting through the threshold without a single word or glance back.

The dishes rose above the table, vanishing before my eyes.

I caught the contents of my dish just before the plate disappeared into the strange vacuum.

Then the translucent female form turned to air with everything else, leaving me alone and cold in the living area with a random shroom loaf clutched to my chest.

Silence.

Stillness.

Nothing.

Not even a breath—because I'd stopped inhaling and exhaling.

How had everything gone so wrong in one day? I stared down at the food in my hands.

Tomorrow would hopefully provide new opportunities.

Or possibly be a whole lot worse.

Yeah, probably that.

AFLORA

"I HAVE A SUPPLY LIST," Zephyrus said as we left Kolstov's suite the following evening. The Midnight Prince was nowhere in sight, and I suspected I wouldn't be seeing him again until next week.

Assuming I'm still here. I sighed, shaking my head. *Who am I kidding? Of course I'll be here.*

The Earth Fae relied on me to uphold the connection to the earth source, which meant blocking any and all dangers. Including myself. And I couldn't deny that the potential binding of my abilities to Shade jeopardized my ability to lead.

What if he can access my elemental gifts? I wondered, following Zephyrus down the stairs. "Does my collar keep Shade from tapping into my earth source?" I asked out loud. "Or is he wearing one, too?" The thought of that actually had my lips twitching. *Oh, I really hope they collared him…*

Zephyrus paused to glare at me. "Were you over there daydreaming while I've been speaking?"

I grimaced. He *had* been talking. And, uh, yeah, I'd not heard a word of it after his supply list comment.

The look he gave me confirmed that the answer was written across my face and he didn't approve. His hand wrapped around my throat, his opposite palm going to my hip, as he pushed me up against the wall. My feet awkwardly found purchase on one stair, holding me upright while he captured my gaze with a lethal stare.

"When I speak, you listen. Understand?"

I swallowed. He stood over a foot taller than me, just like Kolstov. And Zephyrus also possessed the muscles of a man who had spent most of his life hardening his exterior.

Warrior Blood, I recalled from our earlier conversation. While I didn't know the complete definition, I could garner the importance of that distinction. Along with his comments about being a Guardian.

My Guardian.

This was not a male to piss off, and yet… "Do you manhandle all your students in this manner?" I asked him, tilting my head to the side.

His chest crowded mine, and his thighs—*holy crap, those thighs!*—pressed me harder into the wall. "I don't know. I haven't started my new job yet. Ask me again next week."

"You're a new professor?"

"Headmaster," he corrected. "And yes, it's a recently assigned post." His tone held a note of bitterness to it.

"What was your previous post?"

"Why are you so chatty today?" His grip tightened around my neck. "I think I preferred your moping from last night."

"I was not moping," I gritted out, my eyes narrowing. "Let me go."

"Make me."

"This is not proper behavior for a professor."

"Headmaster," he corrected again. "And I haven't technically started yet. Right now, I'm just your Guardian. Which means you'll do whatever I tell you to do, whenever I tell you to do it."

"And you make that point by strangling me?"

His lips curled into a cruel smile. "Trust me, this is nothing compared to what I can do."

I believed him. Yet, for whatever reason, I didn't fear him. His callous exterior presented an ominous front, his cold green eyes just as harsh as the rest of him, but my instincts told me to push back.

"I might be weaker with this cuff around my neck, but I'm still a Royal Fae. That said, I apologize for *daydreaming*. I was thinking about how my bloodline is tied to Shade and wondered if that means he can access my gifts, too. If he can tap into the earth source, I have much larger problems than buying books or school uniforms." Which I guessed was part of his *list*.

A glimmer of respect brightened his emerald orbs. He released me and stepped back, his cloak billowing around his ankles. The lapels were laced with green ink that sparkled beneath the firelight. I studied them, wondering what they meant, when Zephyrus turned on his heel and continued down the stairs.

"The collar around your neck should prevent him from accessing your elemental gifts. It acts as a door, and when it's clasped, that door is shut and blocks your soul from accessing the elements. Which means Shade is also locked out." He reached the bottom level and glanced up at me. "Satisfied?"

"Now you're starting to sound more like a professor," I quipped, giving him a smile. "Thank you, *Headmaster*."

His pupils flared, heat momentarily sparking in the emerald depths. "Hmm" was all he said before turning again and leading the way outside.

Rather than lead the way toward the main gates, he

took a left that directed us into the heart of the campus. Fire flickered on lampposts, gently lighting the charcoal-stoned paths. Obsidian bricks and other types of rock provided the foundation for the buildings, and gothic arches and stained glass lent the scene a palatial appeal that I had to admit was quite pretty.

Burning thwomps and other foreign plants graced the grounds, including black flowers that reminded me of roses and a series of purple-laced ivy that glowed with fiery bugs.

I bent to get a better look, only to be yanked back by Zephyrus. "Don't."

"Why?" I asked, studying the buzzing insects. "They remind me of pixies."

"Fire gnats are disgusting little jackasses who bite. Don't provoke them." Zephyrus released me. "Our wildlife isn't like yours. We coexist because we have to, not because we want to. So trust me, you do not want to touch anything in this realm. Especially not those."

I shivered at the warning, then gasped as a phoenix landed not three feet away from us. Its massive wings billowed in the flames, the eyes predatory.

"Case in point," Zephyrus muttered. "Fuck off." His words seemed to be for the bird, not for me.

The beautiful creature tilted its head, his red irises focused and intelligent. A curious little caw left its throat, causing my lips to curl. Oh, I had no doubt this being was dangerous, but I could respect its gorgeous existence. Not that I had any intention of feeding the bird or stroking it. I knew better than that.

Just as I knew not to disturb the fire gnats.

Admiring nature didn't require any sort of interference.

"You're stunning," I praised.

The phoenix preened as if it understood, his wings expanding to show off the variety of colorful flames.

Zephyrus stepped in between us, cutting off my view, and flapped his cloak in warning at the handsome being.

"I won't tell you again. Fuck. Off."

A hiss of sound preceded the phoenix's departure, leaving me in awe of the way it swooped across the grounds to a nearby burning thwomp.

"Let's get something straight," Zephyrus said, facing me once more. "As your assigned Guardian, my duty is to keep you alive. To do that, I need you to obey my every word. Let's start with this: do not provoke the wildlife."

I bristled at his tone. "I wasn't provoking him."

"Don't engage with the wildlife," he amended.

"That's like telling me not to breathe."

"Then hold your fucking breath," he snapped, causing me to flinch. He cursed and turned away. "Let's go. This list is burning a literal hole in my pocket, and I want this over and done with."

"Yes, sir," I muttered.

"Better," he replied as he continued down the path past a gazebo overlaid with more of that violet ivy. I wasn't given much time to admire the architecture, his long legs leading us into a clearing filled with lava rock instead of grass. My eyebrows lifted at the bizarre textures. Then my lips parted as the ground shifted.

Not rocks.

Animals.

Zephyrus cleared his throat, his hands on his hips, as he glowered at the writhing swarm of birdlike creatures.

Oh my…

They all activated at once, their wings flickering to life and blooming with thin, sharp edges. The air around them pulsed with magic, their chattering beaks and crackling feathers grinding against the wind.

Zephyrus pressed his palm to my lower back, pushing me into the center of the flocking mass. I lifted my arms to shield my face, terrified of being cut by their jagged points. However, they resembled feathers against my skin.

I peeked through my forearms to find us being swarmed by crow-like birds. Black eyes, black beaks, black feathers. Not rocks.

"What in the…?" I trailed off as a keypad appeared. *This is a portal.*

Zephyrus acted before I could catch the movements, his fingers flying over the destination code too fast for me to catch. Not that escape was much of an option for me right now, but having a backup plan couldn't hurt.

The obsidian flurry swam around us, forming a ribbon of solid ink that had me stepping closer to Zephyrus. His palm against my lower back slid to my hip in response—a protective move that didn't go unnoticed for either of us because his gaze seized mine as soon as it happened.

Intensity built between us.

Or maybe it was the aura of the transfer shifting us through space.

I couldn't say, but it escalated my heartbeat. His masculine scent invaded my pores, the minty aftershave he wore an intoxicating blanket that swathed me in his Midnight Fae essence.

All to disappear in a blink as we landed in a closet filled with cloaks.

Zephyrus released me immediately, his long fingers flying upward to unfasten the knot at his neck. He added his cape to the others, drawing my attention to the orderly fashion of the interior. Everything was color-coded by the ink etched into the trim of each formal robe.

Dark purple.

Maroon.

Forest green—Zephyrus's location.

Navy.

And solid black.

"What do they represent?" I asked softly, reaching out to stroke the soft textures.

Zephyrus caught my wrist, yanking me back. "Don't. They're charmed to only recognize their master." He seemed to consider. "Actually, no, it's a good teaching moment. Try to grab mine." He gestured to it as if I wasn't aware of where he'd just hung it up.

I narrowed my gaze. "I think I'm good, thanks."

"It won't hurt," he promised. Not that I believed him. "Just zaps a little."

"And that's all I need to know," I replied, heading for what I thought might be the door.

His arm snaked around my waist, yanking me backward. "What part of 'follow my lead' don't you get?"

"You never told me to follow you," I pointed out, glancing up at him. "And stop manhandling me."

"Stop acting impulsively," he returned, yanking me around in the other direction to face a mirror. "We're going this way. The door just leads to other portals." His grip tightened. "And don't even think about exploring them. I will hunt you down, and you will not like the consequences."

"Wow, your faith in me is charming."

He met my gaze in the mirror, one arm still wrapped like a vise around my waist. "I don't have faith in anyone but myself, Aflora. You would be wise to adopt a similar armor." With that, he shoved me through the glass—which gave way just like the entrance to Kolstov's suite at the Academy—and stepped through behind me.

Zephyrus ran his fingers through his thick mane of dark brown hair, the edges taunting his round ears. "Right. This way." He linked his fingers through mine, pulling me alongside him down a sidewalk littered with Midnight Fae.

Wow, I thought, in awe of the shops and busy atmosphere. It reminded me of strolling through the Human Realm, particularly New York City, except the buildings weren't nearly tall enough. Only four or five stories at most, but their glass exteriors were very modern.

Everyone wore business attire, allowing Zephyrus to fit in with his suit. My skirt and blouse from my date-gone-wrong barely passed the fashion test, but it beat wearing Kolstov's clothes.

"Here," Zephyrus said, pulling me toward a random

building with the name *AcaWard* scrawled over the windows.

Clearly, the Midnight Fae didn't believe in doors. They just had enchanted thresholds. Because one moment the chaotic sounds of the outside world bustled around my ears, then in the next moment, we were surrounded by the warm tunes of the interior.

An endless array of outfits stretched out on racks before us. Most lined the walls in rows that climbed all the way up to the ceiling. I frowned up at them, wondering how one retrieved clothing from way up there.

Probably with a wand.

At least it proved to be an efficient use of space.

"Hello, hello," a female voice chimed. "Welcome to AcaWard. How can we help you?"

I glanced around, frowning when no one appeared. Was someone watching us on a camera and talking over a speaker system?

"Aflora needs at least seven Academy-sanctioned outfits, undergarments, and some casual wear. You are to charge the items to the Nacht account." Zephyrus slipped an envelope from his pocket with his free hand, holding it in the air. "All the details required are in here."

The note vanished, causing my eyes to widen.

"I'll return in an hour to retrieve her." He looked down at me. "We've already discussed what will happen should you try to flee. I don't recommend it."

With that, he released me and stepped backward through the glass to disappear in the throng outside.

"Wait—" I tried to follow him out, but the glass didn't give and instead smacked me in the forehead. "Ow!" I rubbed my head, irritated by my inability to leave the shop and offended by it sealing the door on me.

An array of voices erupted around me, all chattering at once.

"Hmm, yes, new clothes are needed. Indeed, indeed."

"A cloak, too."

"Don't forget a wand."

"Oh! Have you seen the new Academy skirts? I'm thinking black and red, to match the Nacht line."

"Royal, yes. Let's look at these notes. Hmm, hmm, more than seven, clearly. Too many courses."

"Shall we mix it with a touch of light blue? To match her pretty eyes?"

"Oh, is she cerulean? Haven't seen one of those in centuries."

"With hints of red, I see."

"How fascinating."

I spun around, searching for the source of the feminine tones, but found myself utterly alone in the shop.

"This way, this way," one of them said.

I felt the nudge against my backside. Then gaped as an invisible *something* grabbed my shirt to tow me forward. "Why can't I see you?" I demanded.

Tinkling laughs served as their reply.

Then they began to comment on my appearance, noting the quality of my dark hair, my clear skin, and my tiny waist.

When one of them touched my breasts, I scowled. "Show yourselves."

More tinkling.

And then they closed me in a ten-by-ten room with a mirror and three walls. No exit.

I tried walking through each barrier but found myself trapped.

Then clothes began to appear on a magical rack behind me.

"Try, try, try!" they all sang in unison.

When they started to unbutton my blouse, I whirled around and batted their figment hands away. "I will undress and dress myself, thank you."

"Oh, feisty fun," one of them murmured.

"Yes, yes. She demands privacy. We'll go."

"Try them all, love! And pick all your favorites. The

note says all expenses are covered."

"Enjoy!"

They blew invisible kisses through the air, the sound caressing my cheeks in an unwelcome wave. I wiped them off with a gag, then froze as silence fell around me.

I counted to twenty before I let my shoulders fall in relief.

Finally.

At least thirty outfits waited on the rack, as well as a dozen or so shoes.

I ran my fingers along each shirt and skirt, noting the fine quality. As an Earth Fae, I always enjoyed making my own clothes from nature. But that wasn't an option here. I needed outfits that helped me assimilate to this realm. The more I blended in, the less people would notice me. And that would become important for my eventual departure.

Assuming I found a way to escape. In addition to a place to run to.

Sighing, I resigned myself to my current fate once more. Might as well pick some outfits that suited my tastes. Besides, all the expenses were covered, right?

Nacht account, Zephyrus had said. I recognized the family name as the one Kolstov belonged to. Which meant he, or maybe his father, was paying for all of this.

My lips curled.

While I'd prefer Shade foot the bill for getting me into this mess, I couldn't deny feeling a little bit of glee knowing my wardrobe spending spree would be billed directly to my primary captor.

Seven outfits?

No, surely he meant seventeen.

And a dozen or so casual ones as well.

"Ladies," I called out, glancing around and waiting.

"Yes, Miss Aflora?" one of the figments cooed.

"I'm going to need at least three times this selection," I said. "And don't forget undergarments, socks, and more shoes. Oh, and wands."

A chittering sound followed, the gleeful noise echoing in the chamber. "Oh, yes, as the madam requires!"

The room expanded around me, an entire row of clothing appearing as if waiting for my very command. A glass case followed, wands gleaming inside.

Yes, this would do.

I rubbed my hands together.

You all want me to stay here for the indefinite future? Fine. But I'll be staying in style.

I smiled at my reflection in the mirror. "Thanks for the new wardrobe, Midnight Prince," I whispered, hoping somehow that message reached his pompous ears.

Zephyrus said I had an hour?

Well, I'd take three.

"Ladies, let's get started," I mused to the magical beings. *This is going to be fun.*

AFLORA

ALL RIGHT. The Midnight Fae Academy uniforms weren't bad. A lot of black, but my shirts were white.

I finished tying cloak number nine around my neck, testing the weight. All the others were too heavy, the fabric choking me worse than the leather collar around my throat. But this one was made of a light silk and fringed in dark red tones.

Smoothing my hands around it, I twirled, liking the way it feathered around my exposed legs. The Academy skirts were a bit short, hitting me midthigh. Hence, I'd requested some knee-high boots to—

"Not bad," a deep voice murmured behind me. "But I personally think you would look better in my family color, which is purple."

I spun around to find Shade lounging in a chair that didn't exist a moment ago.

"How did you...? Where did you...? What...?" I shook my head, biting my lip to keep from issuing another unfinished question at the willow stump sitting a few feet away from me.

"The collar is a nice touch. Does that make you my pet?" he asked, pushing to his feet to draw closer. "Or is Kolstov trying to claim what's mine?" His fingertips brushed the leather around my throat, sending a hum of energy across my skin and eliciting a hiss from his mouth. "Bastard."

Shade grasped the back of my neck before I could even think to react, pulling my body up against his in a move that stole my breath.

Electricity zipped down my spine from his hold and the rioting device around my throat. It didn't hurt so much as send an unpleasant sensation across my skin. "Shade..."

"How are you, love?" he asked, walking me backward into a wall. "Are they treating you all right? Apart from the collar, of course."

Some of my senses started to return as he pressed his body into mine.

He was the reason I had to wear a collar.

Because *he* had bitten me against my will.

And now he had the audacity to show up and ask me how I was doing? Like he gave a damn about my feelings?

"Oh, you!" I planted my palms against his chest and tried to shove him away. "You're the reason I'm in this mess!"

"You seem to be enjoying said mess," he returned, glancing down at my blouse and black skirt. "Playing fashionista on the royal dime. How fun."

"Because I need an outfit for the Academy I have to attend *because of you.*" I attempted to push him again, but he didn't budge an inch.

Instead, he leaned into me more, his hips aligning with mine as he anchored me against the wall. "Still upset, I see." He drew his nose across my cheek, his breath fanning my face. "Allow me to make it up to you, little darling."

"Make it up to me?" I repeated, my nails digging into his blazer. "You've destroyed my life. Possibly even earned us both a death sentence. There is no living way you could make it up to me, Shadow." I was panting by the end of my statement, not because of his close proximity or the way his thigh had slid between mine, but because of the anger heating my blood. "*I hate you.*"

He chuckled and kissed the space below my ear, his palm leaving my neck to grip my hip. "Wrap your arms around me."

"No."

"Mmm." He hoisted me into the air with both hands on my waist. I grabbed his shoulders in response, gasping as he pressed his groin into the apex between my thighs. "Grip me with your legs, baby, or you'll fall."

"Put me down."

"Not a chance." He captured my mouth instead and took full advantage of my shock by slipping his tongue between my lips.

What is happening?
Why is he doing this?
And oh, no, this… can't… be… happening.
Dizziness shot through my mind.
Adrenaline fueled my limbs.
I wanted to *hurt* him.
Needed to fight.
Because this couldn't be allowed to continue!

I clamped down on his tongue, only to be rewarded with the most beautiful taste in response. I froze. Then moaned. *Oh my…* Exquisite decadence filled our mouths, distracting me from my goal and throwing me into a whirl of oblivion that I couldn't escape from. Instead, I fell headfirst into it, allowing my instincts to take over.

My legs were around his waist in a second.
My arms encircling his neck.
And his essence coated my lips, my mouth, my *throat.*

I groaned, craving another swallow more than anything else in the world. He gave it to me with his tongue, sliding along mine, feeding me that delicious liquid I desired.

One hand remained against my hip while his opposite rose to my hair, his fingers entangling in my strands as he tilted my head to better receive his kiss.

Some part of me was screaming at us to stop.

But I couldn't hear her over the roar of *need* in my thoughts.

Heat unlike anything I ever remembered feeling seared my insides, pulsing through my veins with one driving thought—*more*.

His arousal grew between my thighs, his slacks rubbing the thin barrier of my lace panties. My skirt was up around my hips, my blouse unbuttoned to reveal my bra, and I couldn't remember how it happened. Except it was my hand running down my shirt, my fingers unfastening the final button.

I shivered. "What are you doing to me?" I felt possessed. Owned. Hypnotized by this male. Yet completely lucid and aware. "How are you doing this?"

"This is all you," he whispered, his lips brushing mine. "You bit me, Aflora."

"To make you stop," I remembered, though I couldn't recall *why*. "I don't like you."

He smiled. "Likewise, baby. But that only makes this so much hotter." His mouth recaptured mine before I could reply, his touch robbing me of my ability to think.

His hands were everywhere and nowhere at the same time.

His kiss a brand against my lips.

His dick throbbing against the place I needed to be touched most.

Too many clothes.

My wrists were caught in one of his hands and hoisted above my head. "Not yet," he breathed. "Not here."

"Not what?" I replied, dazed.

"Shh," he hushed, his refreshing scent surrounding me in a jungle of sensation.

Trees.

Water.

Flowers in full bloom.

The familiarity of the aromas had me sighing in contentment while my body hummed to life with renewed passion.

I kissed him with all of my being, gifting him with the life thriving in my soul, only to be ensnared in his dark web in return. He tugged me under, filling me with a venomous energy that felt wrong beneath my skin.

"Shade," I whimpered, writhing against him.

"I've got you," he promised.

But I didn't believe him.

I couldn't trust him.

Just as Zephyrus said—I'd be wise to develop a similar armor. One outlined in distrust.

My limbs began to shake.

Tears slid from my eyes.

The world rumbled around me, and I couldn't make it stop, even while an inferno built inside me, begging to be released.

It terrified me.

Enthralled me.

Owned me.

Shade's tongue dominated mine, his cock a thick presence against my core, pushing me to the precipice of something terrifying. I clung to him with all my strength, horrified and captivated at the same time. Nothing I could do would stop this. I felt it in my very blood, an unerring compulsion to give in to Shade's ministrations.

A part of me rebelled.

The other part… rejoiced.

I hated him more in that moment than anyone else in my entire existence. Yet my craving for him won.

Ecstasy erupted inside me, drawing a scream from my

throat that was filled with self-loathing and pain. And also represented the most powerful orgasm of my life.

I wasn't a complete innocent.

I'd played with Glacier countless times, and while the Water Fae was good in bed, he *never* made me feel quite like this.

Like liquid ice.

Hot on the inside, frozen on the outside.

A tremor rocked me from head to toe, my rapture subsiding beneath a fresh wave of horror.

I couldn't discern up from down, right from wrong, or passion from hate. Shade's lips were at my neck, his kiss far too tender for my liking. I'd prefer his bite so I could hate him more. Only, he held me with worship in his touch, his warm body wrapped around me in a false blanket of protection.

"I hate you," I whispered, my eyes wet. "I hate you. I hate you. I hate you."

"I know," he replied softly. "I hate myself, too." He nuzzled my throat, sighing. "I'm not supposed to be here, but I wanted to make sure you were okay."

"I'm not okay," I told him, shuddering. "Not okay at all."

He kissed my jaw before pulling back to meet my gaze. "You're strong, little rose," he said softly, the new nickname underlined in a deep caress. "We'll both be okay in the end. You'll see." He pressed his lips to mine once more as he carried me to the chair. Lowering me into it, he hovered over me with a sinful look. "I need to go before Guardian Zephyrus finishes his spell. But I'll see you again soon. In your dreams."

Shade vanished into a cloud of smoke that seemed to take up the entire room, his existence touching every article of clothing and all the walls, until all I could see was darkness.

"Aflora!" Zephyrus's furious voice slapped me across the face, jolting me from the chair. He stood before me with a livid expression, his wand in his hand.

I frowned at him, then whirled around the unfamiliar room. *Wait...* I glanced down to find myself fully clothed and wrapped up in a cloak like a blanket.

My skirt looked brand new, my blouse fully buttoned, and I even had on knee-high boots.

I blinked. "What...?"

"A sleep enchantment," Zephyrus hissed. "That little prick." He shook his head, a curse falling from his full lips. "He's circumventing the rules with mind play. I'd be impressed if he wasn't breaking a hundred protocols to do it."

"So he wasn't... That didn't... I..." My cheeks heated, unable to finish. My damp panties were the only thing on me that matched my supposed dream. So either I'd woken up turned on or I'd orgasmed in my sleep.

Which meant Zephyrus had probably seen it.

Oh, Mother Earth... Warmth touched every inch of my being at the thought of what he'd witnessed.

Fortunately, he didn't seem all that keen to mention it.

"We're done shopping," he said instead, turning on a wave of superiority, an array of bags forming around him. "I assume that's your cape of choice. Same with the wand. The other items will be in your wardrobe by the time we get back." He glanced at my boots and skirt. "A little schoolgirl for our trip back, but I doubt anyone will notice. Let's go."

"Wait, what wand?" I asked. "I didn't pick one."

"Check your pocket, Aflora. One already picked you."

I patted the side of my cape, my eyes widening. "They do that?"

He just gave me a flat look and gestured with his chin toward a mirror. Assuming he meant for me to walk through it, I did and found myself in the cloakroom once more.

My cape billowed around me as I twisted in a sharp circle. "How...?"

"You have so much to learn about our world," Zephyrus replied as he retrieved his cloak and wrapped it around his shoulders with a flourish. "Also, a wand isn't a magical being. It's an extension of our power."

With a wave of his hand, a keypad appeared, and he punched in a code that I caught this time. Of course, it was to the place I didn't really want to go, so not all that helpful.

"We use them as a conduit," he continued, his arm sliding around my shoulders to hold me close while the portal began to whirl around us. "As I said, it's an extension of your power. It helps you focus on a single book on a shelf rather than an entire collection."

Cawing pierced my skull as the crows took over, welcoming us back to the Academy grounds.

In minutes, they were back to their rocky forms, dotting the courtyard.

Flames ignited along the paths again, illuminating the otherwise quiet campus.

"When do students start to arrive?" I asked as he led the way back to Kolstov's building.

"Some are already here but keeping to themselves. The majority will return in five days' time to attend the annual autumn bonfire." He flicked his wrist, sending the bags ahead in a train that moved toward the residence. "Let's take a tour before heading back. We can stop by the cafeteria as well and grab something to eat."

My stomach grumbled at the idea, agreeing.

Aside from the tea he'd forced on me after waking up, I hadn't eaten at all.

"Just be warned," he added, already walking. "The food on Academy grounds is of the human variety. So either you're going to have to learn some meal-conjuring spells or you're going to need to change your tastes. I recommended the latter." He snapped his fingers, a torch appearing in his hand. "Now try to keep up, Aflora. I'm going to give you a crash course in Academy life, and I won't be repeating myself."

ZEPH

I DID NOT MISS THIS PLACE.

The food.

The lounging crows.

The general aura of misery.

In a week, this place would be the definition of hell, brimming with students all eager to continue their studies.

I envied them.

My entire life had been determined before my birth, my duty to a family I'd grown to loathe. Anything and everything Malik Nacht told me to do, I did.

Including taking a job as a headmaster at the Academy when I had no interest or desire to teach.

I took a sip of my coffee, enjoying the way it scalded my mouth and throat on the way down. Pain made me feel alive. Unlike my current surroundings.

Aflora sat across from me, a pout on her full lips as she eyed the contents of our trays. I'd selected an array of my favorites for her to try, yet she didn't seem keen on any of them.

Impossible female.

She didn't belong here any more than I did.

I set my mug down and folded my arms on the table, leaning toward her. "Want a magic lesson?"

We hadn't spoken much during the tour. Mostly just me gesturing at buildings and telling her what courses were held where, as well as pointing out the various residential units. She remained studiously quiet the whole time, probably because she didn't plan to stay here long.

Given what I witnessed inside AcaWard earlier, she'd be here a lot longer than she anticipated. Because Shade clearly possessed a hold over her psyche, something that suggested their blood bond was a lot stronger than it should be.

Which meant their powers were going to grow together.

And that would very likely lead to their deaths.

A disappointing thought, but realistic.

"What kind of lesson?" Aflora asked, referring to my query.

"Well, as you don't seem keen on the food here, I'll teach you an easy spell for acquiring alternatives." And in turn demonstrate why she needed to change her attitude about our sustenance offerings.

Acquisition spells required energy.

Something that would become quite evident to her in a matter of minutes.

I pulled out my wand and set it on the table. "As I mentioned earlier, wands are not the source of magic. We merely use them to help focus the energy. I'll give you an example." We had an entire table to work with, the other twenty chairs around it empty, therefore providing me with the room to exaggerate this lesson a little. "The spell for creating something edible is *Tareero Tamida* and then the item."

Pretty simple, really. But her expression told me she didn't agree.

"So I just say the two words and the food I want, then it pops up."

"Well, you need to put some magic behind it. But yes, that's the general idea."

She frowned at me. "And I use the wand?"

"It's not required, no. As I said, a wand focuses our magic." Her creasing forehead told me she wasn't following. "Here. I'll provide an example. Give me a food item you're craving."

"Uh, I don't know. A sandwich?"

Now I was the one frowning. "You have a sandwich." I pointed to the ham and cheese melt on her plate.

"That's not a sandwich."

"It's definitely a sandwich."

"This has bread and meat and cheese. A sandwich is leafy greens baked to perfection with yammock filling, berries, and sometimes a sliver of hartmint, if you're feeling gluttonous."

Right. I didn't know what any of those things were. "How about another loaf instead?" That I at least knew how to make as I'd eaten one before.

Her lips twisted as she shrugged. "Sure. That works. Can you make a coldberry loaf?"

"There are different types of loaves?"

After studying me for a long moment, she said, "A shroom loaf is fine."

Good because that was the only one I knew how to make. Rather than waste time on explaining the plan again, I just performed the spell. "*Tareero Tamida loaf.*"

One the size of her entire plate appeared, causing her eyes to widen.

"That's huge," she gasped out.

"Yeah. Because I didn't control the size with my

wand." Not exactly true. Children could perform this kind of magic in their sleep and still make an appropriate loaf, but I wanted to exaggerate the results for teaching purposes.

Hey, look at me living up to my headmaster role, I thought sourly.

Wouldn't King Malik be so proud?

Arrogant fuck.

Clearing my throat, I pushed the negative thoughts away and refocused. "Using the conduit, you can control the magical outcome." I picked up my wand and performed the spell again, this time creating a perfectly proportioned loaf. Then I muttered a cleanup spell that dissolved all the food on the table—including the items we'd picked up from the chef—and said, "You try."

She considered for a moment, then nodded. "All right." Taking her wand out of her cloak, she gave it a little wave while saying, "*Tareero Tamida sandwich.*"

Nothing.

Not even a twitch of magic.

I leaned back in my chair and watched as she tried again.

And again.

And again.

All without any kind of result or a single hint of feeling.

After her tenth go at it, she huffed, "This isn't working."

"Clearly."

She stared at me, waiting.

If she expected me to give her more directions, then she had another think coming. I already explained how the process worked. If she couldn't figure out how to apply it, that was on her, not me. Besides, I shouldn't even be here.

"Is my wand broken?" she asked, holding out the magical conduit.

I didn't even look at it. "No." *Because it's not about the wand*, I added to myself. She needed to figure that out on her own. Magic came from the blood. I couldn't really help her find the link. She needed to do that herself.

"Well, that's helpful," she muttered, putting away her wand. "Could you at least explain how I make it work?" she asked slowly as if speaking to an idiot.

I answered her in the same tone with, "You access your magic."

"Right. How?"

"How do you call on your earth essence?" I countered.

"It's a natural connection through my soul."

"Then there you go," I replied. "Class dismissed."

She pointed to the collar at her neck. "I think you're forgetting this."

"You're letting a necklace hold you back? How disappointing." It only blocked her earth magic, not her access to the dark arts. I could admit that out loud, but that would belittle this exercise.

"Holding me back?" she repeated. "It cut me off from my gifts!"

"And?"

She gaped at me. "Wow. You are the worst teacher I've ever met."

"It's my first year," I offered in explanation. "And I technically haven't started yet."

"Well, you're off to a horrible start," she muttered.

I lifted a shoulder, unbothered by her attempt at an insult. This wasn't my career choice. And if I had it my way, I'd be done before I even started.

"So you all expect me to perform magic with a handicap," she drawled. "Oh, but I may not have any dark magic at all, which this exercise seems to confirm."

"Yet you dismantled a high-level spell inside your mind yesterday, which suggests otherwise," I pointed out. "Not just anyone can outmaneuver a Nacht binding charm."

"The little web, you mean?"

"There was nothing little about it." Yet, that she considered it *little* said quite a bit. "How did you dismantle it?" I'd wondered the same thing last night but had been too amused by her attacking Kols with a thwomp. Dangerous, yes. And entertaining as fuck. I was almost disappointed when she lost.

Alas, she always would.

"I found a piece of my light and followed it," she answered vaguely. "I don't see any light now because of this." She gestured to her throat again.

"That cuts you off from your elements, not the dark magic growing inside you." Which I sensed humming just beneath her skin. Another hint I could provide her with, but to what purpose? The best way to learn was by doing, not being led. If she wanted any hope of surviving in our world, then she needed to start thinking and acting for herself. Not relying on others to protect her.

Even if that was technically my job for the time being.

She shook her head. "This is a waste of time."

"Is it?" I drawled. "I had no idea."

"Wow. This is really not the right career path for you."

I smiled. "Your reasoning skills are outstanding, Aflora." I leaned forward. "And you couldn't be more right."

"Then why are you here?" she demanded.

"Because I'm serving my duty to the crown as prescribed." *Whether I like it or not,* I added to myself. But enough about that. "Regarding your powers, Midnight Fae pull through our blood, not our souls. So try that instead."

There. I'd tossed her a bone. Now no one could accuse me of not trying to help.

"Through my blood," she repeated, her tone skeptical. "Right."

"Look, if you don't want to try, then eat the shit offered up at the buffet and let's head back. I could use a nap, and you have a pile of textbooks to start reading." Not that any of them would help her.

This poor girl was utterly fucked.

And so not my problem.

Then why are you trying to teach her? some unhelpful voice in the back of my mind asked.

I shoved it away. I wasn't helping her, just providing some guidance to get her started.

Aflora glowered at me, her blue eyes glittering in a way that reminded me of sex.

Hot.

Passionate.

Fierce.

Sex.

The kind of fuck I enjoyed.

Not. Happening.

Except I always did favor the forbidden. And nothing could be more forbidden than the female sitting across from me. With her full, pouty mouth, delicate jaw, slender throat, and, mmm, that body. She might be wrapped up in a cloak right now, but I'd already noticed her ample assets—pert tits, slender waist, and a heart-shaped ass.

I wasn't blind.

Aflora was a stunning woman. And strictly off-limits for a myriad of reasons.

Which only made her more appealing.

"*Tareero Tamida sandwich,*" she said suddenly, her tone underlined in power.

My lips parted as a giant, wrap-like green blob appeared, its front end landing between us as it stretched across the entire length of the very long table and down onto the floor.

Aflora's narrowed eyes quickly widened. "Oh… wand."

Yeah. Wand.

But I wasn't so much worried about the still-growing sandwich as I was concerned about the pale shock spreading across her cheeks. "Aflora—"

She began to tremble, her cerulean irises rolling into the back of her head as the energy wilted from her small frame.

Shit.

I jumped out of my chair and across the table—and the ever-growing monstrosity on top of it—and landed at her side in time to catch her before she went down.

"*Qalto*," I snapped, my spell overpowering hers and dissolving the green atrocity into dust.

Aflora moaned, her consciousness fighting for life as her body gave out completely.

"This is why I recommend you eat our food," I informed her softly. "Magic requires strength, and strength comes from proper nutrition."

If she heard me, she didn't reply.

With a sigh, I lifted her into my arms. "I guess we'll continue this lesson later."

Whenever she woke up.

AFLORA

FIVE DAYS OF READING and I still didn't understand how dark magic worked. It felt unnatural and wrong, like I had to access an inappropriate part of myself to activate my abilities.

Because I don't belong here, I thought for the millionth time.

Not being able to ignite the Midnight Fae influence inside me was probably a good thing. It meant this forced bond with Shade wouldn't amount to much. Maybe it would disappear soon.

When I suggested that hopeful sentiment to Zephyrus yesterday, he'd remained as stoic as ever, never giving anything away.

He was the worst teacher in all the fae kingdoms and totally unapologetic about it.

Obviously, neither of us wanted to be here. Which gave

us something in common. Not that it brought us any closer.

No, Zephyrus was a closed book.

And I didn't try to pry him open.

Instead, I spent most of my time reading alone in my new room. When my stomach complained, either I joined him for meals in the living area or we walked to the cafeteria. At some point he'd gone shopping, or perhaps had food delivered, some of which were items I recognized. However, most were human meals.

Ugh.

My insides still crawled from the breakfast he'd forced upon me. Eggs with cheese and onions. *An omelet,* he'd called it.

Gross.

I preferred to label it as *torture,* but I ate the monstrosity because he refused to make anything else, and my wand didn't want to cooperate. Turns out, his whole lecture about magic requiring energy was right. The less I ate, the worse I performed.

While part of me preferred not to be able to access the dark powers, the other part of me recognized that I needed the magic to survive in this world.

Because yeah, Midnight Fae Academy was proving to have a dangerous campus. Not only were those snakelike vines watching my every move, but I also had all types of wildlife eyeing me with curiosity. And I learned pretty fast that none of the plants or animals in this realm were kind.

My shoulder winced with the reminder of the fire gnat I met last night.

Not a pretty lightning bug, but a beast with sharp teeth and a fiery after-bite.

Zephyrus had watched the entire thing with a bored expression, not once helping me. When I demanded to know why, he merely shrugged and said, "It won't kill you."

Just thinking about it brought a scowl to my face.

Again.

Headmaster Zephyrus served as proof that beauty on the outside did not equate to beauty on the inside. Because his exterior sure was gorgeous, but inside him lived a dark, unhelpful jackass of a man who considered me more of a burden than a project.

Well, fine. He could take his uncooperative behavior and shove it up his muscular butt. Not that I'd spent a lot of time admiring said butt. Or thinking about how many hours he had to clock at the gym to maintain such a fit physique.

Right, so that was a lie. But not many Elemental Fae were warriors, so Zephyrus's fighter build intrigued me a little. *Strong* didn't seem like an adequate enough adjective for him. He practically oozed power from his pores without even trying. Kind of like Kolstov, but in a different way.

With a shake of my head, I pushed away thoughts of the two males and focused on the textbook in my lap. It explained Midnight Fae hierarchy and all the bloodlines. Zephyrus had told me there were only five, but according to my book, there were actually six types of Midnight Fae.

I spent yesterday reading up on the Elite Bloods and Kolstov's family legacy as the oldest royals of that line. As primary conduits for the dark-magic source, Elite Bloods were considered the most powerful of Midnight Fae kind, hence their leadership over all the others.

The Warrior Bloods were particularly gifted in physical strength and agility, allowing them to serve as Guardians of the Elite Bloods. Ergo, Zephyrus's role. What I still didn't understand was why he'd been relegated to the Academy when his family had a long-standing history of protecting the Nachts. From what I'd read, him being here was a demotion of epic proportions. If he wasn't such a jerk, I'd ask him.

Opening my book, I started reading up on the next bloodline.

The Death Bloods.

Shadow's family served as the monarchs, with Aswad as the current king. Their powers were linked to necromancy and the harsher sides of dark magic. It seemed they also maintained access to the source, but in a much different way, through the art of—

A crash inside the suite jolted me upright and off the bed.

The sound of feminine laughter followed.

I frowned. Zephyrus had mentioned that students would be moving back in today. Something about a bonfire kickoff later tonight. Apparently, it was the thing to do. I'd considered using the massive distraction on campus as a potential time to escape, but I had nowhere to go.

The fact that Claire hadn't reached out to me yet confirmed the Elemental Fae Council's fear in having me return. Given what recently happened in that realm, I understood. The last notion they would want to entertain at the moment was a potential hybrid Elemental-Midnight Fae.

Except I didn't feel any different.

Other than the fact that I couldn't access my earth.

I really hoped Sol and Claire were holding the source together in my absence. They were the only others in existence who could access earth magic in a similar way to me. Their connections weren't as strong as mine but should be enough to help the Earth Fae maintain their powers.

Blowing out a breath, I started reading again, when male voices trickled down the hallway.

Kolstov, I thought, recognizing the deep tone.

A knock sounded at my door, followed by, "That's my five-second warning, princess. Try not to be naked again."

I glowered at the door. "Dick," I muttered, putting my book off to the side and standing just as he followed through on his five-second promise.

105

His bright gold irises slid over my shirt and jeans, amusement shining in his depths. "I'm almost disappointed to find you clothed."

Uh-huh. "Well, I *am* disappointed that you're back," I returned, adding a saccharine smile at the end.

He chuckled. "Yeah, I missed you too, sweetheart."

I rolled my eyes. "I bet."

"Stop flirting and introduce us." The smooth voice came from the hallway just as a male joined Kolstov in the doorway. I recognized him from my textbook.

"Trayton Nacht," I said. "Huh. So the photos really do update in real time." I'd wondered that when the images kept shifting around last night, some sort of magic allowing them to update with each passing moment.

"Have you been studying already?" Kolstov asked, a teasing note to his voice. "I suppose you did have a lot to catch up on."

Not this again. "Yeah, I've had some time in solitary this week to read, and since my wand doesn't work, I decided to study the different bloodlines instead."

He leaned against my doorway, arching a haughty brow. "Learn anything interesting?"

"Yeah, the Death Bloods have more intriguing powers than the Elite Bloods." I'd read in the texts that the two types of Midnight Fae had been at war for centuries, and Kolstov's darkening expression confirmed it.

Score one for Aflora, I thought, smirking inside.

"I suppose you're obligated to say that as the illegally chosen mate of the future Death Blood Monarch. Pity you couldn't have been claimed by a worthier bloodline."

And Kolstov evens the match by volleying an equally hurtful statement back at Aflora, my mental voice added, killing my inner victory lap. "Like yours?" I countered. "No, thanks."

"Don't knock it 'til you try it, baby," he drawled.

Trayton shook his head. "Stop flirting with our new roommate."

"That's like telling Kols to stop breathing." A petite

female popped up at Trayton's side, her white-blonde head barely clearing his shoulder. Her bright blue eyes met mine. "I'm Ella. Let me know if these two assholes are bothering you, and I'll set them straight."

Trayton gave her an indulgent grin as he wrapped his arm around her waist. "Yeah? Tell me how you plan to do that."

"Now who's flirting?" Kolstov put in.

"Oh, I'm not flirting." Trayton faced Ella and started to back her up against a wall. "We're way past our flirting stage."

Ella snorted as she grabbed his lean hips. "Always so romantic."

"You love me anyway."

"Do I?" She tapped her chin thoughtfully. "Sometimes I don't know why."

"And you chose the room beside theirs," Kolstov murmured to me, having entered my space. He glanced around with a curious gaze. "It's boring as fuck in here."

"I'm sorry. Was I supposed to decorate?" I asked, batting my eyes. "Because I missed that memo."

He pulled out his wand. "Allow me to help."

I grabbed his wrist before he could wave it around. "No. I don't plan to stay long."

"Yeah?" He stared down at me with those piercing irises, causing my breath to catch in my throat.

Why were all the Midnight Fae so good-looking? Even his brother was a sight to behold.

"Where do you plan on going?" Kolstov asked softly, taking a step closer.

I didn't release his wrist, even though I probably should have. But his nearness had me frozen before him. His rich, masculine scent swathing me in a cloud of intoxicating male.

"I…" I trailed off, my throat constricting tightly.

His gaze dropped to my lips. I licked them on impulse, my mouth going dry. Something about Kolstov called to my inner fae. His power was a worthy mate to my earth essence, only because we both possessed royal bloodlines. I'd felt it when our energy danced in the living area a few days ago.

But he wasn't an Elemental Fae and therefore not truly an ideal match.

Even if my instincts said otherwise.

"Hmm, I think you do want a taste," Kolstov whispered, his free hand going to my hip. "If you're good, maybe I'll allow—"

"Why is my new suite next to yours?" Zephyrus demanded from the doorway. "The whole purpose of this new assignment, according to your father, is to provide students with my superior knowledge. Students, being Warrior Bloods, not Elite Bloods."

Kolstov released me, his wrist easily leaving my grasp as he spun around, giving me his back. "We both know it's a temporary assignment."

"My living next to you? Or my playing the role of teacher?" The bitterness in Zephyrus's tone matched his expression.

"The latter."

"Right. Because you plan to fix it when you become king."

"Are we really going to have this argument again?" Kolstov suddenly sounded tired. "Come on, Zeph. You know why this happened."

The headmaster's eyes narrowed for a long moment before he turned and left without another word.

Kolstov sighed, following him. "You can keep punishing me all you want. It won't stop me from—"

"Don't," Zephyrus interjected. "Just. *Don't.*"

"Then stop being a dick" was the reply.

"Fuck you."

A crashing sound made me jump. I poked my head around the door just in time to see Trayton leaving a freshly kissed Ella behind in the hallway. She blinked after him, then glanced at me. "Welcome to the Nacht family drama. Never a dull moment."

Sounds of a scuffle came from the living room, which suggested the guys were fighting. An image of Zephyrus pinning Kolstov entered my mind, provoked by the first time I'd seen them together.

Zephyrus struck me as the stronger of the two, but I'd tasted a glimpse of Kolstov's power, and yeah, they were definitely evenly matched.

"Don't worry. Tray will make sure they don't destroy anything too valuable," Ella said, moving past me into the room. She glanced around, much like Kolstov had. "Boring maybe, but I get it. You don't want to be here. Shade's a fucking prick for biting you."

My lips twitched. *Finally, someone who gets it.*

She faced me, adding, "My mate at least introduced me to the Midnight Fae realm before biting me."

"Introduced you?" I repeated, her statement confusing me. "You mean you weren't born here?"

"I'm a Halfling," she informed me, then paused as if waiting for a reaction.

"So you grew up in the Human Realm." It was a guess based on her earlier claim about entering the realm.

"I did." The challenge in her tone confused me.

"Did you know you were part fae?"

"No, not until Tray told me."

My eyebrows rose. "Well, that must have been quite a shock."

"Yeah, I imagine it's similar to being bitten against your will and forced to attend an Academy in another realm." She glanced at the book on my bed and smirked. "Ah, the Midnight Fae factions. What chapter are you on?"

"I just started reading about the Death Bloods."

She nodded. "Want a crash course in the bloodlines? It'll be faster than reading that boring thing."

"You're offering to teach me?" I shook my head at how stupid that sounded out loud. "Sorry, the others haven't been very… helpful." Technically, Zephyrus had tried a little. And Kolstov, well, he was just being a pompous ass about me not studying Midnight Fae kind while growing up.

Ella snorted and collapsed onto the edge of my bed. "Kolstov's a bit preoccupied with his future, and Zephyrus is, uh, not teacher material."

"Yet he's a headmaster."

"Yeah, he's going to make our lives hell this year," Ella muttered. "Anyway, enough about that. What you need is a quick overview, something I'm very equipped to provide considering I had to learn all this myself recently." She patted the bed beside her. "I promise I don't bite. All my blood intake is through food."

I gaped at her, the comment so tongue in cheek that it took me off guard.

Which caused her to laugh. "Your expression is priceless and probably similar to mine when Tray first told me about Midnight Fae drinking blood. Oh, but that reminds me. Lesson number one: Don't call them vampires. They hate that."

"Yeah, Kolstov may have mentioned that after I called him a bloodsucker."

Her lips twitched. "Bet he loved that."

"Not so much."

She laughed. "Well, don't let him bother you. He's a womanizing jackass, but deep down, he has a heart. You just have to really dig to find it."

I finally joined her on the bed, feeling somewhat at ease for the first time in almost a week. Something about Ella relaxed me. Maybe it was her calm demeanor or, more likely, her frank assessments. I enjoyed her candor and her politeness.

She didn't judge me for not knowing everything about the Midnight Fae.

And I appreciated it more than she could know.

"Okay, so let me break this down for you," she said,

tucking one leg underneath her while the other bounced off the side of the bed. "There are five main bloodlines. You know the names?"

I nodded. "Death Bloods, Elite Bloods, Sangré Bloods, Warrior Bloods, and Malefic Bloods."

"Do you know what they do?"

"I've only read that Elite Bloods maintain the central source of dark magic and Death Bloods access the harshest resources from a different entry point. They prefer lethal magic and dabble in necromancy." I picked up the book. "One thing I don't really get is how they access the source indirectly. That was the part I was reading when you all arrived."

Ella picked up the book and tossed it to the side. "Yeah, no. Trust me, you want the verbal lesson, not the text one. All bloodlines access dark-magic sources, but the Elites have the most access, which is why they're considered royalty. They're the strongest. All those black lines pulsating on Kols's neck and arms, leading to his heart? Yeah, that's the source transferring reign to him one stroke of power at a time. Scary shit, if you ask me."

I had noticed the writhing inky vines along his neck and hands but didn't realize they stretched up his arms. "Is it permanent?" I wondered out loud.

"No. Apparently, it disappears after he ascends." She shrugged. "I guess we'll see. Anyway, the Death Bloods access the darkest sections of the source. They literally thrive on Death Magic. So, like necromancy, as you said. It's rumored they're just as powerful as the Elite Bloods, which explains why Malik and Aswad hate each other."

The two reigning monarchs, I thought, recognizing the names.

"Then there are the Warrior Bloods, like Zeph, who specialize in defensive magic. They're usually carved out of stone in the sense that they are all hard lines, muscular, athletic, and stoic as fuck. So if Zeph was a dick this week, don't take it personally. They're all like that. And he's particularly moody after having been removed from Kols's personal guard. The whole headmaster position is a demotion of sorts."

"And why did that happen?" I asked.

Ella's lips twisted to the side. "Uh, so, Kols and Zeph... they like to share women. And let's just say, they shared the wrong one. Things went to hell from there."

"They both fell in love with her?" I guessed.

Ella laughed loudly and shook her head. "Oh, God no. Nothing like that. Kols? Love? That's like a bad joke." She shook her head, her shoulders vibrating from suppressed laughter. "But yeah, nothing like that. Anyway, the Sangré Bloods are next. Their power lies in intelligence. They're pretty much wizards when it comes to playing chess." She pointed to the collar around my neck. "That was developed by a Sangré Blood. I can tell by the power swirling around it."

Her not-so-subtle change of subject back to our lesson left me curious about the truth between Zephyrus and Kolstov, but I allowed her to continue.

"So the Sangré Bloods are highly intellectual," I inferred.

"Yep. You'll be able to identify them by their bald heads. They draw these patterns on their skin, and the more intense the design, the more powerful the fae. It's sort of their way of showing off, or that's the way I see it, anyway. The Warrior Bloods wear their muscles and scars, the Sangré Bloods paint beautiful patterns on their heads, the Elite Bloods dress in expensive jewels and robes, and the Death Bloods love their skull shit."

"Sounds... charming."

She scoffed. "Yeah. Shade is the lead asshat on campus, but trust me, the rest of them are just as dark as he is."

"Great. I can't wait," I deadpanned.

Her lips curled. "I like you. As much as I know you don't want to stay, I'm looking forward to having your around for a bit. You can help me keep Tray and Kols in line."

"Yeah, I doubt they'll listen to me at all."

"Oh, I'll teach you my ways," Ella promised. "You'll see. We can tame them together."

I doubted that but smiled anyway. "So what about the Malefic Bloods?"

"Ah, yes, the final of the five. The Malefic Bloods specialize in offensive magic. They're like the polar opposite of the Warrior Bloods. The latter defends, the former prefers spells that create damage. When I first learned all this, I called them the malicious ones, to help remember that their magic is dangerous and often intentionally cruel."

Right. Avoid that sect of Midnight Fae, I noted to myself. "Is there a way to tell them all apart? I mean, the Sangré Bloods will be obvious, from what you've said. What about the others?"

Her blue eyes captured mine, a grin forming in their depths. "Actually, how about we continue this lesson tonight during the bonfire. That way, I can show you more than tell you."

"Zephyrus mentioned the bonfire."

"Yeah, it's an annual tradition," she replied, bouncing off my bed. "It's actually pretty fun. But a word of advice? Don't drink the beezlepunch. You'll regret it." She started toward the door. "I'm going to make some sandwiches if you want any. I'm sure the idiots will be starved from throwing all that magic around. Feel free to join us whenever you're ready."

AFLORA

I DIDN'T JOIN ELLA for sandwiches but did agree to follow her down to the bonfire with Trayton. Kolstov and Zephyrus had disappeared, whether together or apart, I wasn't sure. I also didn't care.

Or that was what I kept telling myself.

I *shouldn't* care.

They were just two hot fae handling their own problems. It had nothing to do with me. My curiosity as to what the hell happened between them paled in comparison to my need to survive this new world.

Yet, a part of me kept hearing Ella's casual statement about how the two men used to share women.

It wasn't uncommon in the Elemental Fae realm for us to mate more than once, especially when a fae had access to multiple elements. Our new queen had access to all five elements and therefore required five mates to satisfy her ever-growing power. Yet, that wasn't what Ella had meant.

She'd implied they shared women for pleasure.

And now I wondered what that entailed. Because being sandwiched between those two beautiful, fierce males? Yeah, that painted a pretty hot picture.

One I quickly doused water on because it would never happen.

At least, not outside my head.

Because in my head, it was definitely already happening.

And I really, really needed it to stop so I could properly focus on whatever Ella was saying beside me. Something about the bloodline colors.

Despite everyone wearing casual clothes, they all seemed to be dressed in similar shades.

"The Malefic Bloods wear solid black all the time. They never wear color," she said, nodding toward a group of Midnight Fae socializing on one side of the bonfire.

"Because we're at the Academy?" I wondered out loud. I'd opted for one of the Academy-regulated black skirts and a plain white button-down top. Nothing too fancy, but appropriate for the school grounds. Ella had chosen jeans and a tank top. Most of the others were in their cloaks, the females in skirts, the guys in slacks.

Except for the Elite Bloods. They all seemed to be showing off their fashion sense with a variety of different colors. I'd recognized them almost immediately because of the power swirling around them—it reminded me of Kolstov.

"No. They wear black everywhere regardless of the event or occasion. It's their signature color." She shrugged. "All the bloodlines have one. Death Bloods are purple. Sangré Bloods are navy. Warrior Bloods prefer a deep green, like the color of the LethaForest that surrounds our campus. Elite Bloods wear dark red. And Malefic Bloods…" She nodded toward the same group, finishing her statement.

115

Wear black, I translated. "What's a LethaForest?" I asked, glancing around the open meadow and searching for trees. We weren't near the campus buildings anymore, but we weren't in a woodsy area either.

"Beyond the walls," she explained. "We're still in Academy proper. But if you go past the gargoyle-guarded gates, you'll quickly find the LethaForest. Don't go in there alone. There's a bunch of scary shit that lives in there, and it's filled with wild thwomps." She shivered with the statement, something that caused Trayton's lips to curl down as he approached with two glasses of some sort of drink.

He handed her one. "Are you okay?"

"Just warning Aflora about the LethaForest."

His frown disappeared into a knowing grin as he held out the other cup for me. I accepted it with a softly uttered "Thanks."

"You're welcome. And yeah, Ella isn't a fan of things that go bump in the night. When I mated her, I didn't realize she was afraid of phantoms. Had I known…" He let that hang, and Ella elbowed him in the side.

"Shut it. You grew up in this world. I didn't. And those *phantoms* are freaky as fuck."

He lifted a shoulder. "That's why I don't go near them."

"Yeah, yeah. I'm never going to live that down, am I?"

"Nope."

She rolled her eyes, refocusing on me. "I may have gone exploring my first year here. And I may have found myself surrounded by ghostly knights with swords that weren't corporeal, but very real. They were not happy with me for disturbing their nest, or whatever they called it."

"Haven," Trayton corrected. "You totally slept through our Wild Creepers course last year, didn't you?"

"No. But your world is full of so many make-believe critters that it's hard to keep them all straight."

"Uh-huh. I think—"

I dropped my cup as Shade appeared across the way, flanked by two male Midnight Fae. His gaze instantly met mine, his icy blue eyes smoldering from the embers of the flames separating us.

"Grr, I have things to say to you," I growled, mostly to myself since Shade couldn't hear me yet.

"What?" Ella's forehead creased.

Trayton bent to pick up my glass, the contents all over the obsidian grass below. I couldn't even take a moment to consider how improper that color was for *greenery*. "Aflora?" he prompted, arching a brow.

I could see the pair watching me from my peripheral vision, their expressions ones of matching confusion. Until Trayton followed my stare. "Oh."

Yeah. Oh. "Hold my flowers," I said, taking off toward my now smirking Midnight Fae *mate*.

"Hold her flowers?" I overheard Ella repeat behind me. "Is that supposed to be like holding a beer?"

"Maybe?" Trayton replied.

I ignored them.

My colloquialisms clearly didn't belong in this realm. Just as I didn't. But nothing could be done about that now.

Except maybe kick the tulip arse of the Midnight Fae who had forced me into this situation.

He watched my approach, amusement dancing in his features. "Hello, gorgeous."

His expression and words infuriated me so much that I couldn't stop my fist from landing right in his face.

A hush fell over the air around us, shock displayed on the faces of those flanking Shade. I didn't care. I wound up my fist, ready to hit him again, only to find my wrist caught in his hand.

His smirk died behind a mask of annoyance as he used his grip on my wrist to yank me into his hard body. "It seems you need a lesson on how to properly greet an old friend."

"Old friend?" I huffed a laugh. "Yeah, you're certainly

not that."

My knee angled upward, aiming for his groin.

But I hit his thigh instead.

His eyes narrowed threateningly. "Who taught you how to fight? A flower?"

He whirled me around in a cloud of smoke that clogged my lungs and blinded my vision. I spun, searching for freedom, only to find my back pressed against something hard. Squirming, I tried to escape, but another wall hit my front, two strong palms grasping my hips and holding me in place.

"Let me go!" I demanded.

"Too late for that, princess," he replied, his lips against my ear. "You're already mine."

I grasped his shoulders—confirming Shade was the wall in front of me—and tried to use the surface at my back for leverage to shove him away.

But he remained immobile, his strength overpowering mine far too easily.

A whimper caught in my throat. He'd ensnared me in less than a minute, capturing me in this thick, smoky blanket. "Don't you dare bite me again," I snapped, feeling utterly helpless and infuriated at the same time.

"You came at me, baby," he whispered menacingly. "What kind of mate would I be if I didn't punish you properly, hmm?"

"I'm already being punished, you willow stump!"

He chuckled, shaking his head against my neck. "Darling Aflora, we really do need to improve your vocabulary." He kissed my racing pulse, sending a shiver down my spine that seemed to settle in my lower belly.

No, not a shiver.

A tremble.

One that ignited a subtle quake inside that terrified me even more.

Because it meant some sick and twisted part of me enjoyed his touch.

I squeezed my eyes shut, forcing that sensation to subside. *No. No. No.*

His teeth grazed my skin, stirring goose bumps down my arms. "Please don't," I begged, my nails digging into his cloak.

If he bit me again, it would deepen the bond. Kolstov said Shade had only initiated the bond and a second bite would seal it. Then a third… I shuddered, unable to finish the consideration because I couldn't allow that to happen.

Or any of it.

I needed to stop him.

To fight.

To *escape.*

He murmured something that I didn't hear beneath the chaos rattling around inside me. The noose around my neck kept me from accessing my earth essence. But somewhere within, there was a link to dark magic— because of Shade. I just needed to use it against him.

Pushing away from reality and ignoring the shadowy smog cloaking my vision, I searched deep in my mind for some sort of link. Anything that didn't belong. Anything that I could *use.*

His tongue danced up the column of my throat, his touch temporarily drawing me back to the hands on my hips and the growing arousal pressing into my lower abdomen.

The flame inside me inched higher, yearning to dance with him in an intimate way that neither of us could afford. It had to be the bond. This compulsion to give in to him sexually and do whatever he requested.

I clenched my jaw, refusing to cave.

I'm stronger than this.

Don't let his mind tricks overwhelm you.

Focus.

With a deep breath, I dove back into my mind, frantically searching for a path to follow that would lead me out of this complication. Because giving in to him and these indecent urges wasn't an option.

Tying myself to him more would harm us both.

Not that he seemed to care.

"I don't want to hurt you, Aflora," Shade murmured. "I know I have, but it was never my intent."

"Lie," I choked out, torn between what he was doing and saying and my desire to fight.

"No, darling. I've never lied to you, nor will I ever lie to you." He kissed my jaw, working his way to my mouth. "You can hate me—and you should—but I promise there's a reason."

"What reason?"

"Fate," he replied cryptically before sealing his lips over my mine.

I refused to open for him.

Refused to kiss him back.

Refused to fall into this lustful trap.

He made no sense. Had ruined my life. Wouldn't give me any details on what he wanted. And now had me trapped against some tree or wall, surrounded by a thick essence I couldn't see through. Were we still at the bonfire? Or somewhere else entirely? He seemed to be able to teleport, in addition to controlling my mind. What else could he do?

Heck, was this even real?

I'd dreamt of him almost every night this week, waking up in a variety of orgasmic states, all brought on by his mouth and hands. Were the dreams a response to his bite? Or was he manipulating me?

I hated that I didn't know.

Hated more that I didn't know how to stop him.

His tongue danced along the seam of my mouth, requesting entrance.

I denied him.

His grip on my hips tightened, causing me to wince. I grabbed his neck and dug my nails into his scalp in response, needing to harm him in some way.

Yet all it did was make him smile against my lips. "I love that you're not giving in," he admitted softly. "Proves you were the right choice all along. An easy mate would bore me significantly."

"I'm an *unwilling* mate," I snapped. "You ra—"

He took advantage of my retort, sliding his tongue into my mouth and stealing my breath away. I nearly bit down, then remembered what that did in my dreams. His blood made me crazy with lust.

No.

Allowing his kiss made more sense.

Only, I didn't want any of this, even if my body seemed to crave his touch.

I returned to my inner search, navigating the complex webs of my mental state for anything out of place. When I found nothing, I dove into my soul, desperately seeking out my link to earth.

So dark.

Black.

Wrong.

Wait, what's that? A glint of cerulean blue light caught my focus, drawing me nearer. It blended into the inky abyss but began to glitter as I approached. Tugging on the thread, I followed it into the deep recesses of my spirit.

A chill slithered over me, followed by a wave of warmth as Shade deepened our embrace. For as much as I hated him, I had to admit the male knew how to work his tongue. I couldn't help responding, my body arching into his as if being pulled upward by a string.

"I hate you," I muttered against his mouth.

"You've said that before," he acknowledged. "And I've admitted to hating myself for what I've had to do to you."

"Yet you won't tell me why."

"Because I can't." He recaptured my lips, silencing our conversation, and drew his palms up my sides as if memorizing my body for the first time. And maybe he was. I really had no way of knowing if he visited my dreams or if they were all in my mind.

I couldn't even tell if this was real or not.

The glimmer of cerulean drew me deeper, dividing my focus between Shade's touch and the mysterious puzzle unfolding inside my soul. Something was unraveling, a lock of sorts that I seemed to be distorting with this odd wisp of beautiful blue.

"I can feel that," Shade whispered. "Whatever it is you're doing."

I ignored him.

He couldn't possibly be this deep into my soul.

Dancing in the darkest recesses of my being.

"We're mates," he added. "My bite sealed us together for eternity. The sooner you accept that, the better."

"I'm not a Midnight Fae," I replied, irritated all over again.

"Are you sure about that?" he countered, causing me to blink up at him.

The smoke had dissipated, allowing me to catch his azure irises. *I am pressed up against a tree*, I thought, finally able to see my surroundings.

We weren't anywhere near the bonfire.

So either he'd teleported us or I was lost in a dream state again.

"Release me, Shadow."

"I can't."

"That seems to be your favorite phrase," I replied coldly. "You can't tell me why you bit me. You can't release me. You can't explain—"

"You talk too much." He kissed me again, causing me to growl in frustration.

The cerulean rope in my mind tightened suddenly, causing me to stiffen just before a wave of power rippled across my skin. Shade flew backward, landing on his ass a few feet away, his eyes wide in shock.

And the tree behind me withered to dust.

I gaped at the bright blue flames dancing along my

palms, then shivered as they disappeared.

"What the fuck was that?" a sharp male voice demanded.

"Her power awakening" was the drawled reply.

I spun around to find Kolstov glaring at me and Zephyrus leaning against another tree. "I didn't mean to do that," I said, a note of pleading in my voice. "I just wanted Shade to release me."

"Well, it worked." Zephyrus seemed amused.

Kolstov definitely did not share that opinion.

Neither, it seemed, did Shade as he shoved off the ground to stand at my side. "Touch her, and I'll fucking destroy you."

I blinked, surprised by the protective quality in Shade's tone. He'd just been taunting me moments ago, refusing to explain anything and kissing me without my permission. Now he wanted to stand up for me? How ridiculous.

"I'd love to see you try," Kolstov replied, folding his arms. "You're handicapped and alone."

Shade lifted his arms, revealing the leather cuffs against his wrists. "Oh, you mean these?" The bands disappeared a second later. "Yeah, I deactivated those almost as soon as Chern put them on. But thanks for the accessory."

Energy rippled around Kolstov, his expression thunderous. "Do you have a death wish, Death Blood?"

"Is that meant to be some sort of oxymoron?" Shade asked conversationally. "Because you'll have to be more direct. I skipped a lot of my language courses throughout the years. Well, those and other classes."

"Your arrogance is going to get you killed."

Shade grinned. "Is it? Good to know."

"Can someone tell me what just happened?" I asked, interrupting their little testosterone-filled fight. "Why did I turn blue?" The fire had since dissipated, but I felt it roaming through my veins, waiting for me to call upon it again.

"Blue?" Kolstov repeated. "I saw purple."

Zephyrus frowned. "It was red to me."

The two males shared a glance as Shade looked down at me. "Blue?" he asked softly, his tone different from the one he'd used with the other males.

"Yeah. Bright blue."

"Like a lighter shade?"

I nodded.

"Interesting," he mused, glancing back at Kolstov. "Are we going to have a problem here?"

"We already have one," the prince replied on a snarl. "You bit her against her will."

"Is that what she said?" he returned, sounding far too entertained. "Well, she might be right. But our laws still make her mine. Fascinating how that works, yes?" His smile was cruel. "It is your family who stands behind those archaic politics, Kolstov. Can't go breaking the rules now, can we?"

Kolstov appeared ready to murder Shade.

But his words were rolling around in my thoughts.

Kolstov's family allows the males to claim females in the manner Shade did? Without reprimand? Why?

"Elemental Fae choose their mates," I said out loud. "It's a much better practice. And I will choose mine."

Shade chuckled, his expression indulgent. "An adorable thought, but impractical in our world. You already belong to me, Aflora."

"I don't belong to anyone."

He grabbed the back of my neck, pulling me to him. "Keep denying it, baby. That makes our dance so much more fun." He pressed a quick kiss to my lips before releasing me and refocusing on Kolstov. "So I'll ask again. Are we going to have a problem here? Because she's mine and I protect what's mine."

"I don't need you to protect me," I corrected him. "I've survived a lot worse than this, and I'll continue to survive, thank you very much."

He ignored me.

As did Kolstov.

Some sort of strange conversation happening between the two males.

"It was a minor explosion of power," Kolstov said after a beat. "She's safe from reprimand."

"Good." Shade's shoulders seemed to relax a fraction, suggesting he'd been tenser than I realized.

"Why would I be reprimanded for protecting myself?" I asked, confused.

"In a normal situation, you wouldn't be. But nothing about your circumstances is normal. Any and all signs of you morphing into an abomination will be considered and taken into account by the Council." Kolstov arched a brow at me. "I don't think I need to tell you what will happen should they decide you've grown too powerful as a result of this mating."

I swallowed. *Oh.*

"Well, this has been fun," Shade interjected. "Aflora and I will be going now."

Wait, wh—

"No." Zephyrus finally pushed off the tree, his expression still bored yet somehow holding an edge. "I'll escort her back to the Elites, as she's under my protection."

"Yeah? And who protects her from Kolstov should he decide to make a regal decision in regard to her life?" Shade countered.

"Perhaps that's something you should have considered before you jeopardized her life for your own selfish need," Zephyrus returned, avoiding the question. "Let's go, Aflora."

I stared at all three of them and shook my head. "Yeah, no. I'm good. I'll just escort myself, thank you."

I turned on my heel, heading toward, uh, darkness. Then spun around again, only to find another thick layer of ink painting my vision. Not because Shade was messing with my mind, but because he'd taken us somewhere without a lot of light.

When I turned around, it was to find three pairs of amused gazes.

"Lost, sweetheart?" Kolstov prompted.

My jaw clenched. "Just point me in the right direction." As soon as I said it, I realized the error in my words.

Even if they gestured a certain way, I couldn't trust them to tell me the truth. With my luck, I'd end up in that LethaForest Ella mentioned earlier. Or somewhere worse.

Gritting my teeth, I caved and refocused on Zephyrus. "Fine. Escort me back."

His lips actually twitched as if he approved of my downfall.

Dick.

"This way, *princess*," he said, gesturing to the path behind him.

I didn't reply or look at the other males as I followed the headmaster in silence.

Maybe Shade and Kolstov would kill each other in my absence.

One can only dream, I thought. Then grimaced at the realization that everything Shade had done to me tonight had been real.

And with my luck, he'd probably go much further as soon as I closed my eyes.

"This world stinks," I grumbled to myself.

"Sucks," Zephyrus corrected. "Or you could say it's shit."

"What?"

"Consider it a vocabulary lesson," he tossed over his shoulder. "I am a headmaster, after all."

I rolled my eyes. "Yeah, you're a brilliant teacher."

For a brief second, he almost appeared entertained by my jibe.

But it disappeared a second later behind his usual expression of stoicism.

"Do me a favor, Aflora. Try not to explode in class

tomorrow. Another display of power like that could be your death sentence."

With that, he led me back to Kolstov's suite without another word.

Ten minutes later, he left me in the living area, and I felt even more alone than I had every night this week.

Because his words had served as a not-so-subtle warning, one that told me my life was very much in danger here. Something I already knew, but the reality still stung.

How could I control a power I knew nothing about?

And worse, what if I couldn't control it at all?

KOLS

"DID SHE WONDER HOW WE FOUND HER?" I asked as I entered Zeph's suite without knocking. His gargoyle hadn't batted an eye, which told me I was welcome.

Zeph confirmed it by entering the living area with two bottles of beer, one of which he tossed to me. I caught it by the neck.

"Aflora was too consumed by her explosion of power to ask questions," he replied, collapsing into one of the room's recliners. "If she thinks about it later, she'll probably assume we followed her from the bonfire."

That wouldn't necessarily be too far from the truth. When her locator jumped positions, I knew something had happened. Tray's text message confirmed it when he said Shade had used a smoke spell to remove her from the bonfire. The bastard clearly didn't know how to abide by any rules. Not only had he removed his cuffs—something he should not have been able to do—but he'd also interacted with Aflora after being expressly told to leave her alone.

"I should report him," I said out loud, referring to Shade.

Zeph popped the cap off his beer and took a long swig, his throat working with each swallow. "Wouldn't do much."

Leaning against the wall a few feet away from his chair, I sighed, "I know." If I reported Shade, they might expel him. Then he'd just lurk around the shadowy edges of campus anyway. "What game is he playing with her?"

Zeph set his bottle off to the side, his expression thoughtful. I'd almost forgotten about this side of him, what with all the animosity he'd thrown my way these last few months. Part of me hoped our earlier brawl meant we were finally moving forward. The other part of me knew better.

Things between us would never be the same.

"You really saw purple flames?" He glanced at me.

"Yeah, the kind I'd expect from a Death Blood." They were vibrant and violet flared.

"Well, I saw red, like the kind of flames you create."

We frowned at each other. "And she called them bright blue," I added. "Which is impossible. No Midnight Fae burn bright blue."

"Maybe she meant navy, like the Sangré Bloods?"

"How the fuck would that even be possible?"

"No idea. But she's not exactly normal. Could it be an influence from her elemental power?" Zeph suggested.

I flicked the top off my bottle and took a long sip while considering that. Then slowly shook my head. "She's an Earth Fae, not a Fire Fae. The flames are tied to her awakening connection to dark magic."

"Suggesting her mating bond with Shade is indeed turning her into an abomination," Zeph pointed out.

We both fell silent, me drinking my beer, Zeph swirling

his around on the table in that thoughtful way of his.

"Fuck, this isn't good," I finally said. "This isn't good at all."

"Are you going to report it?"

I nodded. Then I shook my head. "I don't know what the hell I'm going to do. It might still be temporary. Maybe she expelled what little power she has inside her and now she'll go back to normal." I heard the lie in my words, saw the confirmation of it written in Zeph's features.

"It's not like you to play the naïve card, Kols."

Kols. Not Prince Kolstov or Kolstov, but Kols. He hadn't used my preferred name in months. I swallowed another sip to keep myself from commenting on it or allowing him to see the glimmer of hope that small word provided.

We might not be able to go back, but I wasn't opposed to moving forward.

Zeph was the one who cut off all ties.

Not me.

"I know you want to fuck her, just like you do every other hot, unattainable female to cross your path," he added, destroying the moment. "But that shouldn't hold you back from doing what you have to do. Just do the deed and end her afterward."

Such a cruel approach. Although, I knew he didn't mean it that way. Not completely, anyway. Zeph thrived on logic. And to him, feeding the lust before completing the task struck him as practical.

Except nothing about this assignment was practical.

"I can't just kill the last remaining Earth Fae Royal," I reminded him. "And maybe my approach is naïve, but I need to hope this power mingling will just go away."

"Wrong. What you need to do is prepare for the inevitable. Her power is growing. I've been watching her all week, and she's not growing weaker. She's growing stronger. Almost as if Shade's bite flipped a switch inside her. Something's not right, and her little power display tonight proves it."

He picked up his bottle and finished it off in a few deep gulps. Then he waved his hand over the glass, refilling it with a muttered spell.

I pulled up my phone, checking the app linked to Aflora's tracker, and noted her presence next door. She hadn't tried to run yet, which actually made me admire her a bit. It implied that she put her people before herself. To return in her current state would thwart the balance. She also wouldn't be safe there given that the Elemental Fae recently took down an insane abomination. They wouldn't be all that accepting of her return.

So maybe it wasn't so much that she put her people first as it was her survival instinct kicking in.

Regardless, the intelligence in her decision to stay boosted her appeal in my eyes. Which was exactly the wrong response overall because I could not—and should not—entertain the possibility of fucking Aflora.

She was a forbidden fruit.

Off-limits.

As Zeph already said, *unattainable*.

Yet I couldn't deny the urge to kiss her earlier. I'd also enjoy sticking one to Shade in the process. The asshole had disappeared into a cloud of smoke before I could give him a piece of my mind. However, I felt his residual presence all the way back to my building, suggesting he'd followed Aflora.

"He seems to care about her," I mused out loud.

"Who?"

"Shade," I clarified. "He traced after you and Aflora to the Elite Residence."

Zeph considered for a second, then lifted a shoulder. "I think he cares more about the bond than he does her. If something happens to her, he'll be the one living in pain for eternity."

"Probably should have thought about that before biting her," I grumbled.

"True, but I think there's a bigger scheme behind it all." Zeph set his mostly full bottle down and braced his arms on his thighs. "Shade's a dick, don't get me wrong, but that fucker doesn't do anything without a reason."

"I don't know. He seems to do things all the time just to piss everyone else off," I muttered in reply. "That's part of what makes him such an ass."

"Yeah, but those are small irritants. Taking an Elemental Fae mate—specifically, Aflora—is a catastrophic decision for him and her. Why would he do such a thing? It has to be more than just wanting to piss off his father, or your father, or the Council. He's up to something."

Which brings us full circle, I thought, recalling the way our conversation began about what game Shade was playing and why. "Something tells me we won't know until his plan unfolds."

"Which is precisely why I suggest you say nothing and observe. Let's see what he does with her."

"You want to use the Royal Elemental Fae as bait?"

He flipped his hands, palms up. "Shade signed her death warrant the second he bit her, and we both know it. This whole observation game is just for the paperwork so they can validate killing her. We might as well figure out what the hell Shade is up to in the process and make use of what little remains of her life."

I released a humorless laugh, his words a repeated punch to the gut. "You're a cold son of a bitch. You know that, right?"

"I'm thinking defensively. It's what I do."

"Yeah, and while you're great at it, could you for a moment try to remember that she's a person, not a pawn?" *Technically, she's a future queen*, I corrected myself. *Much more important than a pawn.*

"Shade put her in this mess, not me. I could choose to pity her, or I could choose to use her to ensure he never pulls that shit again. I vote for the latter. You should, too."

"It's not black and white, Zeph."

"Why? Because you want to fuck her? Just get your dick wet, sate the need, and move on. It's what you do best."

My jaw ticked at the barbed insult. "Right, and you're not at all interested in fucking her?" I knew he was, because I'd caught the flare of intrigue in his gaze while looking at her. Oh, he hid it well, but I knew him better than he gave me credit for. A few months apart would never change that.

Besides, we both had a type, and Aflora checked all our boxes in spades. She also posed one of the biggest challenges I'd ever encountered, mostly because flirting with her was akin to flirting with death. One wrong move and we'd end up on the chopping block right beside her. Which only made her more alluring as a prospect since it added the element of true danger.

"We're not talking about this," Zeph said, his voice deepening.

My lips quirked up. "You're right. We don't need to. I already know you want her. And you brought it up—twice—not me. I'm just throwing the ball back in your court. If you want to share her, just say the words."

"Stop."

"Why? Because I'll push your limits?" I taunted. "Because the whole headmaster role adds yet another element of the forbidden to an already intriguing situation?"

His green irises swirled with embers. I'd either just royally pissed him off or turned him the fuck on. Probably both.

Zeph enjoyed harsh sex.

Anger was his aphrodisiac.

Fighting served as foreplay.

And we'd fought a lot these last few months, both mentally and physically.

Our earlier quarrel still simmered between us. He'd gotten in a few good hits, but so had I, and it'd left us both infuriated and a little bruised on the inside. Hence, I'd opted to avoid the bonfire. But the alert on my phone, activated by Aflora's collar, had sent me to Zeph's door. Then Tray's text had forced us both outside.

Now Zeph and I were alone again.

Two decades of experience hanging between us.

Five years of that spent between the sheets with multiple women and occasionally just each other.

I didn't date or do girlfriends. Yet Zeph had always been my one constant.

Until six months ago when we seduced the wrong chick. She'd used the sexual distraction to try to take advantage of me and my power, and she'd caused a lot of damage in the process.

Needless to say, my father had not approved of the outcome or Zeph's inability to "properly protect me."

And here we were.

"I need you to leave," Zeph finally said, his hands balled into fists. "Now."

"No." What we needed to do was have this out once and for all. Six months of this bullshit was long enough. "What do you want me to do, Zeph? Apologize again? Promise you I'll fix it? Because I've already done both of those things. What more can I do? You want me to suck your cock all night? Let you take me up the ass? Go seduce Aflora for us both? Find a human that fits nicely between us? Tell me what I need to do to fix this."

"You can't fucking fix it. You let me take the fall for *your* choice."

"I told my father that I picked her and invited her into our bed. He blamed you for not vetting her. Which, yeah, is sort of your job as my Guardian."

His gaze narrowed. "He denounced me in front of the fucking kingdom over a fuckup we both shared equal blame for."

I flinched at the memory of my father's cruelty. Because yeah, he'd been a major dick over the whole issue.

Then turned around and told me to grow the fuck up. "We both suffered that day."

"Yet you'll still ascend, and I'll remain here as a headmaster. And don't tell me you're going to change that. I don't want any favors from you."

"You're my best friend, jackass. It's not a favor. It's a reality. No one can replace you as my Guardian. I refuse."

His lips curled into a harsh grin. "Yeah, well, I can and will refuse the assignment."

I matched his grin with one of my own. "You can try, Zeph. But we both know my word will be law."

"Which makes you just like *him*," he retorted. "You must be so proud."

Fuck, I hated when Zeph took on the asshole act. "I'm not my father."

"Then prove it and stop threatening to force others into positions they don't want to be in."

The bottle almost slipped from my fingers, his words hitting home. "You really don't want to be my Guardian anymore." Not a question, but a statement. "All because of one fucked-up experience?"

"It was more than a fucked-up experience, and you know it. We were reckless and stupid, and lives were lost in the process when that bitch borrowed your access to the source. How can you not feel guilty about that?"

My lips opened and then closed. Because I suddenly understood.

This wasn't about punishing me but about punishing himself for a failure he felt responsible for.

"Those women died because of Dakota, not because of you or me."

"You really are naïve if you believe that. It's your duty to the Midnight Fae realm to protect that access, and you didn't. Just as it was my duty to protect you from harm, and I failed when I let that bitch into your bed." He pushed off his chair and rolled his neck. "I'm done for the night. It's your turn to play babysitter. I'm going for a run."

"Zeph—"

"No." He cut me off with a thunderous expression. "I'm done, Kolstov. Absolutely and resolutely. It's time for you to believe that and move on." He pushed past me, heading toward the door and not once looking back or even asking me to leave. Instead, he left, his angry aura burning the air in his wake.

But for the first time in months, I knew why.

He wasn't mad at me.

He was mad at himself.

No, he was mad at *us*. For all the damage we'd caused. And while I understood the guilt and responsibility for what had happened, I also knew dwelling on the past fixed nothing.

Instead, I'd learned from the experience.

I rarely fucked Midnight Fae before the event, and now, I never would.

Only humans.

And I intended for it to remain that way, even after I mated Emelyn.

I shuddered at the thought of her and our intertwined destinies. Not fucking her would be the easiest task of my life.

Unlike Aflora...

I pulled out my phone again, noting she was still next door. Probably in bed. It'd be far too easy to join her and use her as a distraction from my growing frustration.

Except, with her increasing powers, it was possible she could also access my source.

Which firmly placed her in the *will never happen* pile, where she belonged.

"Fuck," I muttered, rubbing a hand over my face.

I set my bottle down in Zeph's sink and gripped the counter.

I could really use an outlet of relief right about now. Rather than fuck around like I'd intended to this last week, I'd spent the majority of my time with Cyrus and Exos—

two Elemental Fae Kings—talking about Aflora. They were adamant that I protect her, stating she wasn't just a Royal Fae but also a friend of their Claire. Which meant any harm befalling the beautiful princess would put me on the shit list of a queen and her two kings. Not to mention her other three mates.

Talk about a rock and a hard place, I thought, sighing. Right, well, standing in Zeph's kitchen wasn't going to do anything for me. Knowing him, he wouldn't be back tonight.

I'd work on him more tomorrow.

Because, while I agreed with his bait idea, we needed something more solid that allowed us to keep Aflora safe.

Even if her death was indeed inevitable.

AFLORA

"ALL RIGHT, THIS IS WHERE I LEAVE YOU," Ella said, stopping in front of an ominous-looking building with tall, black, moving spires. Well, not moving, exactly. More like the vines wrapped around it were moving.

Because of the snakes.

I suppressed a shudder.

"You just go up to the gargoyle there, give your name, and he'll allow you to pass," Ella added, gesturing to a snarling stone statue a few feet away.

"Yeah, he looks friendly," I muttered.

Ella snorted a laugh. "They're all like that. They think they own the campus." She started to walk away backward while saying, "I don't recommend kicking one. I made that mistake early on, and it tried to eat my foot off. Annoying little assholes, if you ask me." She shrugged and turned away with a wave. "Good luck."

I wrapped my cloak tighter around me as if it were a blanket rather than a piece of my Academy wardrobe. The jabbing of my wand in the inner pocket made it impossible to forget the true purpose.

Nibbling my lip, I wandered up to the gargoyle and said, "I'm Aflora of the Elemental Earth Fae."

Two pinpoints of bright red scanned over my outfit, the unfriendly expression turning even meaner. "Your energy signature is a puzzling mix of magic—part Royal, part Midnight Fae." The grating of stones deepened the being's voice, giving it a harsh quality that made me flinch.

"I have a class in here today for death magic," I told it. "If you would please allow me entry, I'll be on my way."

"Such a polite one. So abnormal. Just like your magic. You're a bit of a quandary, aren't you?" Those sharp points of red light met my gaze. "This is not the course or field for you."

"Just let her through, Sir Schmahl," Shade said as he materialized beside me. "As my chosen mate, she has Death Blood running through her veins. This is an appropriate course for her, even if she's too weak to handle it."

"Too weak?" I countered, focusing on the willow stump to my left. "I'm not weak."

"We'll see, won't we, love?" He refocused on the bristling gargoyle. "Come on, Sir Schmahl. You know you want to see the outcome of this little test just as badly as I do. It'll be fun to watch her fail, won't it?"

"Hmm, yes. Yes, she will fail," the gargoyle agreed.

"Seriously?" I gaped between them both. "Bullying me on my first day of classes? How charming." It didn't escape my notice how many times I'd called Shade *charming* in a sarcastic sense.

"No bullying, just speaking practically," Shade replied, his dimples flashing. "What do you say, Sir Schmahl? Are you up for a bit of rebellious fun?"

"If she dies, I am not responsible" was the gargoyle's

dark reply.

The door swung open beside him, showcasing a tunnel lined with torches. *Great. The inside matched the ominous exterior.*

Shade pressed his palm to my lower back, giving me a nudge. "Don't worry, Sir Schmahl. I'll clean up any messes she creates."

A snort followed that comment. Or maybe it was just the gargoyle shifting positions. I couldn't really say, the sounds the being made hard to decipher.

"Come along, pet," Shade whispered against my ear. "I'll escort you to the lecture hall."

I bristled but didn't argue. Mostly because I had no idea where we were going. The schedule Zephyrus had given me didn't list room numbers, just buildings. And on our tours this week, he said nothing about where to go once inside each castle-like structure.

Shade's warmth seeped through my cloak, his peppermint scent swirling around me in a wave of refreshment. Every inhale increased my alertness, waking me up to this new world of Midnight Fae while also soothing me in a way it shouldn't.

It's the bite, I told myself. *He's hypnotized my blood.*

"The halls change," he said, his hand moving to my hip to stop me from taking another step. He placed his arm around my lower back in a decidedly intimate manner. When I tried to move away, his grasp tightened. "Hold on."

"Stop manhandling—"

Shifting rocks cut off my statement, freezing me in place as the corridor warped into a new dimension of dungeon-esque walls. My throat went dry at the windowless wooden doors and the flames crawling along the different torches.

"Every student creates a different path," Shade explained softly. "Our age dictates what course we should take and leads to the appropriate classroom. You can see ours outlined in purple fire down there." He pointed ahead to the violet glow.

"Are all the buildings like this?" Because if they were, this was going to be a very long week of finding my courses.

"There are similarities, but every subject has its own nuances. Defensive arts, for example, requires you to battle a figment to enter. Your experience and skill are determined by how well you do, and you're placed accordingly. So I suspect you'll be in a beginner-level Warrior Blood course." He winked down at me.

I scowled. "You know nothing about my abilities. And it's not my fault your Council handicapped me." I pointed to my collar, then recalled his statement last night about his cuffs. "Wait—"

"Oh, no. I know where you're going, and no, I won't help you remove it. Prove your own worth and figure it out yourself. I have faith in your failure, baby."

Ugh! "You're such an ignorant, impossible jerk of a willow stump!"

He laughed loudly, shaking his head. "I can't take you seriously with words like that, Aflora. Try calling me an asshole and we'll talk."

"How about I call you a bloodsucker instead?" I threw at him, livid by his callousness and hot and cold behavior. "A manipulative, impulsive *bloodsucker* who uses cruelty as a flirtation tool."

His smirk died. "Careful."

"Or what?"

"Or you'll piss off every Midnight Fae in this building. That term isn't one we allow here."

I scoffed at that. "Well, it's what you are, so I'm not sure why you'd shy away from it. *Bloodsucker.*"

He studied me for a long moment, his evil grin returning. "You know what? I changed my mind. Go ahead and use that term. Let's see what happens."

With that, he turned and headed toward our supposed

class. It was probably a pitfall directly into hell, yet I followed him anyway.

And paused on the threshold when I found a normal-looking lecture hall inside with desks and chairs and windows that overlooked a courtyard of burning thwomp trees.

This place was like a riddle. The hallway resembled an underground cavern meant for criminals, and this room reminded me of something from a human college campus. There was even a chalkboard at the front.

I stepped inside, half expecting it to morph into a nightmare, but nothing changed.

Shade had taken a seat amidst a group of students, their expressions filled with adoration as they spoke to him.

He must save his "charming" act for me, not the others.

Or maybe they enjoyed that side of him.

I sat on the opposite side of the room, keeping him in my peripheral vision while assuring an ample amount of distance.

As more students entered, they greeted him with a variety of weird handshakes, some bumping his fist, and all took seats near him, leaving me very alone. Which was fine. I preferred it that way.

At least until they started glancing at me and whispering things to him that made him chuckle.

I narrowed my eyes. This game of his had proven to be very dangerous, mostly because I didn't know how to properly play it. He bit me, seduced me, pretended to protect me last night, and guided me today, all the while issuing insults, and now it appeared he was making jokes about me.

Were they taking bets on how quickly I would fail?

Well, I'd just have to prove them all wrong.

Except I had no idea what I was doing or how to use my wand.

And the choker around my neck resembled a noose.

Shade's words echoed in my mind. *"Prove your own worth and figure it out yourself. I have faith in your failure, baby."*

Pompous jackwad, I thought at him now. His goading fueled a fire inside me, one that blended with the cerulean energy I'd created last night. I felt it humming beneath my skin, having not quite died even while I slept. As if it now belonged despite the foreign sensation of its presence.

I studied my fingers, half expecting to see them glowing, when a loud crash at the front of the room sent my focus upright.

A burly male appeared from a cloud of smoke, his cape flapping around him like bat wings. An appropriate entrance considering his small head. It didn't quite fit his robust physique. Not fat, so much as solid. His neck bulged with strength, his thighs the size of my waist. And he had to stand at least a foot taller than me.

He reminded me a bit of Sol, causing my heart to skip a beat in my chest. Not in the way it used to when I had a crush on him, but in a familiar way. The male had practically raised me with his mother's help. And his sister had been my best friend before she died.

It felt like a lifetime ago.

A distant memory when faced with my current reality.

Which included a pacing giant at the base of the classroom, his hands holding a scroll. Everyone had gone quiet, waiting for him to speak.

A pair of midnight irises scanned the room, landing on me.

Here we go.

But rather than say anything, he shrugged and went back to his scroll. The parchment went up in bright purple flames a moment later, and he clapped his hands. "Welcome to Advanced Conjuring. Most of you are familiar with my teaching methods. For those of you who are not, I prefer pair teaching. Now, get your wands ready and we can begin."

All the students pulled out their conduit tools, so I did

the same.

"You know the spell," he added. "Well, maybe not." That last statement was for me, something he confirmed when he met my gaze. "When I count to three, wave your wand in a crisscross pattern three times and say *Sharikana*."

I nodded to display my understanding, but he'd already looked away.

"And go," he said.

Echoes of the spell chanted from around the room, and I quickly followed suit, only to startle as energy zipped around me. A lasso of sorts formed around my wrist, the magical substance roped directly to Shade across the room.

His lips curled and he blew me a kiss.

I tried to yank myself away from him, which only tightened the connection and sent a piercing whistle through the air.

Cringing, I ducked into my desk and nearly dropped my wand.

Then felt Shade's subtle tug back. A taunt. And it shoved me right over the cliff into a puddle of fury.

Angling my wand at him, I snapped, "Let me go."

Which did absolutely nothing other than amuse him.

So I sent a blast of blue fire down the rope, directly to his wrist.

He jumped out of his chair, dropped his wand, and wrapped his hand around the flaming line. This time I fell out of my chair when he yanked.

I screamed and sent another blast of my cerulean magic at him, until the link severed.

And a raging professor stood before me. "Have you lost your damn mind, girl?!"

Yes, I thought at him, wiping my hands against my black skirt and fixing my white blouse. "He lassoed me," I explained dumbly. Because he had to have seen that, right?

"Because that's the purpose of the spell!" the professor roared. "*Pair magic*." He gestured around the class, indicating the ropes tying other students together. "Your magic chose his magic. Then you tried to burn him up with your power, which is not acceptable behavior for my class."

My jaw hit the floor. "My magic chose his?" That was impossible. I would never in a million years choose that willow stump!

Another realization struck me just as quickly. *My spell worked. Oh, this can't be a good sign. It's supposed to stop, not start working.*

Pixie sticks, this was bad. *Very* bad.

Shade stood a few feet away, his entertainment over our situation clear in his icy gaze. "Perhaps we should try again, Headmaster Irwin? It seems Aflora isn't interested in being my partner for the year."

The robust male spun on his heel. "The spell cannot just be undone, Shadow. She's your partner, and you will learn to work together. Starting in detention after we're done here today."

"Detention," I repeated, familiar with the term but never having experienced it.

"Yes. Where you will work on pair-bonding exercises until I'm satisfied you understand the purpose of teamwork."

He uttered a spell and waved his thick branch of a wand, and the world righted around me as he sent me back to my chair with some sort of floating spell. I tried to bat it away, uncomfortable with the inky presence coating my being, but it disappeared as soon as my butt hit the seat.

Shade was not provided the same treatment.

He merely collapsed beside his desk into a lazy sprawl befitting a king.

I hated him.

Loathed him.

Could not stand the mere sight of him.

And now I was stuck with him as a mate *and* as a class partner.

This year could not get any worse.

AFLORA

I LIED.

This year could absolutely get worse.

As I found myself literally bound to Shade's side in Headmaster Irwin's version of detention, all I wanted to do was die. But we had an essay to write—together. He'd joined our hands with some sort of magical pen that required our agreement on the words for it to work.

The topic? *Define partnership.*

I gritted my teeth as Shade tried to write something about partnership falling to the stronger of the pair to lead.

When the script vanished, he sighed and glared down at me.

"You try."

"Screw you," I tossed back.

"He won't let us leave until we're done."

"Then I guess we're living here now." A childish thing

147

to say, but there was absolutely no way I could work with this monster. "You only have yourself to blame, really. Not like I asked you to bite me."

He snorted. "Are we back to that old argument already?"

"It's not old," I countered. "It's very fresh and new and *wrong*."

His arm flexed against mine, the rope tying his left limb to my right limb tightening with the movement. There was another band of magic around our torsos, gluing my right side to his left side. Every time he breathed, I felt the strap pull against my chest.

This would have been intimate with anyone else.

With Shade, it only made me want to kill him.

But we were forbidden from drawing our wands.

Not that I knew how to use mine anyway. Today's class had consisted of a series of insane tasks involving conjuring deathly objects like skulls and bones and *hearts*.

As Shade had predicted, I failed every task.

Mostly because I refused to try. Playing with the dead went against every principle I possessed as an Earth Fae. I conjured life, not death.

Shade, however, excelled in a frightening manner. Each spell he uttered resulted in perfection, his aura an essential cloak of darkness. If only I could turn him into a ghost and make him disappear.

"Look, if I promise to tutor you, will you stop acting like a brat?" he asked, his genuine tone almost comical.

Except his words had me seeing in shades of red.

"You are the absolute last fae in all the realms I'd seek tutoring from. And I am *not* acting like a brat."

"That entire statement was the definition of *brat*, Aflora," he replied, sounding tired. "I'm the best conjurer in this Academy. Hell, I'm one of the best, period. Saying no to my tutoring offer is both impractical and stupid. You're only denying me because you're mad at me. Hence, brat-like behavior."

"Well, excuse me for being a little miffed by our current predicament. *You* put me here."

"And what's done is already done. It's how we use the past to move forward that defines us, and so far, you're not impressing me."

"Aw, well then, it's a good thing I'm not trying to impress you, Shade," I replied sweetly, batting my eyes.

His jaw popped from clenching his teeth, the first sign of frustration I'd ever seen in him. "We need to finish this damn assignment, Aflora. Unless you intend to join me in more intimate locations like the bathroom or the shower." His gaze dropped to the top button of my blouse. "Actually, that sounds like a beautiful plan. Shall we go?"

I tried to elbow him but couldn't, thanks to the binds.

Instead, I growled at him low in my throat. "Not happening."

His lips twitched as he bent to press his mouth against my ear. "That's not what you say in your dreams, little rose."

I gasped and tried to face him, only to be yanked right back into his side by the powerful spell. "You are in my head!"

"No, I'm in your *blood*." He kissed my neck before I had a chance to realize his intention, then nipped my pulse. "You're mine, princess. Forever. Now either work with me or let's go play in bed."

"Never."

"Stop lying to yourself," he said softly. "I know how you really feel and so do you. The sooner we get past this brutal courtship period, the better. Because I'm dying to fuck you."

"Shade!"

"What?" he demanded, his blue eyes glowing with power. "Would you rather I lie, too? Pretend my cock isn't hard as granite right now from your flowery perfume and seductive curves?" He snorted. "And I don't even like flowers. Yet all I can think about is exploring your petal-

149

soft skin and dipping my tongue into your damp pussy. Because let's be honest, we both know you're wet. I can *smell* it, Aflora."

My jaw nearly hit the floor, his crude words doing things to me that they most certainly shouldn't.

And with Headmaster Irwin lurking in the other room.

Oh, Mother Earth, save me from this cruelly handsome fae!

"Mmm, and now it's intensifying," he mused, leaning in to nibble my neck once more. "Did Glacier not speak to you like this, baby? With intention and lust-filled promises?"

I shivered, his nearness messing with my mind.

Until his words fully registered.

Glacier. I couldn't recall ever mentioning my *boyfriend's* name. Well, ex-boyfriend technically. He never prioritized our time together, our last missed date being the final straw for a lot of reasons. Not least of all because of Shade kidnapping me.

"How do you know about Glacier?" I asked, my voice taking on a husky quality I pretended not to notice.

"I know everything about you, Aflora," he whispered into my ear. "You've been mine for longer than you know."

"What does that even mean?" All these cryptic words about a fate he seemed to know everything about were driving me crazy. "Why did you bite me?"

"Because I was told to," he replied against my jaw, his free hand coming up to cup my face.

I allowed him to guide my mouth to his, only because I was too flustered to stop him. And a small part of me wanted to taste him again, to feel the caress of his lips against mine.

Because Shade knew how to kiss.

Really, *really* kiss.

His tongue mastered mine in a single move, silencing the conversation between us while providing me with a distraction I didn't realize I craved.

He had this bizarre hold over me, one that drove logic out the window and replaced it with mind-numbing *need*.

In this state, I longed for another bite. Not that I'd admit it out loud. Although, something told me I didn't have to. Shade claimed to be in my blood, but that somehow linked to my mind. I could feel him infiltrating every square inch of me, taking over my existence with his own.

"I hate what you're doing to me," I admitted on a whisper, my attempt to pull back thwarted by his hand sliding into my hair and holding me in place.

"Your racing pulse and arousal say otherwise," he replied, taking my mouth once more.

His earlier kiss paled in comparison to this one. He'd gone easy on me before. Now he demanded submission with each stroke of his tongue, his grip falling to my nape, where he squeezed and held me in place for his domination.

The binding around us seemed to slacken a little.

His arm moving against mine.

But I was too busy trying to keep up with the assault on my mouth to consider what else was happening.

He'd stolen my ability to breathe, his lips turning violent in a way I should hate. Yet my legs clenched in reply. My abdomen coiled. And the intimate parts of me wept for attention.

Wet didn't begin to cover it. Why was this turning me on so completely? Because of our bond? Another spell? Or did I enjoy this love-and-hate pull between us?

I whimpered, conflicted.

My mind loathed this male.

Whereas my body succumbed to his every touch, almost as if he'd trained me in my dreams to respond this way.

His lips curled against mine. "There. That wasn't so hard, was it?" he asked softly, causing my brow to crumple.

"What?"

He brushed his mouth against my cheek before settling back into his chair. "We're done," he called out.

I blinked at him.

Then down at the paper he'd written *while* kissing me.

It disappeared before I could read it, and Headmaster Irwin appeared in the doorway holding the essay. His surprised expression told me whatever it said was not what he expected and probably not something I'd agree to at all. Shade had done something to override the lesson, in addition to kissing the life out of me.

"Very well," Headmaster Irwin said, releasing us from his bonds. "I expect better behavior during our next session." That last bit was aimed at me before he disappeared into a cloud of smoke.

Shade stood and stretched, his impressive bulge inches from my face.

He wasn't lying about the *hard* part.

"My tutoring offer still stands for whenever you decide to consider logic over emotion," Shade said, then caught my chin and lifted my gaze to his. "As does my shower and bed offer." With a wink, he turned toward the door. "I suggest you follow me, little rose. Or you'll end up lost in the building until the students start arriving tomorrow, which will throw off your schedule completely."

He disappeared through the glowing doorway, not giving me a second to gather my thoughts or my things.

Except they were all gone.

Headmaster Irwin had passed out a class text and notebook during the class, along with pens. The others had left with them. But mine were nowhere to be found.

I chased after Shade and found him waiting against the wall, his books and mine tucked under his arm. "How...?"

"As I said, conjuring is my specialty." He canted his head, causing his dark hair to fall over his forehead and into one eye. "They'll be in your room when you get back. Consider it my version of an olive branch. Accept it at your own peril."

He didn't allow me to reply, merely continued down the corridor. I stayed close to his side, pausing when he did to allow the walls to shift. Then breathed a sigh of relief the second we exited into the dark evening.

Until I found Zephyrus waiting with a scowl beside the gargoyle.

"What the fuck took you so long?" he demanded, scowling first at me and then at Shade.

"Detention," Shade replied. "She attacked me with green fire. Impressive, really, but does make me wonder where she's getting that Warrior Blood influence from." He cocked a brow at the headmaster. "Any ideas?"

I frowned at Shade. "It wasn't green. It was blue. And you deserved it."

"I think you might be color-blind, babe. Maybe we'll check that out later." He tossed a grin over his shoulder, apparently deciding this conversation was over despite his question to Zephyrus. "See you in your dreams tonight, little rose."

"Stay out of my head!"

"Blood, baby," he reminded me, the words a whisper against my ear despite the distance his legs had put between us.

I batted at the vacant space, trying to get rid of whatever residual presence or spell he'd left in his wake. And found Zephyrus staring at me with an arched brow. "Blue fire?"

"Yeah, blue."

"Can you show me?" he asked.

Sighing, I held out my hand, calling the power to my fingertips. And of course, nothing happened. "I think Shade sucked out all my energy for today," I muttered.

Zephyrus considered me for a long moment, then nodded. "Perhaps tomorrow, then. We're late for the dining area anyway, and you need to eat."

"Is it your job to feed me now?" I wondered out loud.

"No. I just want you to survive," he replied. "Follow

me if you feel the same way."

Unable to fight that logic, I did what he asked.

Ate a disgusting humanlike dinner in silence.

And found my books waiting for me on my bed when I returned to my room. Beside them was a black rose and a note that read: *Sweet dreams*.

AFLORA

DAY TWO OF MY SCHEDULE centered around Warrior Class.

Because apparently Midnight Fae enjoyed fighting.

At least the wardrobe worked for me—stretchy black pants, a T-shirt, and my hair thrown up into a ponytail. I even had on tennis shoes. All the guys were similarly dressed, including Kols and Shade. Only the Malefic Bloods wore black T-shirts instead of white.

"You were right," I said to Ella. "The different types are becoming easier to identify." The Sangré Bloods were the easiest with their colorful heads, then the Malefic Bloods because of their penchant for obsidian. The Death Bloods I recognized because of class yesterday, and the Elite Bloods seemed to be gravitating toward Kolstov.

The Warrior Bloods weren't in this class because it was defense basics and they would slaughter us all. Or that was how Ella explained it, anyway.

Regardless, I was ready for a physical course. I had a lot of pent-up annoyance to burn, thanks to Shade's mental gymnastics last night. He'd taunted me with his tongue over and over, never letting me orgasm, and I woke up panting and hot and *very* frustrated.

His smirk now told me he knew it, too.

"I can't tell if you want to fuck him or kill him," Ella remarked, following my glower to the source of my anger.

"Kill," I said. "Definitely kill." I tugged on my collar, irritated by its presence. I'd give anything to be able to create a tree and use its branches to smash the willow stump's head into the ground.

Of course, it'd probably be a burning thwomp.

Uh, yeah, I didn't want to play with those again.

A hush fell over the students as Zephyrus appeared in a pair of loose pants and a sleeveless shirt. He didn't acknowledge me or Kolstov, just picked up a thick wooden stick from the ground, gave it a twirl, and ignited both ends with green flames.

"You all know who I am. You all know why you're here. Defensive magic is a key part of your continued education. But I'm not going to waste your time teaching you spells from a book you can read. Instead, we're going to practice them. However, before I can assign you to groups, I need to assess your skills. So today will be about what you know and what you can handle."

Ella and I shared a glance.

I was pretty sure what *group* I'd be assigned to.

"We'll go for old-fashioned duels with winner and loser circuits. I've already assigned your first pairings." He snapped his fingers, and names began scrolling through the air in emerald script crafted from fire.

"Ha. Well, our friendship was short-lived," Ella remarked, pointing to our pairing. "You'd better bring more than flowers to this fight, earth chick. I've been practicing with Tray." She wiggled fingers lined with dark red magic, her gaze taunting in a playful manner.

Her teasing warmed me slightly, making me relax just a bit.

Until the first fight began.

Vibrant sparks flew through the air as physical attacks were blocked with defensive spells.

Defensive spells I didn't know.

"Uh, this is going to be a really short fight," I told Ella.

She smirked. "I know. But I promise to go easy on you. Trust me, I was a newbie not too long ago. I get it. We can review some common defenses tonight or during one of our break days."

I nodded absently, my focus falling to Shade as he stepped into the ring with a lanky Malefic Blood. The male narrowed his gaze. "I'm so glad we're paired, Shadow. I've been dying to kick your ass all week for disgracing my sister."

"Is that what she told you?" Shade mused.

"That would require her to be able to speak, which—"

"Stop flirting and get to it," Zephyrus said, interrupting the Malefic Blood.

"Gladly," the lanky male replied, a sharp, translucent blade appearing in his hand.

I jumped as he charged Shade in a whirl of power, his aim going right for the other male's heart. It was a brutal attack, one clearly meant to kill.

But Shade sidestepped with ease, stirring a dark cloud in his wake and wrapping it around the other male's throat. "If you want to play like that, then properly challenge me," he said sharply, yanking on the hold and bringing the male to his knees.

"Enough," Zephyrus snapped.

Shade released the male with a little wave of his hand and shrugged. "Stiggis started it."

"Bastard!" The Malefic Blood flew through the air toward Shade, additional weapons falling into his hands, but he ran headfirst into a wall of magic and bounced backward to collapse to the ground.

My eyes widened as Zephyrus put away his wand, the block disappearing with it. "Chig, take this idiot to the medic."

"Yes, sir," another Malefic Blood said, his body width twice the size as that of the male on the ground. He lifted the unconscious man and tossed him over his shoulder as if he weighed nothing, then headed off the field.

"I'll move you into the winner's circle, Shade. But I expect to see defensive magic in your next match." Zephyrus dismissed him before he could comment and gestured for the next pairing to come forward.

Which was Kols and a petite female wearing a wicked smile. "Ready, future lover?" she asked him, her catlike eyes glowing red with power.

"If you think I'm going to go easy on you, Emelyn, then think again."

Her resulting laugh reminded me of nails on a chalkboard, her expression nowhere near amused or kind in any way. She flipped her long black braid over her shoulder and fell into a fighter's stance. "I've been practicing."

"I'm sure you have," Kols replied, his stance relaxed as they squared off. "Give it your best shot, Jyn."

"Is her name Jyn or Emelyn?" I asked Ella in a low tone.

"Emelyn Jyn," she replied, her tone sour. "She's Kols's future mate."

My eyebrows lifted. "She is?" Didn't he say something about not doing girlfriends?

"Yeah. Assigned by the Council. Some sort of agreement between Malik and Lima."

"Yes, our Council fancies arranged pairings," Shade added as he came to stand with us. "I was assigned to Cordelia, Stiggis's older sister."

I frowned at him. "Then why did you bite me?"

"Why indeed?" he mused, his lips curling. "Maybe I

wished to avoid my arrangement. Or maybe it was for another reason entirely. And maybe, if you're a good little rose, I'll tell you one day." He touched the tip of my nose with his index finger and sauntered off just as Kols pinned Emelyn to the ground beneath a wall of power. It reminded me of the one Zephyrus had used to block Stiggis's attack on Shade.

Emelyn screamed in pain, but Kols didn't stop.

And Zephyrus merely watched.

"Isn't he going to stop him?" I demanded, torn between Shade's commentary and the action unfolding before me.

"Who? Zeph?" Ella asked, snorting. "Yeah, no. He'll let this continue until Emelyn gives the signal, which should happen in about three, two, there it is."

A cloud of red smoke puffed out around them, and Kols released the brick of magic. "Practice harder, Jyn," he said, walking away.

"We're next," Ella informed me.

"Great." I followed her into the ring and noted how several fae fell silent around us, their intrigue palpable.

Too bad for them this would be a short show.

"I have no idea what I'm doing, so go ahead and start," I said, owning my inexperience.

Ella smirked. "Already am, princess."

I almost asked what she meant, when I *felt* her energy swathing me in a cloak of immobility. The thought of being bound triggered me into action, that blue light within me igniting to life and easily cutting through her invisible ropes while also memorizing the magical feel of them.

Using the knowledge, I tried to weave my own spell to wrap around her and nearly smiled when her legs locked in place.

"Holy shit, you're a fast learner," she said, pulling out her wand. "*Italaka.*"

My spell dissolved.

I took out my wand as well, unsure of how that would

help me, and waited for her next attack. Which came in the form of a water figment shaped like a lion. I jumped to the side as its jaws yawned wide, its teeth far too real. They reminded me of crystal fragments. Sharp, precise, and turning right for me.

A cerulean wave of power billowed out of me, destroying her fragment and sending Ella to the ground.

Zephyrus stepped in with one of those walls, except it went around me while he and Tray knelt to check on Ella. I stood frozen on display, unable to move, and confused as hell.

"Did I do it wrong?" I asked, but my words echoed around me in my makeshift prison. I pressed my palm to it and jolted at the zap. Then cocked my head as the energy signature seemed to unravel in my head, allowing me to absorb the knowledge just like I did with the binding spell.

Strange, I thought, even as I memorized the spell Zephyrus had woven and, more importantly, how to undo it.

Closing my eyes, I disentangled the threads, removing the enclosure and allowing me to hear the chaos erupting around me.

Questions and accusations flowed from every inch of the courtyard, followed by someone screaming, "Zephyrus! She's escaping!"

He spun around to find me free of his cage and narrowed his green gaze. "You. Come with me. *Now.*"

I wasn't given an option to comply, some sort of invisible noose tightening around my waist and yanking me forward.

Kolstov fell into step on my other side, his jaw tight. "Why didn't you tell us you could do that, Aflora?"

"Do what?" I asked. "All I did was dismantle her water monster."

"You attacked her with WarFire," Kolstov snapped.

"What? I don't even know what that is."

"It's the giant purple ball you just threw at my brother's

mate," he returned through his teeth.

"Purple?" I blinked at him in confusion. "It was blue."

"And again, I saw red," Zephyrus added, opening a door to a nearby building and ushering us inside. "What role do you want? Peacekeeper or guard?"

"Peacekeeper," Kolstov replied. "I'm the only one with the right bedside manner for it." His focus fell to me. "Do exactly what Zeph tells you to do, or I'll be left with no choice but to reprimand you publicly."

He turned on his heel, leaving us just inside the archaic stone structure. I gaped after him, startled by both the threat and the plea in his gaze as he uttered it. "I don't understand."

Shade materialized beside us, his amusement palpable. "Well, that was exciting. You sure do know how to make friends, little rose."

"Did you know she could do that?" Zephyrus demanded.

"No, but I'm thrilled by the prospect."

"Would someone tell me what I supposedly did?" I cut in before the headmaster could reply.

"WarFire," Zephyrus said. "You created WarFire and threw it at Ella. It's a lethal flame meant to kill. And it requires high-level magical skill, something you claim not to possess, but that little act suggests otherwise."

"I…" I wasn't sure how to reply to that. "All I did was destroy her water lion."

"What color did you see?" Zephyrus asked, ignoring me in favor of Shade. "I saw red. Kolstov swears it's purple. You?"

"Green," Shade replied. "Just like yesterday."

"It's cerulean blue," I insisted, annoyed that they kept talking about the color of my flame and not focusing on what the heck just happened. "Is Ella all right?"

"Cerulean…?" Zephyrus repeated, trailing off and sharing a glance with Shade. "That's impossible."

"Why are you all so obsessed with the color? You're

telling me I almost killed Ella. Is she okay?"

"Tray's healing her," Shade replied, still holding Zephyrus's gaze. "And I agree; that's impossible."

"Do you have Quandary Blood in your history?"

"No. It's a dead line."

"I know that."

"Then why bother asking such a question?"

"Just tell me what's going on," I interjected, tired of these conversations about colors and bloodlines. There were more important things at play here. "How could I possibly create WarFire? I don't even know a standard defense spell."

"WarFire is an advanced offensive spell." Zephyrus finally gave me his attention again. "It's exceedingly difficult to conjure and requires a lot of energy. It's also extremely illegal."

"Great." I threw up my hands and paced in the small stone space, wary of the dusty walls and cobwebs in the corners. *Beautiful place*, I thought, pinching the bridge of my nose. "You realize Earth Fae don't fight, right? We're very peaceful beings."

"Could have fooled me," Shade murmured.

"I learned how to duel at a young age because of my birthright, but I rarely took defensive or offensive skills in school. My method of fighting is through power. *Earth* power. And we don't create fire."

"Yet here we are," Shade replied, leaning against the wall with his arms folded. "How did you pick up her bondage spell? Or did you read that in a book?"

"I don't know. I just... absorbed it."

"Which is how you dismantled Zeph's force field?" Shade guessed.

"Is that what that was?"

"Yes." Zephyrus narrowed his eyes at me. "A powerful one, too, that you took down faster than anyone I've ever seen."

I swallowed. "Oh." That wasn't good for a lot of

reasons. Well, none of this was good. It showed a growth in dark magic, which I definitely didn't want. "I really am becoming an abomination, aren't I?"

"So it would seem," Zephyrus replied, not mincing words. "The question remains: Is it permanent or temporary?"

I had no answer for that and neither, it seemed, did Shade. He merely remained as nonchalant as ever, not a single inkling of remorse tainting his features.

Because he didn't care at all that he'd put me in this situation.

"What about you?" I asked. "Are you growing elemental gifts?"

He lifted a shoulder. "Everything feels normal to me, apart from my link to you. That's new."

"Yeah, you put it there."

"I remember."

"And you don't care at all that you did it."

"Of course I care. Why else would I be willingly standing in this outdated shack of a former classroom with you?" He pushed off the wall to stalk toward me. "This isn't exactly the most comfortable of spaces, but I didn't want to leave you alone with Zeph and Kols."

I glared up at him. "I'm in this mess because of you."

"I know."

"And you're completely unapologetic."

"Am I?" he countered, cocking his head.

"Are you?" I demanded.

"Shall we play the 'maybe' game again?"

"Ugh!" I wanted to slap him. "You're impossible and cryptic and such a… a… bloodsucking willow stump!"

He chuckled and shook his head. "You're so close, Aflora. So close."

Apparently, *bloodsucking* had lost its damning effect from yesterday, leaving me as the butt of his joke yet again. "Fine. You're a fucking asshole," I told him, the words tasting wrong in my mouth.

And of course, they only amused him more. "Oh, I do like that word from your lips, little rose. Say *fuck* again."

I threw my hands up in the air and turned to Zephyrus. "Can you make him leave?"

"It would be a waste of a command. Shade doesn't follow rules."

"Indeed, I don't," the Death Blood confirmed. "Besides, I'm here for your protection against the angry mob outside. If Kols can't calm them all down, we're going to have a fight on our hands. And I'm not ready to lose you yet."

"Don't feign selflessness." Zephyrus folded his arms, causing the muscles to clench and flex in the process. "We both know you just want to avoid the pain of losing a mate."

"I never claimed otherwise," Shade replied casually. "But my reasoning is neither here nor there. I'm here to protect her, and protect her, I shall."

"Or I could just create another ball of *cerulean* flames," I muttered, not really meaning it.

"Do, and I'll kill you myself," Zeph warned.

A chill swept down my spine at the truth in those words.

His green eyes glowed with sincerity, too.

I swallowed and nodded. "Then maybe you could use this time to teach me how to control it."

"I'm going to need more than a few minutes for that lesson." He considered me for a long moment. "But I'll talk to Kols about your schedule. I think your independent study should be reevaluated and scheduled with me. You're going to need all the defensive-magic help you can get after that little display out there."

Shade nodded, his agreement clear.

Something told me my reply wouldn't matter, so I remained quiet and waited instead.

What felt like hours later, Kols joined us once more, his expression wary. "Ella's fine. Tray's irritated, but understanding. And the others, well, let's just say Aflora hasn't made any friends."

Not like I had any here anyway, I thought sourly.

"No one is escalating the issue, but I had to agree to enhance her collar with more power restrictions," he added.

Zeph's chocolate-colored eyebrow inched upward. "How are you going to do that?"

"I have no idea." He looked at me. "For now, I need you to stay in the suite. No going to the cafeteria. No socializing."

"What about class tomorrow?" I asked.

"You'll be with me, so that'll be fine. But going forward, we need a better device to keep your powers in check."

So, a tighter leash. Awesome.

I sighed. "All right." While I hated the prospect of it, I understood the reason behind it. If my powers continued at this rate, I might actually hurt someone, and then I'd never be able to live with myself. Restraint made sense. I'd rather bear the pain myself than inflict it on another.

"You're not going to fight me on it?" Kols asked, his expression surprised.

I shook my head, swallowing. "I know what an abomination can do, Prince Kolstov. If that's truly what I'm becoming, restraint is a requirement." My shoulders fell as I looked toward the door. "If you lead me back to the suite, I'll stay there until you tell me otherwise."

Because escape was never going to be an option at this rate.

Not with the fire still licking a hot path beneath my skin, begging to be unleashed.

The power inside me seemed to be searching for an outlet, a way to explode. There had to be a way to temper it. Because if not... I shivered, refusing to consider that outcome.

I will survive this, I promised myself. *Somehow.*

165

KOLS

"I SWEAR TO GOD, if you apologize again, I'm going to hit you with another jaws creation," Ella threatened as I finally returned home.

Dealing with Aflora's little power display had cost me more than I wanted to admit. Mostly because of Emelyn. She'd gone to her father, which meant I'd been called into an emergency Council discussion regarding Aflora's development. I assured them all that I had her under control and reiterated the complication of her status as the last Earth Fae Royal. Killing her now would provoke a war. They needed to come to terms with the Elemental Fae Council before that could even be considered as an option.

Several wanted to lock her up.

But my father stood by my side and reminded everyone that this task served as one of my ascension trials.

An ascension trial that was proving to be my most

difficult test yet.

Aflora sat on a couch beside Ella, her shoulders caved inward as she held a mug of hot chocolate between her delicate hands. "I had no idea I could do that."

"I know."

"Maybe I shouldn't go to any more classes," Aflora continued. "The power seems to be growing, not dying, and that can't be a good thing."

"Classes are a requirement," I interjected, making my presence known since neither of them seemed to hear me walk through the door.

Aflora jumped, her blue eyes rounding as she looked up at me.

Ella didn't react at all. So maybe she had noticed my arrival.

"How'd the meeting go?" Tray asked as he walked out of the kitchen with a beer. He did a good job of hiding his anxiety over what happened today, but I caught the hardening of his jaw as he took in Aflora's close proximity to Ella. That wasn't an incident any of us would soon forget, even if Ella seemed fine now.

"I have an upgraded collar for Aflora to wear," I replied, pulling the item from my pocket to show him and the rest of the room. "But they've agreed to let her stay for now, as long as she continues to attend her courses as scheduled. Her independent study day will be with Zeph, where he will attempt to teach her more about defensive arts and control."

"Bet he loves that assignment."

"Actually, he volunteered," I replied.

Tray's dark eyebrows shot up into his hairline. "Did he attend the meeting?"

I nodded. "He served as a witness in her trial."

"Wait, there was a trial?" Aflora asked. "Why wasn't I allowed to testify?"

"Because you're a female," Ella muttered. "The Council is full of sexist assholes." She looked pointedly at me and Tray with those words, the argument a common one between us.

"It's how our world functions," I replied, more for Aflora's benefit than Ella's. The latter already knew full well how we did things around here. "Only males are allowed to present to the Council. If you have something to say, you send your mate."

Aflora snorted. "Because I can trust Shade to speak on my behalf." She shook her head, giving me a look. "I'm technically a queen, Prince Kolstov. I speak for myself."

"From what I understand, you still haven't accepted your ascension, which makes you a princess," I corrected. "And as I said, our Council does not allow females to attend our proceedings." As I agreed with her concerns regarding Shade, I didn't comment on that part. But I did feel it was necessary to add, "That said, Shade did speak on your behalf today. And he did well."

Her lips parted. "*What*? What did he say?"

"It's not important. What you need to know is, the Council ruled to allow you to continue attending classes, but they want you to wear this upgraded collar. Shade, Zeph, and I have also been charged with monitoring your power growth, so you'll be partnered with at least one of us in each class." I glanced at Ella and Tray. "Do you mind giving us a minute to sort out the power exchange? Just in case there is a fallout from the swap?"

Normally, I wouldn't mind their presence, but I wouldn't risk Ella again.

Tray clearly agreed because he set his beer down without a word and walked to his mate, extending a hand.

"Really?" she said, giving us both a sardonic look. "Aflora's not going to explode."

Neither of us replied because we both knew that Aflora could indeed explode at any moment, and I was the only one powerful enough to handle the fallout.

"It's fine," Aflora murmured, pushing off the couch. "Let's go to my room instead. I won't fight the exchange."

After her easy capitulation earlier, I assumed she'd say something like that. Because Aflora put everyone else's safety above her own. This collar could very well suck the life right out of her, for all we knew, and yet she would willingly let me put it on her if it meant she'd suffer instead of those around her.

I admired the hell out of her for that.

Because I would do the same thing in her situation.

It was the responsibility of a royal to put others first. Which, consequently, was exactly why I loathed Emelyn Jyn. She only thought of herself, not others. When I told my father that, he merely shrugged and said it was my future duty to keep the woman in line. So, yet another task to fall on my shoulders in my future role.

Pushing the annoyance away, I focused on Aflora's thick black hair falling in waves down her back as she led me to her room without another comment. She really was beautiful, in an otherworldly way, with her creamy skin, soft curves, and heart-shaped ass.

Any other lifetime, and I'd bend her over her bed, plunge deep inside her, and make her moan my name for hours.

But this life denied me the ability to follow through on that lust-crazed fantasy.

I caught her hand as she entered her room and led her to mine instead, desiring the familiarity of my personal space for the conversation we needed to have.

She didn't fight my nonverbal request, just allowed me to take her into my quarters and shut the door. Stopping a few feet inside my room, she turned and watched me warily.

"I have no idea what this is going to do when I put it on you," I admitted in the stillness between us.

Her throat worked as she swallowed. "I guess there's only one way to find out."

"Actually, I see there being two approaches here." Hence the reason I wanted her in my room for this discussion. I was breaking about a dozen rules, but the idea came to me while on my journey home.

Collaring her felt wrong. Like a steep path I didn't want to risk going down because I probably wouldn't enjoy whatever I found waiting for me at the bottom.

However, I'd give her the choice of where we went from here.

"My concern with this upgraded collar is that it's going to handicap you completely, leaving you unable to defend yourself." Something I suspected she was going to need now that she'd proven herself capable of producing WarFire. That was an advanced, difficult skill to master. And she'd displayed it beautifully in the worst possible way.

Aflora stepped backward to my four-poster bed and sat down without an invitation. Not that she really needed one. "If you don't put it on me, I could lose control and hurt more people."

"Yes," I agreed. "But how are you going to learn control if you are shackled so completely?" I pushed off the door to join her on the bed and handed her the upgraded device. She flinched as it shocked her skin, much the same as it'd done mine when Chern had given it to me. "You can feel it, right? How it's sucking the power right out of your fingertips?"

Her throat worked again, her tongue slipping out to dampen her full lips. "I'll do what I have to do."

"I know." I reached out to tuck a lock of her dark hair behind her ear, then ran my fingers over her current collar. "But sometimes the safe way isn't the right way."

Bright blue eyes met my own. "What do you mean?"

"I mean that in order to survive, you need to learn control, and none of us can teach you that while you're handicapped." I allowed my hand to drop to cover the device in her palm. A zing of discomfort immediately drove up my arm. Placing it around my neck would suffocate me entirely.

I suspected it would utterly destroy Aflora, likely belittling her to a near-human state.

"How about we hide the collar for now and save it as a backup plan. Then, in the interim, you can work with me and Zeph on how to master your new gifts. It won't be easy, and we certainly won't perfect this overnight, but with a little trust and guidance, I think we can make this work."

"That's an option?"

"It can be one, yes." It was a huge risk on my part, especially as it went against the Council's decision. But my father had trusted me with this assignment, claiming it as one of my trials, which allowed me to do this my way. And that collar just felt wrong on so many levels.

"Your Council didn't approve this option," she said after a beat, her intelligent gaze reading my face a little too well. "Why would you risk this for me?"

"I'm the future king, and sometimes kings make unpopular decisions." That was a lesson my father taught me at a young age. "This would be included in that category."

I released my hold on the item in her hand, kicked off my shoes, and twisted around on the bed to face her. It placed my back near my mountain of pillows and the headboard. I relaxed against the silky haven, pulling up one knee to wrap an arm around it while my opposite leg dangled off the edge of the mattress.

Much more comfortable.

"Have you never had to make an unpopular decision for your people?" I wondered out loud, studying her and catching the grimace my question evoked. I knew her answer before she admitted it.

"Yes." She mimicked my pose, only she didn't have a headboard to relax against, just air or the dark wood post. She chose neither and set the collar aside, her fingers wiggling as if to regain feeling. I understood because I'd felt the same twinge of loss in my hand from touching that power-sucking choker. "When Chancellor Elana attacked last spring, I absorbed a lot of her dark energy into myself to protect my people."

Well, that was an interesting detail.

"How did you do that?"

She nibbled her lip, then cocked a shoulder upward. "Honestly, I don't know. It was a natural impulse to take the brunt of her assault and dismantle it."

I considered her for a long moment. "Describe to me what you mean by *dismantle*." Zeph had told me what she said about the cerulean flames earlier, as well as her comments about picking apart spells and putting them back together. Her comment about Elana suggested something else at play here. Something that had nothing to do with Shade biting her.

"It's like a web." She twisted her lips to the side, her gaze turning inward as if she were searching for the design inside her mind. "I can see all the strands and pick them apart to morph into whatever I need them to be. Or, like today, I memorize how it was created and replicate it."

Well, shit. "Have you always been able to do this?"

"Yes. No. Well, sort of." She blinked, coming back to me. "I rarely had a need for it before, but I've always been able to think that way about power. It's natural, which is why I reacted to Elana the way I did. And also today. I understood the magic in a weird way, crafting it to suit me, but I had no idea it would produce WarFire. I just released some of the flames burning under my skin."

Her shoulders fell on a sigh, and I fought the urge to reach across the bed and pull her into a hug. I could see how troubled she was by everything that happened today. It marked her as an abomination, a threat to fae kind. Yet she clearly wanted to do the right thing. Unlike some fae in her position who would go after the power to use it to their advantage, to protect themselves at the cost of others.

Aflora wasn't like that at all.

If I told her to wear that choker, she would, even if it

killed her in the process.

And it had nothing to do with her need to survive and everything to do with her desire to lead properly.

"I want to try something." I pushed away from the headboard to sit cross-legged on the bed.

"Um, okay." She copied my position again, facing me with our knees almost touching.

"I'm going to release a spell—nothing violent—and I want you to try to manipulate it without using your wand or your voice. Just like you did with Ella earlier. But don't use any fire."

She nodded slowly. "Okay."

"Good." I held my palms up and indicated for her to do the same. "This is a simple spell for creating an object. You saw Stiggis do it earlier with Shade. Ready?"

"Yep."

"*Ajamee* apple." A bright red apple appeared in my hand. I brought it up and took a bite, waggling my brows.

She frowned. "I thought the spell for creating food was *Tareero Tamida*."

"Ah, yeah, that's one way to do it for food. *Ajamee* will create anything you want." I set my apple on my nightstand and opened my palm again. "*Ajamee* dagger." I visualized the knife I wanted, and it appeared a second later, glistening beneath the moonlight shining through my windows. "You have to envision what you want when you say it, and the object appears."

"Zephyrus told me not to do this without a wand."

"Well, I don't want you to use a wand or your words at all. I want to see if you can make the magic work without uttering a sound, like you did today when dueling Ella."

"But that was different because the magic was used on me. I can't sense your spell at all like this."

"Hmm. All right, we'll go about this a different way, then. Lie down," I said, a dangerous idea forming in my head.

I couldn't touch her the way I wanted to, but I could

use my gifts on her in an entirely different way. I had promised not to unleash a violent spell. I said nothing about erotic ones.

Aflora stretched out her long legs and laid her head on a pillow while I shifted to my knees to sit near her abdomen. "Okay, I want you to try to absorb what I'm doing, the way you did with Ella, and use it back on me." *This'll be fun*, I mused. "Ready?"

She nodded. "Yes."

I hovered my palm over her midsection, noting the way her shirt had ridden up to display a taunting sliver of her creamy skin. I focused my energy there, murmuring a spell meant to induce heat in a sensual manner.

Aflora's fingers dug into the comforter on either side of her hips, a sweet little sound catching in her throat.

"Do you feel that?" I asked softly, compelling the sensation to spread across her stomach and higher to her breasts.

She shuddered, her eyes falling closed.

"Focus on the spell, Aflora," I whispered, using my power to send a wave of it downward to the apex between her thighs. "Try to unweave it and send it back into me, sweetheart."

Goose bumps pebbled down her arms as she squeezed her legs together in a manner I recognized all too well.

It took physical restraint not to bend over and place a kiss above the waistline of her pants. Mmm, then I'd tug down the fabric to explore her dampening arousal with my tongue. I bet she tasted sweet, just like how she smelled. Her alluring scent called to me, confirming her interest and telling me how ready she was to receive.

My spell wove deeper into her, seeking the places on her body that required a skilled touch and heating them even more.

"Kolstov," she breathed, arching up off the bed.

"Kols," I corrected, giving in to the desire to press my palm to her abdomen. I pushed her down into the bed and hovered above her. "Now manipulate the spell and re-create it, just like you did with the binding curse from earlier."

"O-okay," she managed to reply, her voice husky with need.

Oh, this was a hazardous game because now I wanted to hear her moan. To watch her fall apart. To slide my thickening cock into her and bring us both to a climax neither of us would soon forget.

I clenched my jaw to hold back a groan, my balls aching with the prospect laid out before me. It would be so easy to slip out of our clothes and lose ourselves in the sheets for hours. Days, even.

Fuck, I need to get laid.

Preferably by a writhing, dark-haired goddess with bright blue—

My eyes widened, the scene unraveling before me an impossible sight.

Holy shit, it's cerulean.

I could *see* her magic unfolding as she mentally stroked my spell, learning and manipulating the ends and crafting it into a spell of her own.

"You're—" A jolt of heat directly to my groin had me falling to the mattress beside her on a spasm so violent that my heart seriously stopped.

Aflora's beautiful gaze captured mine, her smile that of a seductress with her enchantment wrapped around my dick. Literally. She gave it a stroke, and I grabbed her hip in response, our bodies turning toward each other on the bed. "Fuck, Aflora."

Definitely not a virgin or inexperienced.

Not with a grip like *that.*

"You said to use the spell against you," she replied, her tone still husky but this time filled with feminine pleasure. "How am I doing?"

"Wonderfully," I admitted on a hoarse exhale, jolting as she did it again. My grip tightened as I fought the instinct to push her to her back and truly take over. To kiss her deeply, rip off her clothes, and fuck her until my heart stopped again.

But that sliver of cerulean magic taunted my senses, grounding me in the reality of our situation. Not only had she just learned a spell through touch, but she'd also unwoven it and reapplied it in a way only a Quandary Blood could. And the color surrounding her magical essence proved it.

Aflora was absolutely an abomination.

A problem I would eventually need to slaughter.

If I were smart, I'd end her now and not wait for her to grow any stronger. There was a reason the Quandary line died out.

The Midnight Fae had slaughtered them all.

This female posed more risk to my ascension than anyone I'd ever met.

Yet my instinct had me pulling her closer, not pushing her away.

The urge to protect such a precious gift overwhelmed me, consumed my ability to think clearly. "Aflora," I whispered, my lips suddenly dangerously close to hers. "You have no idea how unique you truly are."

She released her mental grip on my cock, her energy vanishing as she captured my gaze. "I know more than you realize."

"Can you tell me about your parents?"

"What about them?"

"Did they have any Dark Fae heritage?" I wondered out loud, trying to solve the mystery of her creation. Because these talents couldn't have come from Shade. He was one hundred percent Death Blood. "You're displaying Quandary Blood gifts, and I have no idea how that's possible."

"Quandary Blood?" she repeated, frowning.

"The sixth line," I explained, ignoring my twinge of annoyance at her not thoroughly having researched our kind. Every fae kingdom treated politics differently. And she was right about her upbringing being vastly different from mine. I grew up with parents. She grew up fighting for her existence against some unknown plague that later turned out to be abomination related.

How ironic, given her situation.

"My parents were Earth Fae," she said slowly. "Not Midnight Fae."

"Either that's not true"—which was my suspicion—"or Shade's bite somehow infected you with the rarest gifts among our kind. Quandary Bloods haven't existed in over a thousand years."

"What happened to them?"

I wasn't going to lie to her. "We killed them all."

Her eyebrows shot upward. "What? Why?"

"Because Quandary Bloods, when they existed, could manipulate energy in a way no one else has ever been able to do, including turning off any link they desired and leaving the fae powerless. The web you mentioned is your connection to the spell. And—"

"I can undo it and piece it back together," she finished for me, her body tensing beside mine. "That's not normal."

"No, it's not."

"Shade can't do that?"

"Not that I'm aware of," I replied. "It's not a Death Blood function." But I had to wonder if he somehow knew or sensed this gift inside Aflora. Maybe that was why he picked her as a mate—to wreak havoc on our kingdom.

"My family fell into power because of a Quandary Blood," I continued, thinking about the history my father once told me. "There was an uprising that ended in the overthrowing of a Death Blood from rule—Shade's ancestor, actually—and a Quandary Blood transferred the source connection from the fallen royal to my grandfather." Which initiated a millennium of animosity between our families.

"And then you killed all the Quandary Bloods?"

I frowned, considering. "I didn't, but the Midnight Fae did."

"Why? If they helped, then why would you kill them all?"

"Because they were dangerous. As I said, they could dismantle a Midnight Fae's power and render him no better than human."

"Did they do that?" she asked.

"Yes. The Death Bloods used them to try to regain power about a thousand years ago. The Quandary Bloods were dismantled and exterminated in response, serving as a warning to keep the Death Bloods in line."

"Sounds like a rather murderous approach," she replied, her displeasure written into her features. "Maybe some of them were innocent."

"Like you?" I suggested, arching a brow. "Are you innocent, Aflora?"

I gave in to the impulse to press her back into the bed, my thigh sliding between hers as I moved over her, our lips still dangerously close.

"Because I think you're a lot more experienced than you let on," I murmured.

The double entendre was intentional. It applied to both her magical skills and sexual talents. Because the way she'd used that spell on me without even blushing told me a lot about her confidence in the bedroom.

Which only made me want to explore her more.

"I don't even know how to use this power," she whispered, her big blue eyes guilelessly gazing up at me. I almost wanted to call it an act, but I sensed her sincerity in those words. "I have no idea where it came from or why."

"Your parents, most likely," I replied, resting my elbows against the pillows on either side of her head. "Now the question becomes, what should I do with you?"

Kill her was the obvious choice.

But if Shade somehow knew about her bloodline, that

implied a much deeper motive at play than him just wanting to avoid his mating duties.

I could practically hear Zeph in my head telling me to use her as bait, to determine exactly how far Shade planned to go.

That plan seemed more practical with every inhale, and not just because it would grant me answers. It would also allow me to keep this beautiful creature alive for as long as possible.

I still couldn't have her, especially now that I knew what kind of power she seemed to be harvesting in her blood. But that didn't mean I couldn't have a little fun, right?

"We're going to keep this secret between us for now," I told Aflora, nuzzling my nose gently against hers. "But it means you need to do exactly what I tell you in regard to your growing talents. Understood?"

"Why would you do that for me?"

"Because I'm not done with you yet," I admitted on a whisper, my lips brushing the corner of her mouth.

Dangerous.

Very dangerous.

But, oh, it felt good.

Too good.

This female was an ideal mate in every way. Or that was what my instincts told me.

However, my mind knew otherwise.

I'd made a mistake months ago of following my dick into a bad situation.

I wouldn't be allowing that to happen again, no matter how much it hurt to stop this little game.

Which was precisely why I rolled off of her and onto my back, my body tense with the need to do a lot more than chastely kiss her.

"Now would be a good time for you to leave," I said, my jaw clenching with each word. "We'll talk more tomorrow."

Aflora seemed to pause, but I couldn't risk looking at her. Because if I saw even a single ounce of desire reflected in her gaze, I'd do a hell of a lot more than taste the edge of her mouth.

While I adored stretching my limits and testing my resolve, something told me this female would destroy all my maintained control.

Worse, I'd welcome it.

As the door softly shut behind her, all I wanted was to go after her, push her up against the wall, and devour her entirely.

And allow her to do the same right back to me.

ZEPH

"A QUANDARY BLOOD," I mused.

The news didn't surprise me. I had suspected it when we all saw different colors in her fire. That was a trademark Quandary Blood trait, a way to complicate their magic.

"I wonder what kind of wand the figments gave her at AcaWard." I never actually looked at it, but I imagined it held traces of her heritage. "Have you asked to see it yet?"

Kols shook his head, his expression tired. "I was too focused on keeping her magic under control in Elite Class today. Emelyn has decided Aflora is a fun target for practicing her mean-girl bullshit, which put Aflora in an immediately defensive position." He sighed, relaxing into my couch, and lifted a bottle of beer to his lips.

At this rate, we were going to go through my entire stash our first week. Good thing we had two break days coming up. Just had to get through another class tomorrow first, then I could pop into the Human Realm to pick up more. Except it would be on Kols's dime. He came from money. I did not.

"We could ask for her wand now," I suggested. "She's next door, right?"

Kols took a long swallow, his golden irises flaring in a way I recognized. It told me what he was going to say before the words left his lips. "I need a break before I do something stupid."

"Like fuck her?"

"Yeah, exactly like that." His gaze narrowed at me. "And don't tell me you're immune from the pull. We may not have played together in a few months, but I know your type. You want her just as badly as I do."

I lifted a shoulder. "It's not going to happen."

"I know. Now, if only my dick could get the message, we'd be on the same page."

"Your dick always did get you into trouble," I muttered. *Technically, us*, I corrected. His dick always got *us* into trouble.

He set his bottle down on the coffee table and leaned forward to rest his elbows on his knees. "Yeah, if you need to blame me for what went down with Dakota, then do it. But I need your help here, man. This is a big fucking deal. If Shade mated her because he knows what she is, then there's a lot more going on here than just an act of rebellion."

I don't blame you. I blame myself, I thought. But it didn't matter, because he was right. We needed to focus on Shade and Aflora and whatever the hell was going on there.

"What did you read from her when you discussed her Quandary Blood?"

"Genuine surprise and a hell of a lot of confusion," Kols replied. "She's either an amazing actress or she had no idea about her abilities. I'm going with the latter because she seems to think it's Shade's fault. She was pretty adamant that her parents were pure-blood Earth Fae."

"Her gifts prove that to be a lie."

"I agree, but that doesn't mean she believes it. Regardless, it shows innocence. I think she's a pawn in a much larger game. What I want to know is, who is the master on the board? Is it Shade, his father, or someone else entirely? Because we both know the Death Bloods and Quandary Bloods share a dark history."

"Hence the reason your grandfather killed them all off a thousand years ago," I said, recalling the lessons from my history courses here at the Academy. It was a subject that always left me uneasy—the extermination of an entire bloodline to send a message to all the others.

Behave or you'll be next.

The Quandary Bloods were seen as the villains of the story, but I always suspected there was more to the history than what we were told. It was a topic most of us avoided, something I assumed was done with a purpose. If no one questioned the events of the Midnight Fae Dark Age, then the secrets remained safely buried.

Maybe that was Aflora's purpose here—to help disinter some of those rumors.

"We need to keep her alive," I said, lifting my ankle to rest over my opposite knee. "She's worth more than bait." Because she might be the key to unearthing a truth long hidden.

"My father would want her dead immediately." Kols stared at the floor, his expression hard. "I should kill her, Zeph. She's an abomination. I have proof of it."

I considered him for a long moment. "Then why haven't you executed her?"

He continued to focus on the black carpet. "I promised Exos and Cyrus that I would look after her," he admitted softly. "Not because it's the right thing to do, but because I want to." He exhaled a long breath, his golden eyes finally lifting to mine. "I feel this strange urge to protect her,

Zeph. I barely know her and yet..."

"You feel obligated to shelter her from the harsh future you know awaits her," I finished for him, my voice equally quiet.

Because yeah, I understood. That bizarre inclination to watch over her tied into my strange need to teach her, to help her survive. Yet I knew her death was inevitable. The need to take care of her hit me right in the gut, and I had no idea where it came from or why.

"Do you think it has something to do with her being an abomination?" I wondered out loud. "Maybe she has some sort of enchantment woven into her existence that's forcing us to act in her best interest."

"Like some sort of self-preservation instinct?"

"Yeah, exactly." I rubbed the scruff dotting my jaw, a stiff reminder of my need to shave again soon.

I'd let myself go this week as a result of my misery pertaining to my new vocation. Teaching was not for me. I had little patience for idiocy, and half the new students were too green to know their left foot from their right. They'd learn. Eventually.

"It's possible," Kols replied, considering my enchantment theory. "I feel half-crazed with lust every time I'm near her. And before you say I'm always like that, this one is different. The others were just challenges I enjoyed conquering. Aflora poses more than just a challenge. She's a real threat to me and this kingdom. And it goes against all my training to let her live, let alone *help* her."

"You're talking about the choker." I gave him a hard look. "Tell me you put it on her."

"You know I didn't," he muttered.

"Fuck, Kols." This was bad. Really bad. "That was a direct order from Malik."

"You think I don't know that?" he countered, shaking his head. "I realized my mistake about thirty minutes after I allowed it to happen."

"You mean after you jacked off," I translated, knowing him all too well. He'd told me about the heat spell when explaining his findings about her powers.

"Yeah, twice, but that's beside the point. I know it's wrong, yet I still couldn't put it on her this morning. Instead, I focused all my energy on keeping her under control today."

"Which, I imagine, only brought you that much closer to her power." That was how our abilities worked. We fed off the power waves of others. Kols was the strongest among us, the black lines dancing along his arms and chest an indication of his ties to the source. If we practiced our spells together, my strength would grow tenfold. Implying Aflora's would as well.

"You have no idea," he muttered. "My power is hungry for hers, and not just in an ascension kind of way."

"She's an ideal mate, isn't she?"

He picked up his beer and took a powerful pull before nodding solemnly. "I've felt it from the moment I laid eyes on her. Her personality isn't helping matters."

"Meaning?"

"She's selfless and intelligent, has a backbone of steel, and, let's not forget, she's stunning." He set his bottle back down and dropped his head to his hands. "This is wrong on so many levels."

I allowed him to wallow for a moment while I contemplated everything he'd said. A few thoughts kept popping back into my mind, most of them dangerous to utter out loud. Similar to the historical secrets I suspected were hidden for reasons that might not be in everyone's best interest.

However, since we were already having a conversation that could land us both in a dungeon, why not push the boundaries?

"We've been told our entire lives that abominations are vile creatures," I started, considering my wording carefully. "But isn't it how we use the gifts that matter? Not necessarily who our parents are?"

He lifted his gaze just enough to catch mine, his palms still hovering over his mouth. "What are you trying to say, Zeph? Speak plainly."

"Aflora is an abomination, but she doesn't strike me as evil at all. I'd actually call her *sweet*."

"We barely know her," he pointed out.

While I agreed, I couldn't help saying, "You've always prided yourself on being a good judge of character. Would you trust Exos's and Cyrus's opinions of her?"

He lowered his hands, clasping them between his legs as he continued to rest his elbows on his thighs. "Exos and Cyrus would do anything to protect their mate. And their mate is friends with Aflora. That alone means I can't trust their opinions because they're inherently biased."

"All right, well what does your gut say about Aflora? Because mine says the girl grew up playing with flowers, not plotting world domination."

He snorted. "Oh, she's innocent. But not entirely. The way she used that heat spell on my cock spoke volumes about her lack of innocence."

"Always thinking with your dick," I mused, amused despite the serious subject matter. "Just because she knows her way around your pants doesn't mean she wants to take over the Midnight Fae kingdom."

"Yeah, yeah, I get your point. But I would have bet money a week ago that she was a virgin, and before you say that's irrelevant, it's not. If I misjudged her experience, then I could easily be misjudging *her*."

"Fair," I agreed. "However, I never picked up a virginal vibe from her, just a lack of experience with multiple partners. Which is still my assumption in that realm of conversation. Regarding the more important one, however, I don't think Aflora could ever invoke harm intentionally. Hell, she looked ready to cry when you destroyed her burning thwomp last week."

Kols chuckled. "Yeah, she wasn't at all happy today

when Headmaster Jenkins used a crow in her compulsion spell. There were tears in Aflora's eyes when the poor thing died. I lied and told her the bird was a conjured being, not real."

"She believed you?"

"Yeah." His lips curled. "I made her a crow on our way back to the suite. She still has it in her room."

"And this woman is a threat to our kind?" I scoffed. "You're using that bird to spy on her right now, aren't you?"

"Not presently, but yeah, I can see through its eyes."

I smirked. "I'd call you brilliant, but your ego doesn't need stroking."

"You're right. I already know I'm brilliant." He finally cracked a smile. "So what are we going to do?"

"I should think that's obvious," I replied, lifting my ankle off my knee to sprawl lazily in my recliner. Despite hating the location of my suite, I couldn't deny the comfort in the furnishings provided by Kols's family. They kept my fridge stocked—except for beer—and provided me with all the luxuries I grew up with in the Nacht Estate. Not a bad life. I just hated the new teaching part of it.

"We're going to protect her," Kols said, referring to the future plan.

"Yeah. Until we figure out what the hell is going on with Shade." And possibly glean some historical answers in the process. "He tasted her, so he has to know what she is."

Kols bobbed his head in agreement. "The question is, did he know before he bit her?"

"That's my guess."

"Mine, too."

"One thing that perplexes me—"

"Only one?" Kols joked.

I didn't remark on it, just continued my thought. "He had to know we'd figure this out. Why hasn't he tried to keep us away from her?"

"He hasn't had a choice."

"He's Shade," I reminded him. "He's a dick who doesn't play by the rules, yet he's been waltzing the peaceful line all week. Why?"

Kols frowned. "I... I don't know."

Neither did I, hence the reason I brought it up. "We need to keep him away from Aflora."

"Easier said than done. He keeps visiting her dreams." Kols grimaced. "I overheard her moaning his name last night."

I arched a brow. "Overheard?"

"Okay, I may have tried to play with her in her dreams. It's safe and an easy way to burn off some lust. But Shade was already there."

My lips twitched. "Maybe you should try shoving him out tonight and see what happens."

"Don't think I won't."

"Oh, I know you will." Just the thought of it had my dick awakening in my pants because I knew what that scene would look like from Kols's point of view. And yeah, I wanted in on it. But I'd never give in to it. Even if I went to bed the last few nights to thoughts of Aflora's full mouth wrapped around my cock.

I cleared my throat. "Right. Well. I'm going for a run."

"Another one?" Kols asked, arching a brow.

"A man has to exercise."

"Uh-huh." He gave me a knowing look. "Good luck."

"Given that you're the one who has to sleep next to her every night, I think you're in need of luck, mate." I stood and stretched, smiling as Kols observed the movement beneath his hooded gaze. "Feel free to add me to your little nighttime fantasy. You know what I like."

With that taunt—one I shouldn't have allowed to slip from my lips—I left to explore the Academy grounds again.

All the while thinking of a dark-haired beauty with pouty lips and tits made for a man's hands.

189

Thinking about her wasn't exactly a sin.
Even if it felt like one.
Too bad that distinction only made me harder.

AFLORA

"OKAY, so this time, try not to kill me, 'kay?" Ella stood across from me on a mat, her hands up in the air. It didn't escape my notice that Trayton hovered near the edge, his gaze holding a lethal warning in them.

"No magic," he said, his tone holding a royal inflection I recognized all too well.

Annoyance flashed in Ella's features. "She knows, Tray. That's the point of this makeshift gym class."

"Physical training," Kols corrected, joining his brother. They both wore sleeveless shirts that showed off their athletic physique. I could definitely see the family similarities between them in their regal postures and aristocratic jaw structure. But Tray resembled the night, while Kols reminded me of the sun.

A sun I very much missed.

Starting classes in the evening really messed with my

concept of *days*. We finished closer to the time I used to wake up, then slept during the light hours and started all over again each night.

No wonder the Midnight Fae were pale.

Well, except Shade. He had a slight tan, which I suspected linked back to his penchant for disappearing into shadows.

He winked at me from across the gymnasium where he stood waiting for his turn on the mat.

I scowled at him in response.

His dreams at night were killing me, and he knew it. I argued with him every time he entered my head, yet I still ended up mostly naked and writhing beneath him.

Except for last night.

My cheeks burned at the memory of the things I'd done with Kols while asleep. It'd also been in my head, a coping mechanism that helped me force Shade out, and I was a bit embarrassed by how thoroughly I'd used the Royal Fae. He was supposed to be helping and mentoring me, yet I spent the night doing wicked things to his sculpted physique.

A physique that flexed as he took a step forward and lightly took hold of my arms. "You can do this, Aflora. It's just a tumbling exercise. Ella will show you how it works. Just don't call on your fire, okay?"

Mother Earth, even now he was trying to help me and had no idea how I'd used him last night. My hesitation on the mat had nothing to do with fear and everything to do with guilt.

Just don't think about it. Or how good his hands feel on my arms right now. In fact, you should take a step back, I coached myself.

Except I didn't listen at all.

Instead, I looked deep into his golden irises and thought about how they glowed while I went down on him. I swallowed, his taste a lingering memory in my throat. "I can do this."

"I know you can."

With a nod, I forced myself to look at Ella. She arched a light blonde brow. "Oh, are you finally ready? Because I'm bored and growing fairy wings over here."

Trayton snorted. "You wish."

"I do!" She threw her hands up in the air. "Fae should have wings and pointy ears."

My own ears twitched at the thought, and I brushed my dark strands behind them to show off the tips. "I have pointy ears."

Ella spun around to face me, her lips pulling into a huge grin. "There! That's what we should look like. All she needs is wings."

"Fairies have wings," Trayton explained calmly. "And they're not real."

"Well, technically, pixies exist and they have wings." Amusement briefly touched my chest as I thought of Claire's obsession with the little creations brought on by her connection to the spirit element.

"We have our own version here," Trayton muttered. "Ella loves them."

"But he won't let me keep them as pets," she pointed out.

"Because they bite and like to set fires all over the damn place."

"Are you all going to stand around and chat all day or get down to work?" Zephyrus's voice came from right behind me, the heat of his body sending a shiver down my spine. He'd worn gray sweatpants and a white T-shirt today, something several of the females seemed intrigued by throughout the gymnasium. Myself included.

I firmly blamed Shade for my runaway hormones. If he hadn't spent every night taunting me with his touch and tongue, I wouldn't be having all these illicit fantasies about Kols, and I wouldn't find Zephyrus particularly irresistible today.

"Am I invisible?" the headmaster demanded.

"N-no," I stammered, spinning to face him and having

to look up to meet his smoldering green eyes. There was a hint of brown around the pupils that captured my attention for a long moment before I shook my head. "We were just getting started."

He arched a brow. "Yeah? Because it looks like you're all over here gossiping. Maybe I need to reassign pairings." He glanced to the left, his mouth already moving before I had a chance to respond. "Shade! Get your ass over here."

The Death Blood shadowed over to us in a wave of his black smoke, his expression bored as he appeared. "The whole headmaster thing seems to be going well for you, Zeph. Bet it feels nice to be able to issue commands for once rather than constantly taking it up the ass from Kols."

"Oh, please assign me to him," Kols said, stepping forward. "I'll show him what it feels like to take it up the ass."

Zephyrus shrugged. "I was going to give him to Tray, but go for it." He looked at the other royal. "Help me manage the match between Ella and Aflora, then go spar with Fang."

Glancing over my shoulder, I mouthed, "Fang?" at Ella, hoping I'd heard that wrong.

She burst out laughing, nodding. "Yeah, original. I know."

"Stop goofing around," Zephyrus snapped, his hand grasping my hip and forcing my attention back to him. "I need to see what I'm dealing with so I can better plan our independent study next week. Unless you want me to assume that all you know how to do is pick flowers from the ground?"

I bristled at the negative insinuation in his tone. "I'm not a helpless pixie, Zeph."

His eyebrow arched again, saying nothing and everything with that look alone. We weren't familiar enough for me to use his nickname. It just sort of slipped out.

"Headmaster Zephyrus," I corrected softly.

"Don't be a dick, Zeph," Ella cut in, stepping up to my side. "We were just about to start. And we don't need to be managed."

"That remains to be seen," he replied, his eyes still holding mine. "Go on then, pixie flower. Show me what you can do. I'm waiting."

"Do you think it's wise to goad the chick who almost killed me two days ago?" Ella asked, folding her arms. "No offense, Aflora."

"She's fine. She's wearing the new and improved choker, right?" He seemed to see right through me, his green irises gleaming knowingly.

"Right," I said, swallowing. "I'll be fine."

"Then stop stalling and give me a show, pixie flower."

Heat crept up my neck at his words and the tone with which he uttered them. Hard, demanding, and inflexible. Three words that absolutely described Zephyrus.

With a resolute nod, I faced Ella and caught Kols and Shade standing beside Tray, observing the entire exchange.

Great. So I would be giving them all a show.

"Just kick my ass and get it over with," I muttered to Ella as we entered the circle drawn on the mats.

She gaped at me. "Did you just curse?"

"I know how to curse," I said, falling into what I hoped resembled a fighting stance. I'd watched a few Powerless Champion duels in the Elemental Fae kingdom. I knew what to expect. I just hadn't enrolled in any of the Academy courses, preferring solo athletics to combat sports.

"I'm small, but I'm fast," Ella warned me.

"Good, then this will be over quickly." Because I had no idea what I was doing and I refused to hurt her like last time.

It was a miracle she forgave me so quickly. Actually, it made me question her intelligence. But she claimed to like me and said we had a lot more in common than I realized. Not wanting to deny a gift of friendship, I let the lack of common sense slide. After all, it was in my favor.

Her fist flew at my face, causing me to jump backward on instinct. She followed up with a punch toward my middle, which I avoided by spinning out of her reach. "That's how we're going to do this?" I breathed, dodging another fist.

"You said to get this over with quickly. Stand still and I'll grant your wish," she panted, kicking out this time.

"Why the hell would people want to take a course on violence?" I demanded, glancing at Zephyrus. "What purpose does this"—I ducked again, narrowly missing Ella's elbow—"serve?"

"It's physical exercise that also enables you to protect yourself in untoward situations." Zephyrus's arm snaked around my waist as he hauled me backward into his hard body.

"What kind of 'untoward situations'?" I spun and found my wrists caught in one of his hands before I could even consider my next move.

"Midnight Fae frequent the Human Realm regularly." He started backing me up off the mat.

"And there are situations there that require combat?" I asked while trying to find Ella over his shoulder. He thwarted my attempt to seek her intervention by speeding up his pace and practically shoving me backward with his grasp.

There had to be a way out of his hold, which I suspected was the lesson here, but my body seemed to obey him on impulse despite my brain's commands to the contrary.

"Many dangers exist in the Human Realm, Aflora," he murmured as my back met a wall. He pinned my hands over my head, his opposite hand going to my throat. "Weren't you recently captured and overpowered in the Human Realm?"

"By a Midnight Fae," I replied, glaring up at him. "Not a human."

"Hmm, but had you known how to properly defend yourself, maybe you wouldn't be here now," he said quietly, his grip tightening around my throat. "Even now, you're helpless with no idea how to fight me. I can feel your capitulation with every swallow. I *own* you right now, and there isn't a damn thing you can do about it."

The words were soft, his gaze burning into mine.

Everything seemed to fade away around us, the moment stretching as he held me captive in a decidedly inferior position. It should have infuriated me. Instead, it heated my blood, and not in a combat sort of way. Even if I could fight him—which I absolutely couldn't—I wouldn't. Because I *liked* him overpowering me.

The realization swept over me, causing me to melt beneath his hold.

I wanted him to own me, just like he said.

To tell me what to do. To guide me. To teach me in a manner that had nothing to do with this class and everything to do with *us*.

Oh, I'm in trouble.

First, Kols.

Now, Zeph.

And not to mention Shade, who still haunted my every breath.

"You like this," Zephyrus whispered, his heat surrounding me so entirely that I forgot how to properly breathe. Every inhale filled me with his intoxicating woodsy cologne. It left me light-headed and confused and aching for more.

"You shouldn't like this," he continued, his lips falling to my ear. "Is this why you let Shade manipulate you so thoroughly? He gave you a little attention, and you showed him your neck? Are you truly that easy?"

His comment lit a fire in me that ate through the heat his touch had inspired and spurred me into action. My knee connected with his steel thigh, sending a jolt of pain up my leg. That only made me angrier. I stomped on his foot with as much force as I could muster and squirmed in earnest against him.

His hips pinned mine, leaving me utterly defenseless and seething mad. "Let me go."

"But it was finally getting interesting," he whispered, his teeth skimming my earlobe. He nipped me gently, drawing a growl from my throat.

"You're too big to spar with me," I snapped. "It's an unfair fight."

"Fights are never fair," he returned.

"That's what magic is for."

"Ah, but it's against Midnight Fae Council rules to expose our kind in the Human Realm. So what would you do in this situation, pixie flower? Would you let a bigger male take advantage of you? Or would you use magic on him and bury the evidence?"

I stopped trying to free myself and instead met his smoldering gaze. "Are you asking if I would let him hurt me or kill him instead?"

"A male in this position would do more than just hurt you," he replied softly. "He'd destroy you."

"Then I'd have no choice but to truly defend myself."

"Then do it," he encouraged. "Defend yourself."

"You just said magic isn't allowed in a fight like this."

"We're not in the Human Realm."

"No, we're in Defense Without Magic class," I retorted. "Stop trying to convince me to break the rules, *Zeph*."

His mouth went to my ear again, his breath hot against my skin. "We're all breaking rules here, princess. That collar of yours is just the beginning of the quandary we've found ourselves in, yes?"

I froze. My lungs ceasing to work.

And he pulled back with a knowing smirk. "We have a lot of work to do, Aflora. I expect you to come prepared for our independent study course. I suggest you use the next two days off to study."

With that, he released me and stalked out of the room.

I gaped after him, as did several other students.

Kols flashed me an apologetic look, one that confirmed Zephyrus's statement.

He'd told the headmaster all about my bloodline, as well as the collar around my neck. Not that I could blame him, as the two of them were clearly close even when arguing. But it left me even more alone than before, reminding me that I had no allies in this realm. Whatever assistance Kols provided, it would likely come at a cost.

Because he would always choose his own over me.

Just as he should.

I'd do the same thing in his situation.

Which meant I could only trust him to an extent, if at all.

My shoulders stiffened, my spine straightening. I wouldn't let this knock me down.

Zeph was right. I had to fight for myself to survive this, which meant I needed to learn how to properly defend myself. Both in the Human Realm and in this one. Because someday soon, my life would very likely depend on it.

AFLORA

SEVERAL WEEKS OF CLASSES sped by without incident, mostly because I locked myself away in my room constantly to study. I had a lifetime of material to read in order to catch up in all my courses.

Death Magic class.

Warrior Magic class.

Elite Magic class.

Defense Without Magic class.

Break day.

Break day.

Midnight Fae Politics—the only class I seemed to be doing all right in, thanks to Ella's tutoring.

Malefic Magic class—my least favorite.

Independent study day—*ugh*.

Break day.

Break day.

Break day.

Today, I had another independent study day with Zeph. Who was a complete ass and way too hands-on for my liking. Mostly because he inspired thoughts that weren't appropriate. Especially when he pinned me to the mat or to the wall. I occasionally caught a glimmer of interest in his gaze, but it always disappeared before I could confirm it. Which meant I probably made it up in my daydreams.

Who could blame me with my nightly sexual escapades? If it wasn't Shade in my head, it was Kols. Causing me to heat up every time I went near the Midnight Prince. So I was pretty much in a constant state of red because he rarely left my side, always helping me in every class and ensuring my magic stayed in check.

Shade, however, seemed to be leaving me alone. Mostly because he kept skipping class. It annoyed the daylights out of me because I needed him in Death Magic class and he rarely showed up, forcing me to navigate the halls and spells by myself. When I asked him about it in my dreams, he kissed me to silence the conversation.

The only positive was that it forced me to be independent and to learn on my own. A benefit and a curse because I had no idea if I was doing anything correctly. I just went with my gut.

My legs buckled beneath me as Zeph swept his foot in an arc that sent me ass-first onto the mat. "You're distracted," he accused. "Do you think I want to spend my time babysitting you? Either show up or get the fuck out of my gym."

"Your gym?" I huffed, pushing myself back up to a standing position. "Are you finally embracing your headmaster role?"

He snorted and changed the subject. "Show me what you learned in Malefic Magic class yesterday."

I knew he was going to demand that.

After weeks of sparring with him during several class

days and on a handful of break days, I'd begun learning his expectations. He wanted me to apply every lesson to my sparring. Not only did he want me to master control of my power, but he also wanted me to be able to use it defensively.

Or *offensively* in this case.

Steeling my spine, I held out my hand and murmured the conjuring spell we learned yesterday. Ice picks formed around us almost immediately, all aimed at Zeph. His lips actually twitched as he batted them away with a quick defense spell. "Good. Again."

I repeated the incantation.

He destroyed it a second later.

"Once more."

Narrowing my eyes, I decided to throw him off guard and called up a different spell that I'd read about in my books last night. It was from the next chapter and involved fire. A dangerous move considering my history with the element, but my cerulean flames remained in check as a parade of black embers encircled Zeph.

His eyebrows shot up just enough to confirm I had surprised him. In the next breath, he uttered words that dispelled my creation. "Cute," he muttered. "At least I know you can read."

The jibe made me roll my eyes at him. "I'm not an ignoramus."

He considered me for a long moment. "No. You're not."

"Careful, Zeph. That was almost a compliment." I always called him *Headmaster* or *Zephyrus* around others, but I'd taken to using his nickname when in private. He never corrected me, so I took that as his way of allowing it.

"Well, you seem to be taking well to Malefic Magic, so let's try some more defensive moves. Maybe it'll help you not get your ass kicked next week."

"Praise tied to an insult," I mused. "There's the Zeph I've come to adore."

He glared at me. "Stop talking and start focusing."

"I am focused."

"Then knock me down."

I sighed. "Sure." We both knew I couldn't. Not only did he have, like, twelve inches of height on me, but he was also solid muscle and an expert defender. Hitting him was akin to punching a wall. Making him budge even an inch proved impossible every time we did this exercise.

But I'd try anyway because he demanded it.

Using a technique he taught last week in Warrior Magic class, I tried to circle around to his back to knock out his knees.

He moved with me, his arms folded, his expression bored.

Gritting my teeth, I tried the leg sweep he used on me a few minutes ago.

And nothing.

Not even a flinch.

It actually hurt me more than it probably hurt him.

So I ran around behind him and jumped on his back, my arms around his neck and my legs around his waist.

"What the fuck are you doing?"

"Hanging out," I said, my forearms locking around his throat. "When you get tired of holding me up here, you'll fall."

"You weigh practically nothing," he gritted out, his head twisting in a futile effort to see me. "Get down."

"No."

"This isn't useful at all." He sounded livid, which only made me cling to him more. Pissing him off had become a favorite pastime of mine. He was a dick to me, so I paid him back in kind. "Seriously, let go."

I placed my chin on his shoulder and sighed. "I think I'll just stay here until you fall down."

His resulting growl vibrated my chest through the thin fabric of our shirts. He'd worn another of those sleeveless ones that showed off his arms. It was about the only thing

I looked forward to on our sparring days. Oh, and his gray sweatpants. I rather liked those as well.

"Aflora, you have three seconds before I remove you, and you're not going to like how I do it," he warned.

I yawned. "Do your worst, Teach."

Probably not the wisest move to goad my instructor, but he didn't scare me. Maybe I'd adopted too carefree an attitude while attending the Academy.

My life was still very much in danger, and I took that seriously—hence my endless study hours—yet I had to let go sometimes.

And for whatever reason, those times seemed to occur when around Zeph.

And in my dreams with Kols and Shade.

These three men left me—

"Oof," I breathed as my back hit the sparring mat and Zeph sprawled out on top of me, locking my wrists over my head.

I hadn't even felt him move, just suddenly went airborne as he spun me around in a move that should not have been possible.

"Brat," he muttered, his hips pinning mine to the floor.

"Maybe," I managed to say, the word coming out on a winded exhale, thanks to the roughness of my landing. "But I got you"—I inhaled sharply to replenish my lungs—"on the floor."

His irises swirled with dark green, reminding me of the lush forests back home. I nearly sighed, loving that smoldering look and longing to see a real tree again. The dark magic continued to grow while my access to my primary gift remained just out of reach, although lately I'd felt it flaring on occasion, as if begging me to connect to the source.

Kols told me last week that he'd met with Exos while on a break day and learned that Sol had taken up the mantle of managing the source for me in my absence.

I was both pleased and saddened by that news. Pleased

because the male I loved like a brother needed to embrace his earth more, and I'd finally provided him with the push he required to do so. But the act saddened me as well because it meant the Elemental Earth Fae were seeking a way to survive without me.

It was the right thing to do. I couldn't lead them as an abomination. Yet that didn't stop me from wanting to try.

Kols believed I grew up with my Quandary Blood powers and that Shade's bite had just provided me with an excuse to access them. Or perhaps my presence at the Academy was what had truly awakened them.

Except I'd used them before when I stopped Elana.

"What put that puzzling look in your eyes?" Zeph asked, reminding me of his presence on top of me. Not that I'd forgotten. His woodsy scent and hard, masculine body were difficult to ignore.

"Nothing."

"Don't lie to me."

I gave him a look. "Because you never lie to me?"

He actually appeared affronted by the statement. "Actually, I haven't. Everything I've told you from the beginning has been truthful. We both know you're not going to survive here. It's just a matter of time. It makes my efforts futile, but at least I tried."

I laughed humorously. "You really have a way with words, Zeph."

However, he was right. He always spoke his mind around me, never avoiding the truth. That didn't mean I could trust him, but I could at least rely on him to give it to me straight.

"You're avoiding my question. What were you thinking about?"

"Why do you want to know?" I countered.

"Humor me."

I suspected he meant that literally, as he often found entertainment in my comments. This would no doubt be the same. "I was thinking about Sol taking control of the earth source and how I'm happy for him but sad for me. As an abomination, I can't properly lead my people, no matter how badly I may want to."

Zeph considered me for a long moment and released my wrists to balance himself on his elbows on either side of my head. It effectively caged me beneath him in a decidedly intimate manner that he didn't seem to notice. "Do you know why abominations are killed on sight?"

"Yes. They're evil."

He arched a brow. "Are they?" he asked softly, his gaze dropping to my lips. "Are you evil, Aflora? Or have our Councils trained us to fear what we don't understand?"

I swallowed, the warmth from his body seeping into mine, bringing us closer with each breath. A forbidden desire to kiss him entered my thoughts even while I considered his words. "I don't feel evil," I whispered.

"I don't think you're evil either," he agreed, his voice just as quiet, our conversation one we shouldn't be having. "I believe abominations are destroyed because our Councils fear their power. They claim it will disturb the source balance, but I think what they really mean is that it will disturb *their* balance."

"Why are you telling me this?" I asked as his eyes met mine once more.

"I don't know." He started playing with a loose strand of my dark hair, his long finger coiling it around the end. "Something about you makes me want to protect you. I keep fighting the instinct, yet you pull me right back in. It's a puzzle I can't solve, but I suspect it's linked to your power. Quandary Bloods are considered the most lethal of our kind. Yet, again, I wonder if that label was created by the Council out of fear, not practicality."

He pressed his forehead to mine, inhaling deep and sighing against my lips.

"You're improving admirably," he added, his words nearly silent. Then he fractured the moment by rolling off of me and landing deftly on his feet in one of his expert moves. "Class dismissed, Aflora. I'll see you in a few days."

My heart pounded in my chest as he walked away, my breathing ragged from both his words and his nearness.

If my power doesn't kill me, these males will, I thought, unable to move. I felt hot and cold and so incredibly turned on.

And my dreams tonight would only make it worse.

ZEPH

THANK FUCK FOR DAYS OFF FROM CLASS.

I had three days—technically, three and a half since I dismissed Aflora early—to work off this intense need throbbing inside me.

Every damn time I closed my eyes, I pictured Aflora beneath me, writhing on the sparring mat, or my bed, or against the damn wall, all the while moaning my name.

This mounting desire to fuck her was a problem. I nearly acted on it today, my dick rock hard as I pinned her to the floor. Talking had been the only way to remain focused and keep from doing something colossally stupid.

Glaring at my reflection in the mirror, I took in the dark hollows beneath my eyes and the stubble already growing against my jaw. It seemed that no matter how often I shaved, that perpetual shadow existed. One of these days,

I'd just stop and let the beard come.

Maybe.

"Fuck," I muttered.

What I really needed was blood. The supplements on campus were enough to keep a Midnight Fae going, but nothing compared to a fresh human vein. I'd spent the last month and a half living on the shitty substitute because I didn't feel like fucking around.

Tonight, that would change.

A hot vein and a warm, slick cunt were on the menu.

Because I needed to fuck before I did something I'd regret—like go next door, strip Aflora, and take my fill of her.

The damn female had gotten under my skin in the worst way. All these one-on-one sessions only made it worse. I had my hands all over her daily, memorizing her curves and feeling her body quiver against mine.

She read like an open book. It'd be so easy to take her. She wore her interest in her eyes. Not to mention the floral perfume of her arousal, which seemed to be a constant aphrodisiac between us these days.

New plan, I decided, ripping off my shirt and removing the jeans I'd just put on.

If I went to the Human Realm in this shape, I'd last all of a few seconds inside a woman. Especially if I found one that resembled Aflora.

I turned the water on in the shower, gave it about two seconds to heat up, and stepped beneath the cool spray with my arm braced against the marble tile. No amount of jacking off was going to fix this growing obsession. But it would prepare me properly for tonight, then I'd fuck Aflora out of my system.

And think of her the entire time.

It was so wrong, which only made this indulgence more right.

"Fuck," I cursed again, my head falling to my forearm as I gripped my shaft with my opposite hand.

I'd been hard since I set foot inside the gym. Aflora had pulled all that gorgeous hair up into a ponytail, just like she always did. It elicited all sorts of fantasies every time. I wanted to grab hold of all that hair and jerk her head to the side to trail my lips up the column of her neck and nibble her sweet flesh. Mmm, then I'd use my grip to guide her down to her knees and drive myself deep into—

"Hey, Aflora said you cut your session short. Did her magic...?" Kols trailed off as he entered the bathroom, my walk-in shower wide open in an unintended invitation because I hadn't bothered to close any doors. His attention shifted to my hand and the angry hold I had on my cock, his eyes heating at the sight. "Oh."

A single sentiment, filled with understanding.

I stroked myself while he watched, an entire history of intimacy sparking between us in the flash of a second. This intensity between us only grew over the years, blinding us to our actions and how they impacted others.

Now was no different.

I knew I shouldn't.

I knew giving in to this impulse would be a mistake.

Yet I couldn't deny the flaring of his pupils or the sharp intake of breath as his arousal quickly caught up to mine.

He wanted me like he always did.

And right now, I was too far gone to fight it.

I shoved away from the marble, took hold of his nape, and yanked him into the shower. He grunted as his back hit the wall, his gold irises on fire as he boldly met my gaze. I took his mouth in a punishing kiss meant to draw blood, and he gave it back in kind, his palm grasping the back of my neck and squeezing as he fought my dominance with his own.

He'd lose.

We both knew it.

But part of the allure between us was the battle each time we fucked.

I released his nape to grab his shirt, the buttons tearing

beneath my hand as I wrenched the fabric away from his chest. He growled. I snarled. And his shirt fell in tatters to the floor of the shower.

He kicked off his shoes, the leather ruined from the water. His pants and boxers soon followed, leaving us naked and panting against each other. "Tell me about the dreams," I demanded. "Because I know you've been in her head every night."

Kols arched into my palm as I grabbed his dick, his breath shuddering over my lips. "Not every night," he replied. "Just most of them."

"What does she do? How have you fucked her? I want details. All of them." I tightened my grip, giving him a firm, harsh stroke to underline my demand.

"*Fuck*, Zeph."

"That's the idea," I replied, pressing my forehead to his. "Tell me what she likes."

"She likes everything," Kols panted, his back bowing off the wall. "I've had her so many different ways over the last month, and she loves all of it. Sometimes she even takes control, allowing me into her fantasies. Yet she has no idea that I know or that it's all a mutual exchange. She thinks she's using me against Shade to kick him out of her head to indulge in her own desires."

"Mmm, if that were true, then I'd be there, too." Because I knew she wanted me, had seen the glimmer of interest countless times in her beautiful blue eyes.

"I think she's tried, but I'm always the one available," he admitted. "She fucking keeps me up at all hours with my hand on my cock, stroking endlessly until she's satisfied."

"Do you come?" I asked him, our eyes locked together.

"Every time."

"Do you imagine her coming over to lick you clean afterward?"

"Yes."

"Which makes you come again." It wasn't a question

211

but a statement. Because I knew Kols. We both were drinking blood supplements because we hadn't fed properly in ages. And it was all Aflora's fault. Her fucking enchantment, her allure, her sweet floral scent. "She's driving me mad."

"I know."

"Tell me about the dreams," I said again, wrapping my fist around both our cocks and stroking them together. "I want the details, Kols. Tell me how she tastes, how she screams, her favorite position. How does she like to be fucked?"

He swallowed roughly, his palm still on the back of my neck, his opposite hand on my arm as if he wanted to help me guide the pace below. I thrived on control, and so did he. Poor Aflora would be helpless between us, our needs dictating her every move.

And she'd fucking love it.

We'd make sure of it.

"She sucks cock like a queen," Kols said, his head hitting the shower wall as I squeezed our shafts together on a violent upward twist of my wrist. "I haven't taken her ass yet, but I want to. She looks amazing on all fours and cries out when I fuck her from behind. Shit, she's insatiable, Zeph. I can take her for hours, at least in her mind. I made her come four times against my tongue the other night, and she orgasmed a fifth time around my dick only minutes later."

I released a harsh breath, my hand moving faster. "She'd fit perfectly between us."

"I know. Trust me, *I know*." He bucked into my palm, his eyes falling closed. "But it's never going to happen. She's unattainable."

My dick throbbed with his words, which was entirely the point.

He knew how to spur me on.

Just as I knew how to ramp him up.

"If she were here, I'd command her to kneel and watch

us play," I told him, my wrist twisting once more. "Then I'd make her lick us clean when we finished."

Kols cursed, his exhale sharp and heated. "Would you let her come?"

"I'd *make* her come," I replied. "But I'd tell her to do it herself. She hasn't earned our mouths. Not yet."

"Because she's forbidden."

"She's a disobedient brat."

"Who is also completely out of our reach," he added, his taunt sending a hot jolt of lust down my spine. "She's dangerous, Zeph. A toy we're not meant to touch."

"I know."

"Walking down that path would be akin to flirting with death," he continued, stoking my flame even higher. "She's the most complicated challenge we've ever met."

"I know," I repeated, my forehead falling to his. "*Fuck*, I know."

"We can't have her, Zeph."

I growled at his declaration, prepared to fight.

He grabbed my shoulders to shove me up against the other wall, reading my cues as he always did. And I took hold of him to push him back, my grip on us relentless. "You're going to come all over my hand. Then you're going to lick it off."

"Fuck you."

"Not today," I replied with a sharp yank, eliciting a guttural sound from him. I'd let him take me once, after a long quarrel that equated to savage foreplay. But it was almost always the other way around.

"You're killing me," he groaned, shoving me backward once more.

I grunted as I hit the wall, then spun us around to place his back to the hard surface, keeping my chest pressed against his.

He growled. "You're in a fucking mood."

"I didn't ask you to join me," I said, my lips falling to the corded muscle along his neck to skim his pulse.

"No, you grabbed me and ripped off my clothes."

"You knew I was in the shower," I whispered darkly. "You could hear it."

"I didn't expect the door to be wide open."

"I didn't expect you to barge into my suite, but here we are." I ran my tongue over his raging pulse, felt his dick respond with a throb against my palm. "This is what you wanted, right? To fuck around?" It was what we both needed. All because of *her*.

He grabbed my hip with one hand, his opposite palm still around my nape in an assertion of false control. We both knew who was alpha between us. He just liked to fight it. And I loved that he did.

"She screams when she comes," he whispered, arching into my touch. "It's the most beautiful sound. I listen for it every night, knowing her fingers are buried deep in her pussy, and each time, I imagine my cock taking her deep while you drive into her ass." He hissed out a breath as I squeezed in response to the vivid vision painting my mind from his words. "Fuck, Zeph, she'd make the most arousing noises just for us."

I pictured it perfectly, us driving into her from two different angles and taking her to new heights of pleasure, all the while teasing and taunting and making her beg for more. More images flashed through my mind of her on her knees sucking Kols off, my hand in her hair to dictate the pace. Kols going down on her after I've fucked her, my cum on his tongue mingling with her fresh arousal. Aflora licking him clean after he blew his load all over my abdomen, like he was about to do now.

His forehead hit my shoulder, my lips still near his pulse. "Do it."

"You haven't fed recently," I replied, my breath ragged from my hand and our discussion.

"I'm fine. Fucking do it."

My incisors ached at the prospect, Kols's bloodline an aphrodisiac to my senses. As his pledged Guardian for life,

I could drink from him without worrying about the mating link snapping into place, because we were already bonded in a different way. I pledged my fealty to him nearly a decade ago, sealing our fates.

That was what marked this assignment as temporary.

No one could protect Kols like I could.

We were literally linked in an ancient ceremony very few knew about outside of his esteemed lineage.

"Now, Zeph," he demanded, his voice hoarse with the strain of his impending climax.

I sent him over the edge by biting down hard on his neck and piercing his vein. His power flowed into my mouth on a wave of molten energy that revitalized my connection to the dark arts in an instant and shot me into oblivion with him.

Our groans reverberated around the marble walls of my shower, his seed mingling with mine against our abdomens and coating us in the forbidden lust that constantly brewed between us.

That was why we enjoyed this—the wrongness of it.

We were both equally fucked up and embraced the insanity.

Nothing could ever exist here beyond mutual satisfaction, his destiny and mine already tied up in a fucking bow of Council-sanctioned perfection.

A perfection Aflora endangered, which only enticed me more.

She had the potential to change everything.

And destroy us all.

In likely the best way possible.

I released Kols's neck, my eyes finding his as our minds melded together in a temporary infusion. This always happened when I bit him, our mental states fluctuating.

Those thoughts about Aflora hadn't been mine, but his. Only, I echoed the sentiment now that I'd heard it. "You want her to fuck it all up," I whispered, having seen the darkest secret lurking inside his mind. "You welcome her chaos."

"It's a dark fantasy." He licked his lips, his voice hoarse from our joined pleasure. "It'll never happen."

"But you want it to."

"As do you."

I didn't deny it.

Because he was right. The depraved part of me that connected so deeply to Kols longed to see his wicked thoughts come true. Which was precisely why I released him. "Get out." This never should have happened anyway. I owed it to him—to *everyone*—to remain distant and avoid a repeat of the Dakota experience.

And Aflora posed the biggest risk in the history of my existence to Kols's safety.

We shouldn't even be discussing her, let alone fantasizing about her.

Kols narrowed his gaze, ignoring my command to leave. "Look, I get it. You're losing sight of your control around her. But being a dick isn't going to solve this problem."

I ground my teeth together, my urge to punch him rising with every breath. "This has nothing to do with my control." *And everything to do with protecting you,* I added to myself.

"It has everything to do with your control. You want her, and it's becoming harder and harder not to fuck her. The fact that she could derail a future we both despise only makes her that much more intriguing. But we can't. We both know we can't."

"I'm not the one considering that fantasy," I pointed out.

"Maybe not, but you like the idea just as much as I do," he tossed back as he bent to pick up his sodden clothes. "Next time, I'm in charge."

"There won't be a next time, Kols."

He gave me a look. "When did you start lying to yourself?" he asked.

He didn't wait for an answer, instead stepping out of the shower to throw his ruined wardrobe into my trash bin, and grabbed a towel.

"Thanks for the hand job," he said at the doorway. "But we're both going to need a hell of a lot more than that to survive Aflora."

I couldn't think of a single retort, his words truer than anything I'd ever heard.

So I leaned back against the wall, closed my eyes, and allowed the water to trickle over my skin, washing away the evidence of our pleasure.

He left with a towel around his waist, his accusation hanging between us.

When did you start lying to yourself?

The day Aflora first arrived, I thought back at him now, not that he could hear me.

The admission was more for me anyway.

Including the realization that I'd always been interested in the pretty little Royal Earth Fae, even when I claimed not to be.

Only now, my control was slipping, just as Kols had stated, proving he still knew me better than I knew myself.

I'm so utterly fucked.

AFLORA

"UGH, ZEPH IS IN A MOOD," Ella groaned as we finished our fourth lap around the courtyard. He'd started today's class with cardio fitness, claiming it would help fire us up for whatever defensive spells he had in store.

But I agreed with Ella. Zeph was just doing this to be cruel. "It's too hot for this."

"I know," she panted, grabbing her water bottle off the ground and downing half of it in one go. "I swear the moon is really a sun in this place, because fuck, it's burning up out here."

All the exploding burning thwomps nearby didn't help.

Zeph blew hard on his whistle, calling everyone in and pairing us off like he did for each class. Kols joined me in his sweats and sleeveless shirt, looking refreshed despite our heavy warm-up. "He's being a dick," he muttered.

"I know." I just didn't know why. We hadn't seen each

other since my independent study day that he'd ended early. That was five days ago. Usually, I saw him at least once during our break days, but he'd either left the Academy or avoided me the entire time. I suspected it might be the latter since he wouldn't even look at me today.

He stood with his arms folded in the center of the courtyard, his legs braced, as he explained today's exercise in an emotionless tone.

"Playing with familiars," Shade mused when Zeph was done, his arm brushing mine as he moved to stand beside me. "This part should be new to you, yes?" He didn't wait for me to reply, instead adding, "I wonder what's going to show up to protect you. Maybe a pretty flower?"

"Attack me and find out," I taunted.

As I'd practiced the conjuring spell last night during my preparations for today's class, I already knew what would arrive to defend me. And I'd love to watch it claw Shade's eyes out after the dream he'd inflicted upon me last night. I could still feel the scrape of his teeth taunting the flesh between my thighs. And I hated how just the image of it had me clenching my limbs, my arousal mounting all over again.

For as much as I loathed him, Shade knew how to use his tongue.

At least in the mental visions he continued to force upon me.

I asked him last night if it was all just for show, a fantasy he created to live through since his reality didn't measure up. He'd taken that as a challenge to drive me mad, and he'd thoroughly succeeded.

"Mmm, you do know. Now I'm intrigued," he said, referring to my taunt.

"You're paired with Stiggis," Kols reminded him. "So fuck off."

"Sadly, Stiggis isn't in class today. Some sort of family emergency involving Cordelia. Tragic, I'm sure. Anyway, I came over to play with my little rose instead," Shade replied.

"She's my partner, Shade. Find someone else to irritate."

"Hmm, maybe I should just join you both," Shade suggested, a grin in his voice. "Unless you're afraid it might be too much for her to handle, what with the sensations and all that." I flinched at his suggestive tone and the way his icy blue eyes glimmered with knowledge.

"I—"

"Stop fucking around," Zeph interjected, cutting me off. "Shade, work with Kols. I'll handle Aflora's lesson for today." He grabbed me by the elbow, leading me away before either male could reply.

I twisted out of his grip when we came to a stop in the corner of the courtyard and lifted a brow. "Is everything all right?"

"We're not here to chat," he snapped. "Take out your wand and perform the spell so I can see how much I need to correct before the next exercise."

Right, someone's in jerk mode. An ivy plant must have crawled up his butt this morning and latched on.

Not wanting to pry or make things even more uncomfortable between us, I pulled out my wand and muttered the incantation. A gorgeous bird with black and white feathers swooped down from the sky to land beside me, its yellow-and-black beak parting to release a sound of welcome.

I smiled at the beautiful creature. "Good morning to you, too, my darling Clove." I bent to run a finger along her soft feathers, having named her last night. She blinked big obsidian eyes at me, then leaned into my touch, her only confirmation of comfort.

"A falcon," Zeph mused, eyeing my familiar. "I would have expected a snail or something else slow and easy to kill, not a bird of prey."

I narrowed my gaze at him. "I'm not easy to kill."

He snorted. "Yeah. You are." He had his wand out in a flash, the same spell murmured beneath his breath to call his own animal protector to life.

I jumped as a slithering snake appeared, its tail long and as thick as my wrist. But it was the *heads* that grabbed my focus. There were three of them, all split at the proverbial snake neck—if a snake even had such a thing.

My falcon shifted, noticing my unease, the feathers along the wings beginning to flutter with power as the wings flexed outward. "Your familiar is a snake?" I asked, taking an unsteady step backward.

"Obviously."

The black and green scales began to move as the snake slithered toward me, three sets of beady red eyes seeming to glare at my existence. "I don't think it likes me," I whispered, sliding back another few inches.

"It's my familiar, not yours," he replied, folding his arms. "He senses how I feel and acts accordingly."

Which meant his three-headed creation would be in a similar mood to his master.

"Maybe this isn't a good idea," I said, eyeing the murderous glare coming from his familiar. Zeph might maintain a bored exterior, but inside, he appeared to be furious over something.

And that fury was definitely being reflected in his pet snake as it slithered toward me.

My falcon bristled again, letting out a warning caw of a sound that scattered goose bumps down my arms.

"Zeph," I whispered.

"Headmaster Zephyrus," he returned, his tone dripping ice. His snake hissed in response, the three heads echoing the sentiment and causing Clove to screech angrily.

I jumped backward, the two animals lunging for one another at the same time and squabbling across the ground.

"Stop!" I demanded, trying to pull the slithering

monster off my falcon. It had all three sets of mouths latched onto different points, its tail wrapping around the body to squeeze as Clove's talons dug into the scaly rope and tried to use its beak to pierce the slimy beast.

It all happened so fast, the animals quick and sharp and deadly.

They rolled across the courtyard, horrible sounds wrenching from my falcon's throat as Zeph's hideous creation threatened to destroy her. "Make them stop!" I begged him, tears pouring from my eyes. But he merely watched the show with a disinterested expression, his green irises as dead as his soul.

No wonder he created something so vile.

It represented him so completely.

To be able to stand there and watch his *pet* destroy my beautiful falcon without a care in the world.

Her cries slowly died, a piece of my heart seeming to break off and wither away with her.

I fell to my knees, the weight of devastation crushing me beneath a wave of desolation. The textbook didn't talk about this, only commented on the resolute loyalty of our familiars and how they will protect us to their dying breath.

Clove's obsidian eyes met mine with a final blink, her grief at having failed me so palpable that I cried out in anguish. "Please," I whispered, reaching for her and unable to do a damn thing because I didn't know how to help her. How to stop this. How to *kill* that sickly three-headed *thing* destroying my beloved creation.

"You're pitiful," Zeph said, his voice cold and remorseless. "Just like your familiar." His snake gave a victorious twist, and Clove's body went limp, her eyes falling closed.

I covered my mouth to hold back a sob, the sight before me destroying my will to breathe.

What was the point in inspiring life just to have it taken away so coldly?

The monster refocused on me, those lethal eyes

glowing with malicious intent.

"What will you do now?" Zeph asked. "Run away? Build a fortress of flowers to hide behind?"

I didn't reply, my grief suffocating my ability to move. *How could you?* I wanted to ask him. *Why did you do this to me? What lesson are you trying to teach me?*

The snake slithered off my dead familiar, pinpoints of evil watching me with obvious intent.

I just held its gaze, waiting for the inevitable. Even if I knew a spell that could hurt the creature, I wouldn't use it. "I don't take lives. I create them," I whispered to it, defeated and broken. "So do what you must."

"That's why you won't survive in this world," Zeph replied, his voice dark with some unspoken emotion. "There's no one here who will protect you. Only yourself. And without the will to survive, you'll merely perish."

I swallowed thickly, his words battering my already destroyed heart. "Better to perish than to become a monster." I met his gaze and found death staring back at me from his dark green depths. "A monster like you," I added, finally seeing him for the first time.

Whatever demons he harbored, I wanted nothing to do with them.

If he wanted to break me with this exercise, he'd succeeded, but not in the way he probably intended.

"Killing and hurting others isn't the only way to survive," I told him, pushing to my feet and ignoring his bristling pet. If that thing wanted to attack me, so be it. I wouldn't fight back, at least not in the way Zeph anticipated. Instead, I'd go about it my way—by undoing his spell. Maybe I'd tame a new pet in the process. Or maybe I'd die trying.

At this point, what did it matter?

I turned on my heel, leaving him behind.

He called my name. I ignored him.

He shouted after me. I stopped listening.

Several students watched me leave the courtyard. I

didn't acknowledge any of them.

I'm done, I thought. *I just want to go home.*

KOLS

"WHAT THE FUCK?" I demanded in a low voice, stepping into Zeph's path to keep him from pursuing Aflora. After that little display of jackassery, the dick clearly needed a moment to breathe before he made the situation worse.

"Move," he ordered me.

"No."

His green orbs flashed with emerald fire, his shoulders tensed for a fight.

I arched a brow, daring him to hit me. Class or not, I'd happily duel him in front of the entire school. Even if it meant having my ass handed to me. Anything to protect Aflora from more of Zeph's bad mood. "You could have at least told her that familiars can't really die." Well, unless the owner died, too. Then the familiar passed as well.

A muscle ticked in his jaw as he looked over my

shoulder in the direction she'd gone. "She needs to learn."

"Is that how you justify what you just did to her?" I wondered out loud. "Fascinating."

"I taught her a lesson she needed to learn."

"And what was that exactly? That she can't trust you?"

"Yes. Nor should she rely on me."

I shook my head. "Something tells me that lesson was more for you than it was for her," I muttered, turning around.

"Where the fuck are you going?"

"To fix the pretty little flower you just ripped apart," I tossed back at him.

"Class isn't over yet."

"Then fail me," I retorted.

"Don't tempt me, *Your Highness*."

I ignored him and followed Aflora's energy signature toward the Elite Residence. Zeph could kiss my left nut. Then spar with Shade, assuming the Death Blood bothered sticking around. He'd probably disappeared at his earliest chance, choosing to skip class rather than attend. Given Zeph's behavior today, I wouldn't blame anyone from jumping ship and telling the *headmaster* to fuck off.

Dick, I thought, irritated all over again. When I saw Raph, Zeph's pet snake, ripping into Aflora's falcon, I nearly intervened. But then Shade's damn bat went after Night, and nobody messed with my familiar.

Sensing my unease, Night settled on my shoulder, his black wings brushing my neck in a sign of affection. We'd met years ago when I first learned how to conjure him, as would be the case with most Midnight Fae. But Aflora would be brand new to the bond created with the protector spell, which only made what Zeph did that much worse.

"You can help me give her a demonstration, Night," I told my crow. "Then I'll release you to the wild once more." Most Midnight Fae had a relationship with their familiars where they only called upon them in time of need, or in this case, during a course discussion. They were considered a defensive arm, mostly used in combat. But I suspected Aflora wouldn't feel that way about her falcon.

I entered my suite, noted the stillness of the living area, and went straight for her room. She hadn't bothered closing her door, just went to her bed and curled up in a ball to stare out the window.

After everything she'd endured, this exercise had been the one to fracture her strength. Knowing that had my hands curling into fists at my sides, my irritation at Zeph mounting by the second. He'd taken this strong, beautiful creature and belittled her to a ball of sorrow. All because of his own emotions over his losing control around her.

My crow cawed, startling Aflora into a seated position, her blue eyes filled with hope.

Only to die when she found me in the hallway. Her focus went to Night on my shoulder, her expression clouding over. She returned her gaze to the window, her shoulders caving inward in a way I recognized immediately. Usually, that sort of response would send me running. But I stepped forward instead to sit beside her on the bed.

She trembled in response, her quiet sadness piercing the air and prickling my heart.

"You can bring him back," I informed her softly, referring to her falcon. He'd started stirring around the time I'd stepped into Zeph's path, which meant the beast would be back to full health soon. "Just use the same spell, and he'll find his way up here. It just might take a few minutes to get through all the doors. Sir Kristoff will let him through since he's tied to your essence."

"I don't want a new familiar," she said, her voice barely a whisper.

"It won't be a new familiar. We only get one."

She shook her head, her cheeks glistening with fresh tears. "Zeph killed her."

Her? I thought, frowning. I hadn't gotten a good look at the falcon, but Aflora would know better than I would. Just as she would be able to sense that the bond still thrived if she went looking for it.

Night flew off my shoulder to perch on her nightstand, taking my mental cue through our connection.

"Aflora," I murmured, sliding my arm around her shoulders. It was an awkward angle with her legs tucked partially beneath her, but she melted into my side, her body curling into mine as a single tear slipped from her eye.

"I thought the squawk..." She trailed off, her shoulders beginning to shake.

I followed her train of thought. "You thought Night was your falcon." I didn't bother pointing out that falcons didn't sound the same at all. Her heart didn't know the difference because Zeph had broken it with his cruelty.

"I'm sorry. This is... I'm being..."

"A familiar creates an unbreakable bond with its host," I whispered, my lips brushing her temple. "That's why you felt the pain from your falcon, sweetheart. But I promise you he, or rather *she*, is fine. A familiar can't die unless his or her owner dies. Zeph was an asshole for not telling you that."

Well, he was an asshole for a lot of things.

I gave her a reassuring squeeze and added, "Our familiars are created with the protector spell, meaning your falcon was born from the incantation. She's tied to your existence, so she'll always regenerate for as long as you're alive." Which, if I had it my way, would be for a very long time.

I swept her hair over her shoulder to palm the back of her neck and forced her to meet my gaze once more.

"Say *Ahaminee*," I told her. "You don't need your wand, just the spell." It was a more advanced phrase than the one her textbook would have taught her initially, one I only knew because of my unique upbringing.

Becoming King of the Midnight Fae required a certain

amount of defense instruction early on in my life. While I learned some things at the Academy, I mostly attended as a formality or a rite of passage.

Aflora studied me for a long moment as if debating whether or not to put her faith in me. I allowed her the time to consider her alternatives. She either believed me or she didn't.

"There's only one way to know the truth," I whispered, catching the distrust in her gaze. I couldn't blame her for being wary. While I might have gone out of my way to help her these last two months, it wasn't all out of the goodness of my heart. I wanted her to survive for a multitude of reasons, one of which existed in my pants.

Hence our frequent dream sessions.

Which worsened my cravings for her rather than satisfying them, as tasting her only made me want to experience reality with her that much more.

"*Ahaminee*," Aflora said, incredulity written into her tone and features. But there was enough power tied to it for the incantation to work. I felt the spell shimmering over the air, reaching out for her creation and beckoning her to join us.

When nothing immediately happened, Aflora's gaze narrowed in suspicion. "It's not a trick," I promised her. "Just be patient."

Her jaw clenched, but she gave me a stiff nod, choosing to believe me for a little bit longer.

I released her neck to stroke my hand up and down her back, lending her my strength in the process and caressing the energy vibrating around her aura.

It was a dangerous game to allow my power to mingle with hers. An intimacy I shouldn't grant her. One that would infuriate the entire Council if they ever found out. Yet it came so naturally to me that I couldn't stop it, my connection to dark magic thriving when in her presence because of our mating potential.

She relaxed considerably, her expression softening.

"What are you doing?" she asked, her pupils dilating.

"Something I shouldn't be doing," I murmured, my fingertips trailing up to her throat to brush her quickening pulse.

She leaned into my touch, her eyes falling half-closed. "Why does it feel so good?"

"Because it's meant to soothe you." My thumb traced her jaw, my gaze tracking the movement. She had such soft skin, reminding me of a flower petal. Her lips were soft, too. Or I imagined them to be in our shared dreams. They looked soft now, plump and ripe. I licked my own, my mind wandering to a place it shouldn't as I increased the intimacy of our connection.

She shivered, the power humming between us in synchronization. It'd be so easy for her to reach out, to take a sliver of my access to the source, but she didn't. She merely basked in the glow, her eyes now fully closed in contentment.

Until a cooing sound caused them to spring open in surprise. Our link weakened as her focus went to the falcon swooping in from the hallway, her expression opening in excitement and pure joy. "Clove!"

Aflora's familiar landed on the bed and shook out its feathers before peering menacingly my way.

Night cawed out a warning, but I sent a blast of security through our link, calming the animal before it picked a fight with the much larger bird. I wasn't concerned about Night's success—I knew he would win, as he always did—but I just didn't want a repeat of the experience outside.

The falcon shifted closer to Aflora, its black eyes on me the entire time.

"I'm not a threat to your fae," I informed the bird, lifting my hand for inspection. Not that it helped.

Familiars were resolutely protective of their owners, refusing to submit even to a Royal Fae of my caliber.

"The first rule you need to learn is how to communicate with your familiar via the bond you formed at the time of creation," I said softly, careful not to provoke any emotions from her that might inspire retaliation from her new pet. "For example, I'm currently reassuring Night that you and Clove are not a threat to us. You should do the same for your falcon."

"How do I do that?" she asked.

"Here, I'll show you." I slowly covered her hand with my own and opened our connection to begin a new tutorial on familiars and how to control them.

We covered a variety of spells all meant for calling our familiars to us. I also gave her some hints on how to properly defend herself and Clove when needed and even went into a handful of offensive incantations.

A hint of danger niggled at the back of my mind throughout our entire exchange, the notion that the method of my instruction posed significant risk to the crown, but Aflora never once tried to push, only using our link to learn and improve her own skills.

It took several hours, our familiars watching and bonding the entire time.

By the time we were finished, Aflora had propped herself up against her headboard, legs stretched out and crossed at the ankles, with me right beside her. She wore the most satisfied grin, her blue eyes sparkling with life once more and confirming I'd more than completed the task of improving her mood.

She sighed in contentment as her falcon preened between us, its large wings feathered outward in a display of black and white. Aflora stroked the tips, her lips twitching. "You know you're pretty, don't you?"

"I do, yes," I replied, fully aware she meant the compliment for the bird but accepting it for myself as well.

Aflora laughed and shook her head. "You're so modest, Kols."

"Extremely." I waggled my brows at her. "We both know I'm attractive."

"Do we?" She scratched her jaw, her gaze appraising

me slowly. "Hmm, I guess you're all right."

"All right?" I repeated, arching one eyebrow. "Is your vision failing?"

She snorted, her carefree attitude warming me inside.

Because *I* did that.

I put that smile on her kissable lips.

I improved her day.

And it pleased me to no end to see her resulting happiness now.

She held my gaze, her smile slipping into something more heated as she considered me with a growing seriousness. "You're more than all right," she whispered, her tongue slipping out to dampen her lips. "You're very much more."

"More what?" I asked her, aware of the risky tightrope we both stood upon and daring to take a step forward. "Much more what?"

She angled toward me, her palm falling to the small space on the mattress between us. "Handsome," she whispered, her glimmering blue eyes falling to my mouth.

"Just handsome?" I asked, leaning into her magnetic pull.

She swallowed, her hooded gaze lifting to mine. "More than handsome." She brought her hand to my cheek, her opposite one still situated between us. "You're gorgeous, Kolstov."

"No." I cupped the back of her neck, angling her head to the exact place I wanted it, my lips very nearly brushing hers. "You're the one who is gorgeous, Aflora," I corrected her. "Fucking irresistible."

She shuddered, her sweet breath a kiss I could no longer deny. I captured her mouth on her next inhale, my tongue sliding in to duel with hers a hairsbreadth of a second later, and our worlds came crashing down together in unison.

I felt the intrusion deep inside, the rightness of our embrace locking us together in an intimacy that would never end.

She was beneath me in the next moment, my hips settling between hers as I pinned her to the bed. Months of foreplay between our minds led to this, our bodies coming together like two magnets that had finally removed the barrier between us.

That barrier was a reality I felt slipping away.

Cascading us both into a dangerous oblivion neither of us could deny.

"Aflora," I murmured, my teeth skimming her lower lip.

I should stop this.

Should roll off the bed and walk out the door.

But fuck if my body would listen to my mind.

There'd been ample opportunities for her to access my power. Why would she do it now?

Because you're distracted, a dark part of me reminded.

Only, she appeared just as distracted beneath me with her eyes closed, her body arching up into mine, seeking *more*.

I kissed a path down her neck, my incisors achingly close to her seductive pulse.

No, I told myself, quivering deep within. *That's not for you*.

Oh, but the rest of her I could taste. Could lick. Could nibble. Could explore.

"Tell me to stop," I whispered, my hands on the hem of her shirt, clenching harshly against the fabric. "Tell me to leave."

She shook her head, her little pants of need music to my ears. "I've dreamt of this so many times," she admitted, her voice breathy and so fucking sexy. "I want you, Kols. I know... I know the risk. I know this is wrong. I know we shouldn't." She groaned, her nails biting into the back of my neck as she caught my gaze. "But I need to *know* this. Please."

KOLS

AFLORA'S GRIP TIGHTENED as she yanked me downward, her lips reclaiming mine, causing me to lose myself to her all over again.

Only this time, I welcomed the forbidden nature of our embrace.

I reveled in the sweet danger brewing between us.

Allowed it to seduce my senses and jerk me into the licentious promise of pure sin.

Her shirt disappeared, allowing me my first real glimpse at her pale skin. "So beautiful," I mused, kissing a path downward to the lace of her bra. Her blue eyes burned with passion and need, eliciting a smile from me as I licked a delicate path along the crease of her breast. Her nails dug into my scalp, her breaths quickening as I drew the fabric aside with my teeth to reveal one stiff, rosy tip.

I gave it a tentative taste, a groan catching in my throat

at the pure lust dilating her pupils in response.

"More," she begged.

"More what, sweetheart?"

"Just *more*." She writhed beneath me, her sweet body primed and ready from all our nighttime flirtations. I could almost *feel* her need inside me as if we were connected in an intimate pool of thought.

Her whimpers were music to my ears, encouraging me to suck her nipple deep into my mouth. "Kols!" she cried out in response, tossing her head backward on the bed in a rapturous wave.

I nibbled the tip before repeating the action on her other taut peak, my palm cupping her opposite breast and giving it a tender squeeze. Fuck, she was responsive, her entire body vibrating with desire beneath mine from barely any attention to her tits.

All those fantasies taught me what she enjoyed.

But they also gave her insight into my preferences as well, which she proved by hooking her fingers into the waistband of my pants and shoving them downward in a bold move. That exposed my cock.

She didn't apologize.

Didn't look to me for approval.

Just used her foot to guide the fabric down my legs, leaving me bare below the waist. "Fuck, Aflora."

"Yes," she replied, her hands moving to my shirt to tug it upward. "Yes, please."

A growl morphed into a groan in my throat, my forehead falling to her collarbone. "Don't say that unless you mean it."

She trembled, her grip tightening in the fabric still wrapped around my shoulders. "Please, Kols." Her legs wrapped around my waist, placing my shaft right against her heated center. I could feel her warmth and dampness through the fabric of her black stretch pants, her need seeping into my skin as she rubbed herself shamelessly against me.

I cursed.

My dick throbbed.

My balls tightened.

And I nearly forgot how to fucking breathe.

Because I wanted her. *Badly*.

Take her, a dark voice whispered. *Fuck her raw*.

Just the image of it nearly had me coming all over her.

That I could sense her own mounting need only intensified the experience, urging me to take what I wanted, to indulge in the forbidden fantasies lurking between us.

Her heels dug into my ass, demanding action. My lips hovered close to her breasts, my forehead still against her collarbone.

And then she moaned.

The sound went straight to my groin, wrapping around my cock and giving it a figurative stroke that removed reason from my thoughts.

I wanted her.

She wanted me.

We were consenting adults.

This is going to happen.

A forbidden blanket swathed us in a cocoon of lust and illicit cravings, my mind running rampant with all the ways I wanted to take her. But first, like this, with my cock buried deep between her thighs.

I kissed her again, my tongue spearing her mouth, my resolve crumbling into dust.

She welcomed me with a sweet, needy noise.

And the rest of our clothes disappeared with a muttered spell under my breath.

"Oh," she marveled as the magic shimmered over her skin. She arched into me, her hot pussy welcoming my dick in a wet kiss.

"Last chance, Aflora," I warned her, my shaft sliding through her damp folds.

"Fuck me," she demanded, just as I'd taught her in our

dreams.

Because I loved those two words from her lips.

She made them sound so inappropriate, thus serving as a reminder of how wrong this was between us and inviting my darker instincts out to play.

I wanted to do wicked things to her.

Teach her how to fuck in the best ways.

Explore every inch of her.

Degrade her.

Claim her.

Fucking mark her.

Fuck, I was so hard it almost hurt. Every part of me ached to finish this, to make her mine, to claim her so resolutely that no one else could ever satisfy her again.

"Please," she breathed. "Take me, Kols. I need this. I need *you*." The plea in her voice sliced through the final barrier between us, snapping my control in half.

I slammed home inside her, a jolt of electricity zipping up and down my spine. Fuck, I'd never felt so connected to a woman. Her sensations were mine and mine were hers, only heightening the experience and spurring us onward into a wicked dance between skin and spirit.

She screamed as I plunged in and out of her, driving us both into a frenzy of pants and ecstasy that I felt sure everyone on campus had to feel. Because our powers were mingling once more, her gift weaving with mine in an intoxicating manner that I couldn't escape from.

Dangerous.

Must. Stop.

Can't.

Oh, fuck.

Mine.

I fought that last thought, my body tensing against hers, only to be sucked back into her web of delirious energy as her thighs tightened around me. This was wrong. So, so, so wrong.

Ugh, fuck, I can't pull away.

More.
Less.
Destruction.
Beautiful.

My name fell from her lips in a sound of worship that heated my skin, her gorgeous form glued to mine as I fucked us both into a state of oblivion unlike any I'd ever reached. She screamed as she tumbled over a cliff of darkness, yanking me down with her into a rapturous sanctuary of insanity and bliss all mingled as one.

Her pleasure rivaled mine, her mind open to me in a way I didn't understand.

I could sense her earth.

Could smell the trees and flowers she adored from home.

Could feel her safe haven welcoming me home.

What's happening? I wondered, delirious with pleasure and confusion, my cock pulsing on another orgasm inside her and taking me under once more. "*Fuck,*" I breathed, my head falling to her shoulder.

She quivered, her own ecstasy rupturing as a result of mine, our joining so much more powerful than any dream ever allowed us to experience.

Only, it left me feeling cold at the end, my soul instantly sensing a disturbance, a foreign presence that shouldn't be inside me. I immediately locked it down, terror screeching through me at the thought of another woman using me so horribly.

Yet my powers surrounded me completely, the energy signature normal and untouched.

Except that unknown essence remained, clinging to my life source and locking around me in a way it shouldn't.

I again tried to sever it, using my power to attack the bond and freezing when Aflora shrieked below me in pain.

Her eyes flew open, meeting my gaze at the same time. Her lips parted. Mine curled into a snarl. "What did you do?" I demanded.

Because I could see in her gaze that she knew something.

Panic and horror and fear all mingled in her expression at once.

Her lips moved without sound.

Her pupils flared.

"What the fuck did you do?" I repeated, going to my elbows on either side of her head. Our bodies were still joined below, my cock still pulsing inside her. But fury overrode the rapturous oblivion, my mind catching up with the sensation pulsating in my heart. "*How?*"

"I-I don't know," she sputtered. "I... It shouldn't..."

I recoiled from her, going to my knees on the bed and realizing with disgust what we'd just done. "Fuck!" She'd bonded me. Not as a Midnight Fae, but as an Elemental Fae. I could feel the ivy of her earth magic tightening around me, suffocating my connection to the source and drowning me in an essence I didn't want. "Get rid of it. Sever it. *Remove it.*"

"I-I can't," she stammered, her expression one of astute horror. "It's the third level."

"*What?*" I knew how Elemental Fae bonds worked. There were four levels, the first two breakable and the third... not. It marked us as betrothed. Until the final ceremony that forever joined two Elemental Fae souls. "That's fucking impossible." It required agreement by both parties, unlike Midnight Fae bonds that could be completely one-sided when driven by the male.

"I don't—"

"How the fuck did this happen?" I shouted, springing off the bed and trying to get as far away from her as possible. "How did you trick me?"

"I didn't!"

"The hell you didn't," I snapped, starting to pace. "I wouldn't bond you willingly." I had a duty to my kingdom, to my people, that always came first. And I knew better than to allow an Earth Fae to initiate a fucking mating bond.

I was the future king.

A royal.

A damn powerful Midnight Fae.

"You tricked me somehow," I accused her.

I just didn't know how or when. Perhaps it'd all been a ploy from the beginning. A ruse to seduce me into something wicked. That would explain the pull.

"Was this your plan all along?" I demanded as another thought quickly followed, one that threatened to pull me into a murderous state. "Did Shade put you up to this?"

"What? No!"

"Then why would you do this? Are you working with him? Trying to bring shame to my family? To me? To destroy my reign before it even begins?"

Her lower lip wobbled, her blue eyes spitting fire as she scrambled upward on the bed. "Fuck you, Kols!"

"Been there, done that, princess," I retorted, livid with myself for my stupidity. I gripped the back of my neck, took in the sight on the bed again, and turned away before I did something idiotic like light it on fire. "Get out." The words slipped from my lips before I could take them back. Then it struck me how right the demand was, how much I needed her to leave right this fucking second before I killed her.

Because that was the immediate solution—her death.

It'd break the bond.

It'd shatter Shade.

It'd be a fitting punishment for all parties involved, myself included because I suspected losing her would hurt me as well, thanks to this foreign shit she'd put inside my chest.

I growled and palmed my pec. "Fucking get out, Aflora," I demanded, needing her as far away from me as possible before I did something I couldn't take back.

"And go where?" she asked, her voice suddenly much quieter than before.

The temptation to look at her, to apologize, hit me so swiftly that I snarled. Because fuck that. She didn't deserve my concern. She'd trapped me in her forbidden web and ensured I couldn't leave without significant pain to us both!

I hated her.

Loathed her fucking existence.

Wished I'd never met her.

"Get out!" I shouted, uncaring of how deranged I sounded. Molten lava boiled in my veins, my power increasing by the second. If she didn't fucking leave, I'd explode and she'd bear the brunt of that eruption.

Her sob pierced my ears.

I ignored her.

Too focused on the mounting anger threatening to shred us both.

I barely noticed her running past me in a pair of pants and a shirt, didn't once consider how she'd dressed so quickly, and instead knelt on the floor to unleash the power that threatened my very existence. Flames erupted throughout every inch of her room, destroying the evidence of our fucking, and eating through all her belongings in a thorough sweep of power.

Objects could be replaced.

I'd figure it out later.

When I could properly think again.

"Fuck!" I bellowed, red flames encircling me and spiraling and screeching across the room. A blast of power slammed the door to keep it from spreading through the suite, leaving me trapped inside the raging inferno.

I welcomed the heat.

The punishment for my actions.

And crumpled into a broken pile of guilt and sorrow.

Not just because I'd let the Midnight Fae down, and my parents, but Aflora as well.

I deserved to burn.

I welcomed the pain.

"Destroy me," I demanded, my forehead meeting the ground. "Just fucking destroy me."

AFLORA

HOT.

I felt too *hot*.

Like a volcano on the verge of an eruption.

Heat simmered beneath my skin, inching through my veins, causing me to sweat as I ran aimlessly through the midnight air.

Get out.

Fucking get out.

Kols's fury pierced my heart, his anger a brand lashing at my heart with each step.

I could feel his ire, his anger, his *blame*.

But I hadn't meant for this to happen, didn't understand how it was even possible. *He's not an Elemental Fae*, I thought for the thousandth time. *I can't bond with him.* Yet I felt the unmistakable connection tying us together. We'd skipped levels one and two and blasted straight to the third, our link resolute.

Breaking it would be impossible outside of death.

As if the fae required another reason to kill me.

I need to get out of here, I thought, spinning in a circle somewhere outside of the Academy walls. I'd gone through the open gate, uncertain of my destination, and now I had no clue where I was. A stupid move born of emotional turmoil.

How could a beautiful moment go so wrong?

Kols's essence still warmed my thighs, his seed dampening my core.

Mother Earth, that man could move. He'd taken me to a state of incomprehension. Only to be destroyed by fate showing her ugly head.

It left me mated to *two* Midnight Fae.

I screamed an incoherent word into the void of darkness around me. There wasn't a curse alive that could express my frustration. Nor one that could help. Not even an enchantment. Unless something existed that could undo time, but I doubted it.

"What the fuck are you doing out here?" a deep voice demanded, sending me in a spin toward a shadow lurking near a tree.

I could hardly see, the moon hidden above the thick branches of the forest I'd entered. "Zeph," I said, my heart in my throat.

Clove had followed me outside, only to take flight when I started to run, and I had no idea where she went. Probably somewhere with Kols's crow, as both birds had followed me on my mad dash outside. At least they were safe from Zeph's vile snake.

He moved forward, his steps silent over the earth. "Are you all right?"

I startled, his tone holding a note of concern, but I knew better. Besides, it was such an absurd thing to ask because obviously I wasn't all right.

Just the notion of it had me laughing out loud, the urge

to cry hitting me square in the gut.

Answering him would be futile, so I ignored him instead, spun around again, and picked up my path again through the trees.

Only, he caught my arm and yanked me back toward him.

I reacted instinctually, my leg sweeping low to knock him off-balance and my fist cutting upward to strike his jaw.

Both were hits that would have made me proud in defense class. His resulting grunt and growl, however, had me instantly regretting my immediate reaction.

I took off at a sprint, needing to escape him.

But his arms ensnared my waist merely two steps later.

"What the actual fuck, Aflora?" he demanded, his lips against my ear. "Is this about Raph?"

"Raph?" I repeated, lost. "Who's Raph?"

"My tripod snake," he replied softly, his grip tightening as he pressed his nose to my neck. "Why do you smell like Kols?" A soft question, one I couldn't stand to answer.

I hadn't meant for the bond to snap into place.

Hadn't meant to lose myself in the moment.

Get out.

Fucking get out.

"Let me go," I begged, the heat building beneath my skin once more. It'd temporarily subsided due to the shock of his arrival, but it had returned with a vengeance, flooding my veins with liquid fire.

"No." His tone brooked no argument, yet I needed him to release me, this power inside me threatening my every breath.

"Zeph..." I tried to warn him, my breath coming in pants as sweat beaded across my skin. "It burns," I whispered, my limbs beginning to shake beneath the onslaught of energy cascading through my spirit.

"What are you doing?" Zeph asked, spinning me in his arms and catching me as my knees buckled.

"She looks ready to explode, and not in an appealing way," a new voice said as Shade materialized beside us. His palm caught my cheek, his dark gaze searching. "What has you so troubled, little rose? Why do I sense Kols in you?"

"How the hell did you know we were here?" Zeph cut in.

"Her fear called to me," Shade murmured, his eyes still holding mine. "What did Kols do to you, Aflora? Why is his power pouring through our bond?"

I couldn't say it even if I wanted to, my throat tight with emotion and fear as the flames threatened to surface. If Zeph didn't release me, I'd burn him alive. And even if he deserved that after what he did to Clove, I couldn't hurt him. Not like that.

Swallowing thickly, I pushed the heat down, only to have it skyrocket inside me and spark at my fingertips.

"Her eyes are glowing," Zeph said. "Cerulean fire."

"Where's Kols?" Shade demanded.

"Fuck if I know."

"Isn't it his job to keep her powers under control?" He finally released me to focus on the male behind me. "He's done something to her powers."

Is that concern in Shade's voice? I wondered, starting to feel delirious. *Can't be. No.*

"I can sense it, too," Zeph replied, that same note in his tone.

This is bad, I thought, trembling beneath a hum of electricity that ran across my skin. "Burning," I managed to whisper, my knees wobbling violently. "Going to—"

A scream ripped from my throat, cutting off my words, as pain unlike anything I'd ever felt slashed a hole right through my chest. Zeph released me with a hiss, allowing me to fall to the ground in a ripple of cerulean flames that scorched the forest floor.

"*Fuck!*"

"What the fuck is that?"

Their voices mingled, making it impossible to tell them

apart. I couldn't hear beyond the roar of power lapping at my essence and overtaking my soul.

Tears slid from my eyes.

Everything ached.

My heart sped up.

Too much.

It's too much.

I didn't know how to balance it all, to find my equilibrium. It reminded me of my first time accessing the source of my earth power, that necessary need to placate both sides between my soul and the core of my element.

Only, I couldn't find that center.

It kept moving out of my reach and showering me in electricity, humming dangerously through the air, warning me of the wrongness of my presence.

"Help me," I begged, not sure if I spoke the words out loud or muttered them in my mind. "Too hot. Dying."

An agonized cry reached my ears, the sound excruciating, one I belatedly realized was my own. Everything glimmered in shades of blue around me, a rippling effect of my overheated aura.

Focus, I told myself. *Rein it in.*

Only, I didn't know how because I was too full of energized substance to accept any more.

I ripped at the choker around my neck, needing my earth, hoping to hide in the source to find my stability once more.

There, I thought, my element immediately responding despite the device encircling my neck. Whether I'd somehow deactivated it or overrode it, I wasn't sure, but my beautiful gifts responded and grounded me with the familiarity of soil and earth.

I rooted myself to the ground, reveling in my birthright and locking onto my royal line to find sanctuary in my home element.

Every inhale filled me with floral aromas, and every exhale calmed the fire, until finally I surfaced enough to survey my surroundings in a burnt courtyard shrouded in sunlight.

Blue embers danced in the air, drawing my focus to the damage around me.

I opened my mouth, but no sound escaped me, only another whimper of pain as the flames began to build once more inside me.

Oh, no...

My stomach heaved, a cramp building in my lower abdomen and churning with unrepressed power.

"We need to ground her!" someone shouted. It sounded like Kols, but that couldn't be right.

"And how the fuck do we do that?" *Hmm, Shade,* my mind supplied, his presence providing a temporary balm to my rioting soul. *Mate.*

"I have an idea." That still reminded me of Kols, some part of me recognizing his aura nearby. Or perhaps in me. After all, he was my earth mate now. Sort of. Maybe.

What have I done?

Everything went quiet once more beneath another pulsing wave of excruciating pain that crushed me to my very soul. I curled into a ball on the ground, seeking the utopia only created by true balance.

It eluded me, my talents too fierce and untamed to heed any sort of order.

I whimpered, then jolted as a hand clamped onto my throat, giving it a squeeze. "We're going to help you," a deep voice informed me.

Zeph.

He guided me to my back, his palm squeezing when I tried to curl into myself once more. "We need you like this," he explained, his thigh settling between mine.

Skin to skin.

I frowned.

Why am I naked?

"This had better work," Shade said, his lips suddenly by my ear as he stretched out alongside me.

"If it doesn't, there's only one other alternative," Kols replied, his mouth near my opposite ear, his warmth seeping into my side.

"Kols," I managed to say, my throat dry as I tried to look at him, to apologize, to ask where he'd come from or how he'd arrived.

"Don't," he replied, his tone harsh.

Pain splintered in my chest, only to be overwhelmed by the lava pouring through my being. I could try again later. Assuming I survived this next blast of heat.

Zeph released my throat, his hand traveling down my torso to my hip as he settled between my splayed thighs.

"What are...?" Another pulsating shock of heat silenced my question, thwarting my ability to focus on anything other than the quakes rocketing my limbs.

"Now!" Kols demanded. "Before she detonates again!"

Again? I thought, wincing as something sharp pinched my neck. *Shade*, I recognized immediately, our bond snapping more firmly into place with his bite.

"No!" I screamed, but it was lost to the ripple of ecstasy his mouth forced through my system. I shuddered, conflicted between the inferno threatening my being and the euphoria trickling into my veins.

I gasped as Kols bit the other side of my neck, his incisors sliding deep into my vein to suck harshly at my blood.

A cry lodged in my throat, the pain mingling with pleasure as a third mouth met my breast, the kiss almost gentle. The slice of teeth followed against my tender skin, causing my back to bow off the ground. *Zeph*. I felt his claim, his bond lashing at my spirit and sinking literal teeth into my soul. Along with Kols.

All three of them pulled in unison, taking my blood and leaving me weak and defenseless beneath them.

And utterly powerless.

I nearly wept, my impending death the most blissful and rapturous experience of my life.

Until I realized I wasn't dying at all, but living.

Thriving.

Balancing.

They were taking on my excess energy, drinking their fill and leaving me depleted in their wake. Creating a new equilibrium, one that allowed me to breathe again, to think, to realize the gravity of their sacrifice.

They'd all three just taken me as a mate at once.

Drinking my essence in an effort to help me create order within my powerful chaos.

And I had absolutely no idea why.

I opened my mouth to ask, but my lips were suddenly too numb to move.

They were taking too much.

I tried to tell them, to warn them, to beg them to stop, but each pull sucked me deeper into a web of euphoria I couldn't escape from. Two mouths at my neck, one at my breast, and a pulsing need blossoming between my thighs.

As if Zeph knew, he released my breast to slide his mouth down to my nipple, his green eyes meeting mine as he gently teased the tip with his tongue.

I weakly arched off the ground, my body responding while my mind fought to catch up. Only, he sucked my nipple deep into his mouth, causing my brain to flicker out of existence.

Kols chuckled against my neck, his tongue dancing over the wound he'd created. "That's fun," he mused, tracing a wet path up to my ear. "If I didn't want to kill you, I'd indulge in that reaction more."

I shivered, uncertain of how to react to that threat.

"You won't kill her," Shade said, his mouth whispering over my jaw as he moved to hover against my lips. "It'll hurt too much." He kissed me tenderly, his tongue slipping between my lips to give me a taste of my own blood.

Zeph nibbled my breast sharply, causing me to gasp, and Kols mimicked the motion against my earlobe. "What the fuck are we going to do now?" he asked.

"Mmm, you're the future king," Shade murmured, speaking each word against my mouth. "I imagine you'll figure it out. In the interim, I'll tuck our sleeping beauty into my room for the night since you destroyed hers."

"Don't you fucking—"

I never heard the end of Kols's statement, his words disappearing beneath a cloud of smoke. One that seconds later unfurled to reveal a bed adorned in rich purple silk.

Shade's bed.

ZEPH

"FUCK!" Kols shouted, his focus on the space Shade and Aflora had just vacated. "I'm going to fucking kill him."

"That assuming you'll be alive to do it," I muttered, looking around the field. "You fucking mated her, didn't you?"

Kols expelled a long breath, several curses following before he said, "All three of us just fucking did."

"Oh, I know that part." I pressed a palm to my chest, irritated by the strand circling my heart and linking back to a woman none of us had any business claiming as our own. "I was referring to *before* our little quad formation. Aflora was drenched in your power."

Kols grimaced, his palm gripping the back of his neck as he blew out a long breath. "We, uh, fucked."

I gathered as much by her half-dressed state. She'd run

out here without shoes on, her hair a mess, and her shirt on backward. It was part of the reason I'd chased after her from the Elite Residence. The other part was driven by guilt. I'd been hard on her today. Maybe a little too hard.

And now everything had gone to hell.

"I get fucking her"—more than I ever wanted to admit—"but why the hell did you bite her?" I knew Kols. He had better control than that, even around someone as alluring as Aflora.

"I didn't. Not until just now, anyway." He shoved off the ground to his feet, his focus shifting to the damage around us. "Her Elemental Fae bond initiated, taking us to the third level."

My lips actually parted. "That's why I smelled her all over you." I'd known it was deeper than sex, but I couldn't figure out why she practically oozed his magic. Now I understood it. "She mated you."

"She did." Anger colored his tone, but I suspected he was more furious with himself than with her. Kols knew as well as I did that the bond between Elemental Fae required mutual agreement to take form.

Which meant that deep down he'd wanted to mate Aflora.

And that had to be pissing him off.

"It caused our powers to merge," he added gruffly, taking in the destruction. "She exploded as a result."

"Your power sent her over the edge."

"And straight into the deep end." He shook his head, his annoyance palpable. "I have no idea how we're going to fix this. The consequences will be severe."

"They'll absolutely kill her for this, and likely me as well." Because I'd failed to protect Kols yet again. I'd also partaken in the four-way bond, not to benefit Kols but to save an abomination. That wouldn't be forgiven lightly, if at all.

"Yes," Kols agreed softly. "They'll slaughter her publicly to punish the three of us. Then they'll take your life as well to hurt me specifically. And my father will definitely postpone my ascension." He uttered the words in a dead tone, his golden irises flaring with power and knowledge.

I slowly pushed to my feet, then tucked my hands into the pockets of my sweats. "Is that the path you choose?"

He arched an auburn brow. "Are you asking if I'll let them kill you?"

"Will you?"

"No."

"You won't have a choice." Once the Council found out about this, they'd have all our heads on a platter.

"There's always a choice," Kols countered, his gaze holding mine. "Killing Aflora will literally destroy a piece of my soul—thanks to our illegal mating bond—and leave me in a shell of misery. I've seen it done to other fae. It's the worst kind of punishment imaginable." He stepped forward to grab my shirt, yanking me to him. "And losing you is a fate I refuse to ever accept. I won't allow them to take you or Aflora from me."

Aflora, I knew, was more for his own survival. Losing his mate would destroy him, and she'd bonded him as both an Elemental Fae and a Midnight Fae, marking the consequences of her loss as undefinable. It might very well kill him.

However, he could absolutely live without me.

He just didn't want to.

I grabbed his shirt with one hand, my opposite palm going to the back of his neck, and kissed him to return the sentiment.

As much as I sometimes despised this male, I also couldn't live without him.

Even when I wanted to.

He returned the embrace, his tongue laced with Aflora's blood as he delved deep into my mouth in a dominant sweep of power. I returned the move in kind, taking him with a ferocity I knew he couldn't deny, and smiled when he groaned.

Now wasn't the time or place.

I also wanted to add Aflora to the mix. We were all going to hell anyway, so I might as well grant myself the taste I'd craved for weeks.

But first, we needed a plan, and to properly form that, we required time.

"Your father would have felt the disturbance of power," I said, releasing Kols almost as swiftly as I'd grabbed him.

He nodded. "I know."

"Either you tell him the truth and damn us all or you give him a cover story. And if you choose the latter, then we need to do something to hide our connection to Aflora." Because everyone who walked near us would be able to smell her in our blood and vice versa. It would be obvious to them all what we'd done tonight, and word would spread quickly through the ranks. Especially when several Council members' children attended Midnight Fae Academy.

"I can handle the cover story," Kols murmured. "But we need to make sure Shade is on the same page, as he'll be the alibi."

"You're going to tell your father the two of you engaged in an illegal duel," I translated.

Kols nodded. "It'll explain this." He gestured around the burnt clearing that Aflora had created with her explosion of power. "My father will reprimand us both, but it'll be a verbal warning more than anything else. He'll claim it's a rite of passage for us to fight."

A good and fair point. "That'll work, but we need something to hide the bonds."

"That's going to be harder," he muttered.

"No, it's going to cost us," I corrected. "A lot."

"What do you mean?"

"I know a guy," I muttered, massaging my jaw as I considered what I was about to reveal. "He can help hide things, like bonds."

Kols narrowed his eyes. "Like protection oaths?"

"Yeah. Like protection oaths."

He fell silent, his astute gaze holding mine as a myriad of emotions ran through his expression.

Understanding.

Hurt.

Anger.

Pain.

Each emotion hit me in the gut, making me feel worse by the second. Because yeah, I knew the guy as a result of my own research in regard to how to break bonds. Specifically, the protection oath I'd spoken to Kols. He needed someone else, someone better suited, to guard him. And I'd proven more than once now not to be the right man for the job.

Case in point, he'd gone and mated an abomination on my watch.

That marked me as the worst Guardian in Midnight Fae history.

"We're going to discuss how you know him later," Kols finally said. "For now, can you reach out to see if he can help us mask the mating bond?"

I nodded, saying nothing more. He could bring it up all he wanted, but it wouldn't change anything. What was done was done.

"It's a temporary solution that gives us time to figure this shit out." Kols blew out a long breath, his focus shifting to the dawning sky above. A million thoughts ran through his features, each one tied to an emotion I could taste from his aura without him having to say a word.

Because I felt the same way.

This was so utterly fucked up.

When Kols suggested the three of us bite her at once, I didn't hesitate. I'd accepted the solution almost eagerly. *Too* eagerly. To the point where I hadn't once considered the consequences. I'd just wanted to save Aflora.

I should have killed her instead.

It would have made all of this so much easier.

Had I just taken her out when she first arrived, Kols never would have mated her, his future wouldn't be in jeopardy, and he could have lived his life the way it was meant to be lived.

She'd been a weakness to us all from the day she arrived. Part of me hated her for it, hence Raph's behavior in class today. He'd acted upon my aggression toward her, taking it out on her precious familiar.

Wrong, yes.

However, it'd felt good at the time to expel some of my frustration so violently. Until the guilt hit me square in the chest.

The female had some sort of magical pull over all of us, creating a web of dangerous choices that both Kols and I had fallen into almost willingly.

I despised her for it.

And adored her at the same time.

"I'm glad my solution worked," Kols said, his mind clearly following a similar path to my own because I felt the exact same way. "It's wrong, and I hate her, but I hated watching her suffer more."

"Because you don't really hate her." Just as I didn't.

"I know," he agreed quietly. "But I want to."

"I know," I replied, purposely repeating his words.

A moment of mutual understanding fell between us, our minds aligned in that eerie way we'd come to respect over the years. It was why we worked well together, even when we shouldn't.

"I'll handle my father and Shade, while you..." Kols trailed off, his focus falling to the ground. He bent to pick up a discarded wand, his lips curling down. "I guess I'll talk to Aflora, too. This is hers, right?"

I hadn't actually studied her wand much, but it looked right. "Yeah, I think so. But I don't remember her using it."

"She probably summoned it without realizing it." Kols eyed the magical tool with interest, raising it into the light provided by the rising sun, and frowned harder. "Her essence is all over this, so it's definitely hers, but I swear it's changed somehow. See that blue streak? Looks like a crack, doesn't it?"

I studied the sharp gold tip and noted the letters inscribed at the top. "This wand used to belong to someone else. Are you sure it's hers?"

"It's definitely her wand," he said, catching and following my focus to the word. "*Lahaz*. That sounds like a spell."

"Or a name."

"I'll ask her if she knows what it means when I confirm this belongs to her." He tilted the wand again, his brow furrowing. "How have I never noticed the cerulean lines before?"

"Maybe the wand changed formation," I suggested. Magical conduits were known to grow with their masters. "It could be maturing, just like Aflora's connection to the dark arts."

His jaw clenched, his gaze finding mine once more. "She's going to be a handful."

"She already is."

He snorted. "True." With a soft curse, he shifted focus to the clearing again. "Right. You talk to your guy. I'm going to find Shade and give the asshole a piece of my mind. Then I'll make sure we're on the same page."

"And if we're not?"

"Then I really will have a duel to report." He turned on his heel, frustration and irritation pouring off his essence.

All because of a girl.

One neither of us wanted to be tied to.

Yet I didn't really regret claiming her, even though I knew I should.

That nagging little realization followed me as I made my way to the portal and all the way to Ching's place. By the time I arrived, I still had no answers, only a resolute opinion that we'd done what we needed to do and that there was no real alternative.

Which couldn't be true at all.

We'd shattered our futures all for a girl who didn't belong here.

An abomination.

A wrongness.

So why did it feel so right?

AFLORA

Several Minutes Earlier

SILK SHEETS.

Violet undertones.

Obsidian furniture.

It all matched Shade's usual furnishings when he visited my dreams, the notes of his preferences in every minute detail.

I sat on his mattress, too exhausted to fight him or demand he take me to my room. What did it matter anyway? I wouldn't be alive much longer. Might as well go out in style.

My head fell to my hands, my body shaking from the power exchange in the field. I felt all three of them inside me, their presence somehow grounding me. The question became, was it permanent or temporary?

261

Not that it would change my fate.

I was absolutely an abomination, my power surge proving it. "I'm a danger to everyone," I whispered, my shoulders caving inward.

"You are," Shade agreed, as helpful as ever. "But we can help you manage it."

I nearly laughed. Except it came out as some sort of half-sob, half-crazed snort. "Fae, I'm hopeless," I mused, broken. "When did I become this weak shell of nothing?"

"You're not weak, little rose," he whispered, his knuckles brushing one of the hands still covering my face. "You're one of the strongest females I've ever met."

This time I did laugh and lowered my hands to my lap while meeting his gaze. "That's not what you said when we first met. I believe you called me a delicate flower, just after saying someone called me beautiful." I frowned with the memory, my focus sharpening. "*Who* told you I would be beautiful, Shade?"

"Does it matter?" he countered. "What's done is done."

"As I'm going to die soon, I'd like to know who subjected me to this fate. So yeah, it matters. Who in the Fae gave me to you as a mission?" Wasn't that what he'd called me when we first met? A "task"?

"You're not going to die soon, Aflora." He caught my chin between his thumb and forefinger, giving it a subtle squeeze. "We won't let anyone hurt you."

We being him, Zeph, and Kols.

Ha. "Yeah, I believe that." *Not.* Had the three of them helped ground me? Yes. But that didn't inspire much trust, not after my last few months with them. "Why did you bite me?"

I meant all of them at once, which he must have understood because he replied, "To save you from exploding again." His tone suggested his response was obvious.

He was right only because he hadn't told me what I

really wanted to know.

"Why would you care if I detonated? I mean, why not just kill me? I'm a danger to you, to *everyone*. Why help me?" I should be dead. A buried abomination. Destroyed. Not feeling centered within my myriad of power. Not entertaining mate-bonds to *three* male fae.

None of this made any sense.

He sighed, released my chin, and turned toward one of his dressers. I waited for a reply as he opened a drawer. Continued to wait as he opened a second. Then arched a brow when he turned around to hand me a pair of boxers and a shirt.

"I don't want clothes. I want answers."

His gaze slid downward, heat flaring in his pupils. "Well, that's up to you, but I have to admit my focus is a little distracted with you wearing nothing in my room. Particularly after two months of foreplay in our dreams."

Ugh! I'd forgotten I was naked, my attention divided between my fate and my confusion over what just happened outside. "How did I lose all my clothes?" I'd run out of my room with pants and a shirt on. No shoes. But I had no idea how—

"You destroyed them when you blew up out in the field."

I blinked. "Blew up?"

"You went up in flames, Aflora." He dropped the shirt and boxers beside me. "Bright cerulean flames, I might add, and you destroyed the entire clearing. I'd be impressed if you hadn't nearly killed me and Zeph in the process."

My eyebrows flew upward. "*What?*"

He studied me for a long moment, his icy blue irises thinning as his pupils dilated. "There's too much power inside you, little rose. It required a release, only your explosion wasn't enough and you were gearing up for a larger one. So we reacted accordingly."

By biting me, I translated.

"Why?" I asked.

"Why does there need to be a reason?"

"Because I should be dead, Shade!" I snapped, irritated by his continued evasiveness. This hot and cold game with him needed to end. "Just tell me why this is happening. Why did you bite me? Who put you up to this? What's your—"

His lips captured mine, just as they always did at this point in our dreams.

I refrained from biting him, aware of what that would do.

And instead dug my nails into his neck, deep enough to draw blood.

He flinched and encircled my throat with his palm, pushing me down to his bed. "Is that how you want to play, Aflora?"

"I'm tired of playing," I told him, my voice holding a low growl in it. "I want information, Shade. No more of these half answers."

"A half answer implies I've given you at least a partial response, which I mostly haven't."

"Exactly," I said, exasperated.

He used his grasp on my neck to pull me up the bed until my head met a pillow. He settled beside me, balancing himself on his elbow while his opposite palm remained around my throat.

"How do you feel?" he asked in the softest voice imaginable, his warm game on point once more.

"Irritated. Angry. *Murderous.*"

His lips curled, but only slightly. "How about physically? Are you sore? Does anything hurt?"

"Only my brain," I muttered. "What with all the cryptic responses and everything."

His amusement disappeared behind a mask of mild annoyance. "I mean it, Aflora. You went up in literal flames. I thought you were going to burn to ash beneath that wave of power." He almost sounded sad by the prospect, but I knew better than to believe his tone. "Tell me how you're feeling. Please."

I nearly asked if that word hurt him to utter, but instead gave him the truth because I was too exhausted to banter with him anymore. "I feel balanced and tired."

He nodded, his grasp loosening as he trailed his touch downward between my breasts, reminding me of my nude state.

I should have accepted his clothes.

Except it really didn't matter. He'd seen me naked countless times in our dreams.

"Are you in pain anywhere?" he asked softly, rephrasing his earlier question.

"No." *Just my mind.*

Another nod, this one more solemn. He gripped my hip to guide me onto my side to face him as he lowered his head to rest on the same pillow as me. "Has Kols or Zeph told you anything about Quandary Bloods?"

"I know they can take apart magic and rebuild it," I said. "And that they used to work with the Death Bloods until the Elite Bloods had them all killed."

He nodded. "Yes. They fear that which they cannot control."

"Like abominations."

"Just like abominations," he agreed. "Which makes you volatile and dangerous in their eyes."

"Because I'm too powerful for them to control," I whispered. "You said it yourself—I almost killed you and Zeph tonight." I flinched with the words, my heart giving a pang over the thought of harming another soul, let alone two so close to my own.

"But you didn't," he murmured. "I shadowed him out just in time, and you mostly contained your own explosion as soon as it released. Well, apart from murdering all those trees."

If he meant that as a joke, I didn't find it very funny. "Any loss of life is unacceptable. If I can't be controlled, I should be exterminated."

"That's a very narrow view, Aflora," he murmured, his palm sliding up my side, along my rib cage, and back down again. "What if you could learn control?"

"I've been trying that since I arrived, and tonight should tell you how that's been going for me."

"But now you have a support system to rely on."

"I have no one to rely on," I countered. "You never tell me anything of importance. Zeph is the realm's worst teacher. And Kols hates me. Some support system."

"Yeah, he's a shit teacher," Shade agreed, smirking. "But Kols doesn't hate you, and I tell you important things all the time. You just don't hear me."

"Right." I didn't bother arguing with him. No sense in trying when it wouldn't change anything. He wouldn't even tell me why he'd bitten me, let alone who put him up to it.

A tense stillness fell between us, his icy gaze holding mine as he continued to draw his palm up and down my side. Slowly. Purposefully. Tenderly. Goose bumps pebbled across my arms, the intimacy of his nearness eliciting memories of our dreams and the touches that followed this caress. But he didn't try to kiss me. Didn't try to do anything other than softly memorize the curve of my hip and back up again.

"Kols's grandfather ordered the slaughter of the Quandary Bloods shortly after they helped the Nacht family gain access to the dark-magic source over my family. I believe it's because they didn't want to risk that realignment of power ever being undone. It's the ultimate point of contention between the Elite Bloods and Death Bloods. Which is why your existence must be protected."

It was the most information he'd ever given me at once, and still not nearly enough.

"Did you know?" I wondered out loud. "Did you know I could access Quandary Magic?"

He considered me for a long moment before saying, "I

was told of your potential, yes. I didn't believe it until I felt you override the choker your first week here, and I've been doing everything I can to help you hide since."

I frowned. "Help me hide?"

"You didn't think Kols was the only one assisting you, did you?" His lips quirked upward. "He's been in your head just as much as I have, Aflora. Surely you've figured that out by now."

"He helps me during class."

"And at night," he added, a sinister grin entering his icy eyes. Somehow that look only made him more handsome, in a sinful sort of way that made my heart pound.

Then his words registered. "He knows about the dreams." Not a question, but a statement, my lips parting. "But I thought that was because of our bond!"

"No, darling. Dream manipulation is old magic. You make it easy because you don't know how to defend against it, and none of us have bothered to teach you how. My reasoning should be obvious, but you'd have to ask Kols for his purpose in your mind. If I were to guess, I'd say it was his way of fighting an obvious attraction. For me, I just want to play with my feisty little mate."

I scowled at him, which only made him smile harder.

"You're a rare diamond among a sea of jewels, Aflora. I can't blame Zeph or Kols for wanting you. I'm even willing to share, but you are mine first and foremost. Because my claim is deeper. And soon, we'll finalize our mating. Then the truth can be revealed. At least in parts."

"More riddles," I muttered, shifting to my back, only to have his hand yank me back to my side.

"Providing all the answers would weaken you, Aflora. Riddles, as you call them, are what make a Quandary Blood thrive. And there are some facts in life that must be discovered on our own in order for us to flourish. But that doesn't make me any less here for you. I've been helping you from the beginning, more than you'll ever know."

"Helping to torment me and taking me against my

will," I mused. "Such an amazing mate you are, Shade." I couldn't help the thick sarcasm in my tone, my mind at wits' end. "You destroyed my life, and now I'll die because of it. And you won't even tell me why." This time he let me fall to my back.

I closed my eyes, tired of talking to him.

He wasn't going to give me anything useful.

He never did.

"You weren't the only one not given a choice," he said quietly some time later. "We're all pawns on a board serving a higher purpose. A fate that may or may not come to fruition. Only time will tell."

"What does that even mean?" I asked, opening my eyes to find him propped up on his elbow and gazing down at me with sadness in his eyes. "Someone told you to bite me. Did they not tell you why?"

"I already knew why, Aflora. But that doesn't mean I wanted to take you against your will, that I wanted to force a bond on you without even knowing you." He cupped my cheek, his thumb brushing my bottom lip. "If it's an apology you want, I can't give it to you. Because I don't regret it. Not anymore. Not after learning so much about you. I see now why our fates were destined to intertwine."

"Because of my Quandary Magic."

"No, because of *you*." He leaned in to kiss me, his mouth questing against mine. "I know none of this makes sense, that you blame me for everything that's happened, and you're fully within your right to feel that way. But one day soon, you will understand, and you will thank me for forcing this upon you."

"Not likely," I grumbled, the words brushing his lips.

He grinned. "I very much look forward to proving you wrong."

I knew he wouldn't be able to, that it wasn't possible for me to ever thank him for dragging me into this world and destroying my life. But I couldn't stop the rush of heat that overwhelmed me as he kissed me once more.

I hated him.

Wanted to *hurt* him as he'd hurt me.

Yet the fire he lit inside me stoked higher with each touch, lick, and nip between us. It proved that lust and hatred truly were neighbors in the circle of emotions that dictated us all. Because the passion between us burned hotter and hotter every day.

"I hate you," I whispered.

"I know."

"I wish I'd never met you," I added, a hoarse growl in my tone.

"I know," he repeated, his frosty gaze flicking open to meet mine. "But if you hadn't met me, you wouldn't know about your Quandary Blood."

Another kiss, this one deeper, his eyes holding mine the entire time.

"You never would have explored your other powers," he added, his voice darkening in a way that made my belly flip.

His tongue slipped through my lips, tasting, tempting, and tantalizingly thorough.

I bit back a moan, trying not to show how he made me feel. Attempting to shove away the lust he too easily evoked.

However, the thigh parting my legs knew immediately, his pants brushing my exposed sex, my dampness seeping through the fabric of his trousers in an instant.

"Yet your little display tonight would have been an eventuality with or without my influence," he continued in a gruff tone. "However, unlike tonight, you wouldn't have had anyone to ground you." He flexed his thigh in a way that sparked pleasure inside me, my sensitive flesh pulsating with a need he expertly awoke.

"Shade..."

"You wouldn't have possessed any knowledge of what was happening to you, Aflora," he whispered. "Or how to stop it."

I swallowed, his comments all true, his touch evoking a volcano-like reaction to boil in my lower belly, threatening to consume me completely.

"Without my interference in your life, you would have ended up hurting people you loved." He nibbled my lower lip at the same time his thigh pressed into my weeping heat.

This entire conversation should not be turning me on.

He shouldn't be making me this hot.

I threaded my fingers through his thick, dark hair, clinging to him despite my mind telling me to order him to stop.

Resisting him proved to be impossible.

"You make me feel so..." I trailed off, unable to explain it. My body was on fire in a manner similar to before, but oh-so different.

Kols had ignited me with power and sensation.

Shade somehow caressed my soul with icy flames, an impossible element that seemed to only exist between us.

"Come for me, gorgeous," he whispered against my ear. "I can take it."

I wanted to scream for him to release me, to beg him to take me over the cliff, and to kill him all at the same time. The intensity between us boiled over, my world cascading into a glimmer of oblivion so overwhelming that I nearly forgot how to breathe.

And then I was screaming his name as both a curse and a blessing as energy erupted all around us.

He absorbed it all, allowing me to float in a state of rapture that shook every inch of my being, letting me leave my body and return.

"Shade!" The room glowed, my heart beating a chaotic rhythm that refused to slow, until his mouth brought me back to the reality of our moment.

His tongue stroked mine, his hands gliding up and down my sides once more and his warmth heating up my cool, damp skin.

I shuddered, lost to him utterly and completely, while

despising him all over again, yet kissing him as if I required his existence to survive.

"You're beautiful," he praised, nuzzling me in a gesture almost too sweet for our volatile bond. "Sleep, Aflora. We'll discuss more in the morning."

I opened my mouth to argue but found it falling slack from whatever spell he'd woven over me. My eyes narrowed in annoyance, wishing he would stop messing with my dreams and my sleep states.

But he disappeared in a cloud of his intoxicating smoke before I could convey the message.

And my world went black.

SHADE

I SENSED KOLS'S PRESENCE in my suite about a minute before Aflora detonated. He'd somehow convinced Sir Black to grant him entry, something no one else had ever been able to do. I suspected our shared mate-bond had helped.

Although, that didn't explain how the Elite Blood had managed to enter the Death Blood residential quarters.

"Did you issue an edict to allow your entry?" I mused, materializing behind him in my living area. He'd paused in the center of the room, likely because he'd overheard Aflora's cries of pleasure. I'd stop to listen, too, if I were him. She truly was a beautiful creature. Exquisitely unique, and absolutely mine.

A flicker of gold flame brightened his gaze as he outwardly relaxed. "She screams louder for me."

"Does she?" I considered what I knew of their tenuous relationship and smiled. "I'll see if I agree come morning."

"She won't be in your bed much longer."

"Yeah? And where do you plan to take her? Back to your bed? What with her own quarters being demolished to ash and all," I drawled, leaning against the wall that led to a slender hallway.

Unlike Kols, I only had one bedroom. Guests weren't really my thing. Unless they were dark-haired and gorgeous, like the female fast asleep in my sheets. I'd tuck her in properly when I returned.

He frowned. "Did she tell you that?"

I lifted a shoulder, giving nothing away. Because no, she hadn't told me that. I'd *felt* it. Kols's display of power triggered Aflora's reaction, overloading her connection to the source of the dark arts. Her cries for help had stirred me from my sleep, dragging me into the dawn hours in search of my agonized mate.

Never in my wildest dreams could I have anticipated finding her in the LethaForest. It was a miracle she'd survived her trek out there.

A miracle, I assumed, that could be attributed to Zeph's interference. He'd clearly followed her out there and likely dealt with a few threats before approaching her.

Or perhaps it'd all been a date with fate.

Aflora seemed to adore those.

"Don't worry, Midnight Prince, our queen is safely tucked into my bed. No need to disturb her or move her."

"You're not even supposed to be near her, let alone sharing a room with her," he replied, folding his arms and doing his best to appear regal.

"Oh, are we playing a game of who can break the most rules? Because I think you're way ahead of me tonight, Kols. How many oaths did you break by mating her? Or shall we discuss the nightly visits to her dreams?" I pretended to consider our situation and scratched my jaw. "No, those were technically within the parameters of the

273

rules. So how about that collar you never put on her after her little magical display in Warrior Magic class?" Because yeah, I knew all about that.

"Have you been lurking in my rooms?" he demanded.

Another shrug because I'd never give away my secrets. Not to him. Not to anyone. "What do you really want, Kols? There's a naked, gorgeous woman in my bed that I'd like to get back to, and soon, if you don't mind."

"And if I do mind?"

"It won't stop me," I admitted with a smile. "Just as my initial claim on her didn't stop you."

"Well, you'll have to take that up with her since *she* mated *me*."

"Is that how Elemental Fae bonds work?" I asked, feigning curiosity. "Because I swore those were mutual arrangements." Yeah, I knew about that, too. Had sensed it the moment it snapped into place. It'd felt like a fire gnat latching onto our bond and refusing to let go. I hadn't understood it until I'd found Aflora.

The moment her power went up in flames, the puzzle pieces had fallen into place. I supposed that as a mixed fae, she would have multiple partners. Kols wasn't exactly my first choice for this venture, but I should have known destiny would require it.

He had probably foreseen it. Just like everything else.

A muscle ticked in Kols's jaw. "What game are you really playing here, Shade? You had to know about her Quandary Blood origins. That's why you chose her. What I can't figure out is your end goal. Was this part of it? Forming a four-way bond?"

"Who says I have an end goal?" I countered. "Maybe someone else is pulling my strings."

He snorted. "That's impossible. You despise authority."

"True," I agreed. "But that doesn't mean I can't seek to fulfill a higher purpose. Perhaps I want to end this age-old feud between our families."

Incredulity darkened his features. "We both know that's bullshit."

"Do we?" I countered, giving him yet another shrug. "I guess we'll find out."

He took a step forward, his calm façade cracking. "Cut the shit, Shade. Why Aflora? What's your play here?"

"Maybe I like her," I suggested. Not exactly a lie. I did quite fancy—

I ducked as his fist came for my nose, and shadowed out of his reach and across the room just as Sir Black bellowed a warning through the room. The cheeky little gargoyle despised violence. It was the only trait I disliked about him. I mean, who didn't enjoy a bout of savagery? Especially between a Death Blood and an Elite Blood.

Kols ignored Sir Black and pulled out his wand, his expression radiating the intent to do damage. A spell graced his lips just as a loud ring came from the device he held aloft in his hand.

The murderous intent fled from his features, replaced by a grimace as he answered the magical call with a flick of his wrist. "Hello, Father," he greeted in an admirably calm voice. He flashed me a look that told me not to say anything. I idly considered disobeying him on principle but decided it was in Aflora's best interest not to announce my presence. The less we did to draw attention to ourselves, the better.

Because this whole quad-bond thing? Yeah, it wouldn't end well when the Midnight Fae found out.

Part of me couldn't fucking wait. I almost dared them to do something about it. Our collective power as a unit had the potential to overpower the entire damn Council.

But our strongest asset didn't have a clue how to use her Quandary powers yet.

Which brought me to the practical part of myself who knew we were nowhere near ready yet. Hence, I leaned against the wall and shamelessly listened to Kols's side of the conversation. His familial magic allowed his father to talk directly into his ear while the wand was engaged. Similar to answering a human phone but without the necessary device.

Personally, I preferred the physical mobiles and carried one with me to talk to my own father. The less that asshole could get in my head, the better.

Kols and Malik, however, had a very different bond than me and my father.

"Yeah, Shade and I got into it," the Midnight Prince said, causing me to arch a brow. "That's the disturbance you probably felt."

Ah. Clever. Blame the rivalry instead of our Aflora. Not a bad tactic. His father would believe Kols won the battle with ease, disregarding the significance of my power as most Elite Bloods did. That was how I ran under the radar so fluidly. They all sat on their high and mighty thrones assuming themselves to be the rightful heirs to the kingdom while the true royals hid in the shadows.

Royals like me.

One day, I'd make a point of demonstrating how wrong they'd been about me and mine.

But not today.

Instead, I gave Kols a nod, accepting his story and listening while he detailed our makeshift duel to his father. To his credit, he awarded me a few positive hits but then boasted about my eventual takedown at the end. It took considerable effort not to snort at the ridiculous conclusion.

As if I would ever go down that easily.

However, to protect Aflora, I'd allow the outlandish tale to exist. I'd even go as far as to thank Kols for crafting it because it meant he'd decided to protect our mate rather than turn her in. At least for now.

That decision could change in a second.

Yet something told me it wouldn't. I'd witnessed his concern for the Royal Earth Fae on more than one occasion. And tonight, he'd taken that concern to a whole new level of *need*. Suggesting the three of us bite her all at once had required a fair bit of sacrifice on his part, something he'd given without thought. He'd renounced his entire kingdom to ensure her survival.

Because there was no question now that everything would change.

He couldn't properly ascend with Aflora as a mate. Not because the source would reject him, but because the precious Council would deny his candidacy and demand he step down. As he had a twin with a mostly proper mate, it'd be an easy solution for them. There would be a handful who frowned upon Ella being a Halfling, but knowing Tray, he'd tell them to kiss his royal ass.

Then he'd be faced with punishing his twin for saving an abomination instead of killing her.

Kols's shoulders were tight with annoyance, his golden eyes glowing as he accepted whatever his father had just said with a contrite "I apologize for my behavior. It won't happen again."

I nearly said, "Don't make promises you can't keep," but I wasn't in the business of offering advice. Instead, I wandered into my kitchen to fix myself a drink.

Kols met me a moment later, his wand carefully stowed. "If anyone asks—"

"You kicked my ass in an unsanctioned duel," I finished for him as I dropped three ice cubes into a glass. "Got it."

He studied me for a long moment, his expression wary. "How the hell am I supposed to trust you not to fuck this up for us all?"

"Hmm." I found my favorite liquor, took it from the cabinet, and poured myself a healthy amount.

"That's all you have to say? *Hmm*?" He appeared ready to retrieve his wand again.

"You can start by letting me keep Aflora for the night," I replied, giving my glass a little swirl to chill the contents. "We'll regroup tomorrow when you bring her something to wear."

He regarded me with a violent glint in his gaze. "If you touch her—"

"Oh, be assured that I already have," I cut in, adoring the way his skin turned red in response. "But I would never hurt her."

"And you just expect me to believe you? To rely on you to keep her safe?"

"Yes," I said, replying to both questions. "She's my mate, Kolstov. I may enjoy taunting her, but I'd never let anyone or anything hurt her. Why else would I have showed up in the LethaForest? It certainly wasn't for a little late-morning stroll. That's for damn sure." I took a long, necessary sip of my drink, adoring the way the liquid burned the back of my throat.

Kols finally relented with a sigh, his head bobbing back and forth in defeated agreement. "I'm going to fucking regret this."

"You absolutely are," I agreed, but I wasn't so much referring to trusting me as I was binding himself to Aflora. He would definitely have moments of regret, followed by sweet moments of reward that made it all worth it.

Or maybe that was just my fate, not his.

Time would tell.

"Zeph went to find someone who can help us hide the bonds," he informed me, his tone low. "Until we can figure out how to move forward, we need to hide this from the Council."

"And they call me the rebel," I murmured, amused.

"This isn't a fucking game," Kols snapped.

"Everything in life is a game to someone," I returned, stepping around him to enter the living room.

"Does her life mean nothing to you?" he demanded, his harsh tone causing me to pause midstep. "Do you not realize what will happen to you if something happens to her?"

I glanced over my shoulder to meet his gaze. "I don't

care what happens to me," I admitted, my voice a hush of sound that seemed to slap him across the face. "But I do care what happens to her. Which is why she's staying here tonight. I've given you two months with her, Kolstov. It's my turn to care for her in my own way. You can have her back—unharmed—tomorrow."

I didn't bother giving him anything else, just shadowed back to my room and the beauty resting in the center of my bed. If he opted to stay and listen, that was on him.

What I wanted to do now had nothing to do with Kolstov or Zephyrus or the Council or anyone else.

It all centered around Aflora.

Just as it had since my first bite.

I set my glass down on my nightstand, pulled off my shirt, and crawled into the bed beside her. A few muttered words released her from the sleeping spell, allowing her beautiful blue eyes to open.

Palming her cheek, I leaned in to run my tongue along the seam of her mouth. She opened for me as I knew she would, her mind still caught in the land of fog and dreams and her memories convincing her this might be a fantasy more than reality.

I could so easily take advantage of her in this state.

But I wouldn't.

I wanted to earn her trust in a magical sense, not necessarily in a traditional one. I desired her soul. Her heart. Her everything.

She was nowhere near ready to give me more than physical touch, and that was fine. We had time. We'd work up to what I really craved. She might initially despise me for it, but in the end, she'd fall for me.

Which was all part of the fun.

A Quandary Blood needed challenges and puzzles and riddles. I offered them to her in spades, existing merely to entice her, and one day our powers would mingle to create something so beautiful and amazing that the Council wouldn't dare touch it.

Whether or not Zeph and Kols opted to be a part of that was up to them.

So far, they were following the right path.

But I knew from *him* that our road wasn't an easy one, with a multitude of potential dead ends. My purpose in this life was to ensure the female curling into me survived it.

And I would do everything in my power to see it through.

Even if she hated me for it.

I gently nibbled her lower lip before kissing her deeply, cherishing her in the only way I knew how. She was too exhausted to do anything more, and that was okay with me. I'd hold her all night, guard her in her dreams, and continue watching her from the shadows when she woke.

My mate.

My little rose.

My future.

I adore you, I thought at her, not that she could hear me. *I'm so sorry I have to break you, Aflora.*

The only way for her to truly fly was without restraints, which required sacrifices from us all.

And this one would be mine.

KOLS

"WHY DO YOU STILL HAVE AFLORA'S WAND?"
Zeph asked as he entered my bedroom without knocking.
I'd set her magical conduit on the dresser, desiring to keep
it safe for when I went back to her tomorrow morning.

"I didn't get to see her. Shade had already tucked her
into his bed." I grimaced with the words, not at all pleased
about her spending the night with him. Of course, he
hadn't exactly given me much of a choice. I could have
fought him, demanded he hand her over, but decided it
wasn't worth the trouble. As I could sense her emotions
now—thanks to the bond—I knew she was safe. If and
when that sensation changed, I'd do something about it.

For now, I'd let him keep her.

Just for tonight.

Tomorrow was a whole new day for negotiation.

It also gave me time to replace all her belongings and

the bedroom furniture.

Part of me still wanted to kill her for trapping me in this mess with her. Meanwhile, the more logical side of me recognized it'd been a mutual claiming.

I'd wanted her from the moment we first met, and even before that when I saw her at Cyrus's coronation. She was one of the most beautiful women I'd ever seen, her long black hair highlighted with strands of blue. Those gorgeous eyes. Delectable curves. Sinfully sweet smile.

Every attribute she possessed lured me to her.

Coupled with her astounding power and royal bloodline, it was no wonder my fae soul sought her out as a match.

I'd been too weak to fight it, and for that, I would pay the ultimate price.

Hating her was easier than hating myself. That didn't make it right.

"You look like hell," Zeph said, stopping by my bed. I was lounging in the pillows with a bottle of whiskey in my lap. No shirt. No shoes. Just a pair of gray sweats.

"Thanks. I feel like hell." I took another swig, wishing like crazy it would make me drunk already. But the power I'd imbibed from Aflora seemed to be eating at my ability to feel intoxicated.

I'd taken the brunt of her outburst, allowed it to fuel my insides, and fed it directly back into the source. Like some sort of damn siphon.

Zeph and Shade had helped, but they weren't the ones with direct access to the dark arts. So the brunt of it fell on me.

The ink along my arms writhed in contentment, while my insides revolted.

I couldn't believe any of this had happened, had no fucking clue what to do now. I'd straight up lied to my father, something I had never done before. Not over a major situation such as this, anyway. Little lies, yeah. Major ones, no.

"Fuck," I muttered, taking yet another swallow before holding the bottle out to Zeph. "Want any?"

He took the bottle and set it aside rather than taking a swig. "It won't help."

"Tell me about it." I'd been trying to drown my sorrows for over an hour to no avail. "Her power is like a live wire running through my fucking soul."

"Not sure what I can do about that, but my buddy did make us these." He dropped a pair of brown leather bracelets on the bed beside my hip. "Ching said these will help hide our connection from the others."

"Ching?"

"My buddy who specializes in hiding bonds. Apparently, mating bonds are a popular thing to hide, so he already had several tools available at his disposal to create these." Zeph studied the bracelets. "I didn't give him your identity, mostly because I imagine he'd freak out if he knew. Because there's only one reason someone would specialize in this type of magic, and that's to hide things from the Council."

"But he knows who you are."

"He does. Just as he also knows I want out." He met my gaze, daring me to comment.

I didn't.

Mainly because I was too exhausted to fight with him right now.

I just wanted this night to end already.

Besides... "There's no getting out now," I told him softly, my focus falling to the bracelets. "So how do these work?" I asked, giving him a chance to deflect and change the direction of our conversation.

He accepted it. "They're generic concealing spells. Wearing the bracelet cloaks the mating bond, making it impossible to sense or trace."

"What about Aflora? If she wears one, it'll hide her link to Shade, and people will suspect something is up."

Zeph nodded. "Yeah, Ching is making something

special for her. He's going to try to have it done by morning. If not, we need an excuse to keep her out of class."

"I'll just say she was hit by some stray magic during my duel with Shade. No one will question it. Hell, Emelyn will probably be thrilled." The bitch had painted a target on Aflora's back solely because of her affiliation with me. Well, that hatred would become a lot worse when she realized we'd mated each other.

Assuming we lived long enough for anyone to find out beyond the Council.

My shoulders slumped as I sunk deeper into the pillows.

"It's not like you to mope," Zeph said, his tall frame towering over me as he stared down at me from beside the bed.

"Fuck you, Z," I muttered, tugging a pillow over my head. Childish, yes, Unhelpful, also yes. But I just wanted to hide for eternity.

"You realize this connection between the four of us is powerful, right?" Zeph asked.

"Haven't had a minute to analyze it." My words were muffled by the pillow.

A pillow that disappeared when Zeph took it from me. "Stop being a lazy, woeful dick, sit up, and start thinking."

I glared at him. "I don't want to think, asshole."

"Well, too fucking bad, jackass," he tossed back. "We broke a few rules. So fucking what? The mating laws are archaic and you know it. You also never wanted to mate Emelyn anyway. Aflora is a much better match. She's hot as fuck, too. Strong. Powerful. A Quandary Blood. That means, with the right training, she can rewrite all this bullshit in our favor. The only truly shitty part of all of this is having Shade involved. I'd suggest we kill him, but that'd hurt Aflora, which would weaken the bond overall."

I blinked at him. "Who made you King Practical all of a sudden?"

"I've always been the practical one, Prince Crybaby," he returned.

"I am not a crybaby."

"You're lounging in a pile of pillows feeling sorry for yourself instead of realizing the opportunity that exists here. She's fucking powerful. You felt it tonight when we grounded her. The Council is going to lose their shit over it because they can't battle it, unless we bend over and take it up the ass. Which I'm not keen to do. You?"

"What happened to *they'll probably just kill her and then you*?" I asked. "Isn't that what you said just a few hours ago?"

"Yeah, and you told me you weren't going to let that happen. And I believe you. So stop feeling sorry for yourself and help me figure out a solution. As you said, there's no getting out of this now. Let's figure out what to do with it, unless you have a time spinner lounging around that I don't know about."

"That's a whole different realm of fae beings," I muttered, thinking of the Paradox Fae. "But they would be so useful right about now."

"Yeah, except they'd never help us. Actually, they'd probably make it worse."

I snorted. "True." They were deceitful little fuckers who loved to play tricks with time. To ask a favor of them required significant payment, and even then, it was never guaranteed that they would follow through without leaving some devious surprise lying in wait. "Still an avenue to keep in mind," I said. Because all options had to be considered.

"Not really. I think we'd end up bonding her regardless of how we played it."

He wasn't wrong. "I felt the pull from the moment I first saw her."

"Me, too."

We shared a long look that ended in a mutual sigh.

"What I still want to know is what Shade has to do with

all this," Zeph continued. "He knew this would happen."

"What do you mean?"

"He wasn't surprised at all tonight. Just accepting. What kind of Midnight Fae doesn't mind two other men taking liberties with his mate?"

I frowned. "I'm certainly not keen on her being in his bed right now."

"Exactly."

"Yet I allowed it," I added.

"Because you're not opposed to sharing women. But Shade is notoriously alpha in his preferences and not the type to share."

"True." I sat up, my hand rubbing down my face as I thought it all through. "He didn't seem pleased by my suggestion to bite her, though."

"He seemed worried," Zeph agreed. "But not about our claim. He was concerned for her and what would happen if we couldn't get her power under control. There's a difference."

"Yeah, there is," I agreed, recalling the fear in his eyes as he watched her fall apart before us. "He really does care about her."

"He also saved my life tonight when she blew up that first time. If he hadn't shadowed me out, I would have burned right along with her. Only, I'm not equipped to survive cerulean fire."

That was when I'd arrived, having felt her power mounting through our bond. I'd been able to absorb most of her destruction, keeping the energy centered in that courtyard with an electric current stirred directly from the source.

"This is such a mess," I said, blowing out a breath. "I asked him about his motive tonight. He replied with his usual cryptic bullshit."

"Do you trust him?" Zeph asked.

I scoffed out a "No." Because I absolutely did not trust that bastard.

"Neither do I."

"So what do we do?"

"We monitor him. And we protect Aflora." He locked gazes with me as he said it. "There's something about her, Kols. Something important. And it goes deeper than her Quandary Blood."

"She's an abomination," I reminded him. "That could be what you're sensing."

He shook his head. "I keep feeling like she's the key to some long-buried secret. It's just a sense I get. One I want to understand before we decide how to proceed."

Zeph's instincts had proven reliable over the years, and I wasn't about to deny them now.

"We should start by looking into her origin," I said, thinking about her past. "Her parents supposedly died when she was young. Everyone thought it had to do with the Earth Fae plague, which they later realized was caused by an abomination."

"I'd put money on there being more to that story," Zeph replied.

"Me, too." I'd have to involve Exos or Cyrus in this to request some details. Maybe I could ask them for information on her background and claim I needed it to help exonerate her or something.

"You're thinking about asking the Elemental Fae Royals." A good guess, one born of years of knowing each other.

"I am," I confirmed.

"A good start."

I agreed with a nod before saying, "Well, I guess we need to put on these cuffs and hope your friend comes through with something for Aflora."

"He will." Zeph picked up the brown leather bracelets and handed one to me. "Cheers, Kols."

I huffed a laugh. "Yeah. Cheers." I tapped the band against his, then snapped it over my wrist. Aside from a slight humming sensation, I didn't feel any different, but the nod from Zeph told me it'd worked. When he followed suit, situating his into place, I understood.

The slight traces of the mating bonds were gone.

Now we just had to see how long these things held.

Solve the mystery of Aflora's existence.

And figure out what the fuck Shade was up to.

"This is going to be one hell of a challenge," I said.

Zeph smirked. "Yeah. Yeah, it is." He pulled the sheets back on my bed. "Now scoot over. I'm sleeping in here."

I arched a brow. "Your room is next door, *Guardian.*"

"Shut up and move, Kols."

My lips quirked as I obeyed. "Lose the pants."

"In your dreams."

"Or we could play in Aflora's," I suggested, thinking of how fun it would be to fuck with Shade. "Make her moan our names so loud that the Death Blood can't sleep."

A sinister glint darkened Zeph's gaze to a forest-green color. "It's late and I wasn't planning to rest much anyway."

Yeah, it was nearly half past noon outside. "Then let's have some fun. We've earned it after the last twenty-four hours."

"You already had fun earlier," Zeph replied. "Tonight, it's my turn."

"Then have at it. I'll follow along." And jump in when offered the chance.

AFLORA

RICH SPICES.

Peppermint.

Woodsy cologne.

I was swimming in all three scents, my body well used despite hardly being touched. When night fell, all I wanted to do was sleep since my mates hadn't let me rest at all.

They were all vying for placement in my dreams, their seduction resolute and far too tempting.

I loathed them.

Craved them.

Wanted to kill all of them.

Didn't understand them.

"You hate me," I told Kols, his arms wrapped around me as he pulled me back into his chest, his lips falling to my neck. None of it was real. I knew that. But I didn't know how to stop any of them from playing in my head.

"I don't hate you, princess," he whispered.

"You blamed me for our mating bond."

"Because he's an idiot who doesn't know how to take ownership for his own actions," a dark voice said, directly into my ear and overriding Kols's voice in my head.

"What?"

"Wake up, little rose," Shade demanded, his teeth skimming my throat. "We're done playing this game. For now."

My eyes opened, Kols's chuckle a residual sound in my mind.

Violet curtains were parted to reveal a starry night and silk sheets twined with my legs. Shade rested behind me, his arm tucked around my waist, his bare chest to my back, his lips at my ear again. "Welcome back, little rose."

I swallowed, my heart skipping a beat. "Where am I?"

"My room." He pressed a kiss to my neck once more, then guided me to my back to hover over me. "You need more sleep. How about we skip our classes today and stay here?"

"How did I...?" I trailed off, the events of last night slamming into my mind on a vicious assault of reality.

Zeph's three-headed snake killing Clove.

Sex with Kols.

Him sending me away.

Running into the forest.

My powers bursting.

Shade shadowing me here.

Every memory tumbled through me, causing me to flinch as dread pooled dark and thick inside my belly. "What happens now?"

"We sleep," Shade replied. "Assuming you're taking me up on my offer to skip class, that is."

"No." I shook my head in an effort to clear it. "What happens to the four of us? To me?"

"Ah, I believe the plan is to pretend like nothing happened at all." He lifted a shoulder. "I suppose we'll see how well that works, won't we?"

"I…" *What?* "Will that even work? Won't the Council know? What about our bonds?" I could sense all three males inside me, shredding apart my heart with their various hooks. Their magic rioted around my soul as well, as if each one vied for dominance over my powers, seeking to absorb me entirely.

Grounding me, I realized. *They're absorbing my energy to keep me grounded and stable.*

I poked at them in my mind, rearing back when the lines hissed in response. Shade visibly flinched, his lips curling down. "What did you just do?"

"Touched your… bond?" It was a guess. I didn't really know what to call it, but they felt like anchored chains surrounding my spirit, tying me down.

"You can see them?"

I nodded slowly, looking inside myself once more. "Yeah. I think."

"Can you describe them?"

"Like wispy strands of magic coiling around the core of my abilities," I said quietly. "They're pulsing with power. *Your* powers." I reached for the one with a more solid link, noting Shade's essence as I carefully stroked through our connection.

He shivered in response, his blue eyes gleaming brightly. "That's your Quandary Blood ability," he whispered. "I can't see our connection at all. Not like that."

"What do you see?" I wondered out loud.

"You," he said softly, his palm caressing my cheek. "Or rather, I feel you. Inside me. In my mind, my heart, my soul." He leaned into me, his lips brushing mine. "I can sense your emotions. I know when you're in pain or aroused. Not exactly your thoughts, but close. Like our souls are joined in a way that makes you easier to read. And, of course, I can play in your dreams."

Entertainment teased his full lips, causing them to

twitch as I rolled my eyes in response.

"I'm going to prioritize learning how to block you all," I muttered. Maybe Ella could tell me. Or one of my textbooks.

"Mmm, I'll just counter-spell you, little rose. Or maybe I'll just play with you in reality." He drew his teeth along my lower lip, his touch promising.

"I don't know," I replied, wanting to tease him. "You might not live up to my dream expectations."

He chuckled, his breath a kiss of mint against my tongue. "Darling, I'll surpass every single fantasy, including the ones you shared with Kols."

I shivered at the thought, recalling the one the Midnight Prince had inflicted on me last night. "That might not be possible after last night."

"Why? Because he allowed Zeph to join him this time?" Shade appeared darkly amused. "I know my skills, and they absolutely measure up."

"Right now, you're all talk."

"Says the female who came against my thigh last night from just my mouth touching hers," he replied softly, kissing me again, this time with purpose. "Keep this up, little rose, and I'll provide you with a demonstration instead of letting you sleep."

"You'll probably provide one in my mind anyway," I retorted.

He smiled against my mouth. "Likely." Another kiss. "Absolutely." This time with tongue. "Definitely." I drifted off in his arms once more, this time with an odd satisfaction lingering in my chest.

One that disappeared when I awoke alone in his bed to find his half of the mattress cold. A black rose rested on his pillow with a note beside it.

Something came up. Dream of me later, little rose. —S

I snorted. "All talk," I muttered, pushing myself upright to take in the fixtures of his room. They were elegant in a way I sort of expected from him. Dark, too.

All obsidian wood with violet furnishings. Very Shade.

But there weren't any personal items. No photos. No little knickknacks, just the essentials required for living.

Perhaps he didn't spend much time here.

As he skipped class regularly, that would make sense.

I stretched and slipped from the sheets. The boxers and shirt he'd offered me last night were folded on his bathroom counter with another black rose. I took it as an invitation to shower and change, which I did, his shampoo smelling minty and fresh, just like him.

Tying my hair up into a knot with my long strands, I pulled on his clothes and studied myself in the mirror.

My collar was gone.

I hadn't noticed it before.

Had it fallen off last night, or had Shade removed it?

Likely last night, which explained how my Elemental Fae abilities had returned. I closed my eyes and smiled as the source welcomed me with an aromatic kiss from the earth. It sort of reminded me of Zeph and his woodsy scent.

Actually, it smelled almost too much like him.

Almost as if—

"Aflora." His voice came from the doorway, his green eyes wild with emotions. "We have to go."

I frowned at him. "What?"

"There isn't time to explain. I need you to put this on, and we need to run. Now." He held out a collar that was identical to the one I'd lost.

"Zeph, I—"

"The Council knows, Aflora. They're searching the grounds for you. We have to go right now."

"I don't understand."

"Neither do we, but they have a recording of you admitting you're dangerous. We don't know where it came from or how."

"A recording?" I repeated, swallowing.

He handed me the collar as he replied, "Yeah. I only

heard part of it before I ran here to find you."

"What did you hear?" I whispered, my heart beating a mile a minute in my chest.

"You said any loss of life is unacceptable and that if you couldn't be controlled, then you should be exterminated." He shook his head. "We can discuss this more later, but we need to go. They'll be on their way here next."

I absentmindedly clutched the collar in my hand, my mind too consumed by what he'd just said. "That's what I told Shade last night," I whispered, swallowing thickly. "I told him I should be exterminated."

"Well, then we know where the recording came from," he muttered, cursing under his breath. "I knew we couldn't trust that asshole."

But why? I thought. *Why would he do this to me?*

Why has he done any of this? I countered myself. Nothing about Shade could be predicted. Everything he did was for himself first. I still didn't even know why he'd bitten me.

Something came up, he'd written.

Something like running to the Council to tell them about last night?

"Aflora!" Zeph snapped. "We have to go."

Right. Collar. Snap. Neck. Done. An immediate zing went through my body as the magic fell into place, causing me to tremble. Not only had it removed my access to earth, but it had also significantly weakened my cerulean fire. Almost to the point where I couldn't feel it. "What's in this...?" I trailed off, realization dawning. "Wait, is this...?"

The door to the bedroom crashed open, two Midnight Fae charging in with wands at the ready.

Zeph leaned against the wall, his hands in his pockets, as Kols followed what I now realized were Royal Guardians. They wore the Nacht family crest on their cloaks, the green colors denoting them as Warrior Bloods.

Just like Zeph.

"She's disarmed," Zeph informed them, his tone dead

and emotionless. "As requested."

What?

"Excellent. Take her to the Council dungeons," Kols said, sounding as regal as ever.

"Council dungeons?" I repeated, my heart in my throat.

This whole thing had been planned, I realized. From Shade leaving me with the note to Zeph showing up with the collar. And I'd stupidly put it on, too consumed by the comment about the recording.

Now I was defenseless.

And about to be taken to the Council for extermination.

"An anonymous source provided a recording of you admitting to your increased abilities." Kols met and held my gaze. "Your powers will be evaluated by the Council. If they determine this claim to be true, a reassignment may be required."

I translated what he really meant. *Extermination.* Just like I'd said last night. Only, Shade had provided me with a glimmer of hope, something I should have known better than to feel.

He'd tricked me.

They all had tricked me.

Shade recorded a private conversation and shared it with the Council.

Zeph showed up like a knight in shining armor, claiming to want to help me escape, all to lull me into a false sense of comfort while I put on the power-depleting collar.

And now Kols was looking at me like I meant nothing to him. He wanted me dead. He'd told me that last night. It would make his life easier if I didn't exist, would kill the bond between us and free him to pursue his destiny. So, naturally, he wanted me out of the picture. Why wouldn't he?

The spiteful part of me almost laid the accusation at his feet here, but the intelligent side of me held it back. If I spoke out now, he could take my life and claim self-defense. With Zeph at his back as a witness, he'd get away with it, too. Would probably use the guards' lives as cause and claim I had killed them. When, really, he'd do it to silence them.

At least, that was how I would play it.

Which meant I needed to save the declaration for later.

To announce it in front of other Council members.

Because if I was going down, so was he.

Zeph, too.

And Shade, the treacherous bastard.

They were all going to the grave with me.

Kols's pupils dilated, his gaze narrowing with knowledge as if he overheard the plan unfolding in my mind. Or maybe he saw the desire for vengeance flashing in my gaze.

I didn't care.

I let him see my anger.

Allowed him to witness my promise for retribution.

I'm not going down alone, I told him with a look.

Because in the end, they'd pay for what they'd done to me. *I vow it.*

Welcome to purgatory, boys.

You'd better hang on.

It's going to be a wild ride.

KOLS

EPILOGUE

AFLORA GLARED AT ME with a hatred I felt to my very soul.

She thought we'd betrayed her. Yet everything we'd done was to *save* her.

If Zeph hadn't gotten that collar around her neck in time, the Guardians would have sensed her additional bonds, which would have required me to kill them. Because I couldn't risk them going back to the Council with those details.

Seeing Aflora's expression now, it was clear Zeph hadn't been given a chance to explain.

She appeared ready to kill me. I supposed that worked in our favor in terms of believability, but I could see the wheels turning in her head.

If she breathed a word of our bonds, we were all fucked.

Zeph and I shared a look, his expression telling me he'd caught her resulting animosity as well.

Aflora was a ticking time bomb in so many ways, both in what she could say and in her mounting powers. Not to mention Shade, the bastard who fucking betrayed us all.

Our first order of business would be to free her.

Then we'd deal with the Death Blood.

Preferably with a stake through his fucking heart.

TO BE CONTINUED

THANK YOU FOR READING *MIDNIGHT FAE ACADEMY: BOOK ONE.*

Aflora and her mates will return in *Midnight Fae Academy: Book Two.*

As a thank you for reading, I have a little bonus-scene gift for you all. It's the dream Zeph inflicted upon Aflora that last night before everything went to hell in a handbasket…

ZEPH

AFLORA GLARED AT ME with a hatred I felt to my very soul.

Tracing into Aflora's mind was far too easy, the poor girl having not developed a single barrier to keep me out. The Guardian in me knew we needed to fix that oversight as soon as possible, whereas the male in me wanted to exploit the weakness to the fullest extent.

Tonight, I chose the latter.

The taste I'd gotten of her out in the forest wasn't nearly enough, and after weeks—*months*, if I was being honest with myself—of wanting her, I needed to indulge at least once.

Kols rested beside me, his mental presence nearby without being intrusive. He wanted to watch, as he often did when I played with a female.

I allowed it because I wanted him to watch, too.

Eventually, we would share her.

But for this experience, I needed to have her to myself, to learn her, to adore her, to fuck her the way I craved. Well, maybe not to that extent. That would require this to be reality, not a dream. She also needed to work up to my expectations.

Mmm, yes, this would be an introduction instead. A seduction of sorts. A way for her to get to know my preferences, at least on the surface.

"Aflora," I murmured, pulling her away from Shade and into a dreamland that I controlled.

His amusement touched my mind through the quad-bond we'd all formed, momentarily pulling me from the experience, as having him so near felt foreign and wrong. But I quickly ignited a block, keeping him from interfering, and sucked Aflora deeper into my web.

I suspected he allowed it, as it was far too easy to borrow her presence. He'd probably had his fill of her already since she was in his bed tonight.

Or maybe he welcomed the break.

Was she a needy lover?

A curious one?

Shy?

I couldn't wait to find out, the details from Kols having not been nearly enough. I wanted more, craved firsthand experience, and would acquire that from her tonight.

She blinked up at me in confusion, her beautiful blue eyes showcasing a world of questions she didn't voice out loud. When a flash of pain reached her features, I knew why. My heart gave a subtle pang, my regret over being too hard on her during class hitting me square in the gut. But I wouldn't apologize, refused to give her an inch. The world wouldn't go easy on her, and it was my job to prepare her. As cruel as my lesson might have been, it was a necessary one.

However, her introduction to my version of intimacy

would be a softer experience. Scaring her in the real world differed significantly from my preparation in the bedroom.

I gently palmed her throat, choosing action over words, and bent to brush my lips over hers in our first kiss. Technically, it didn't count. Which meant we would have more than one first experience and that only excited me more.

"Zeph," she whispered, a note of wonder in her voice that went straight to my groin.

Innocent, I thought, amused. Except Kols told me she sucked cock like a queen, which meant she could play both innocent and seductress.

The perfect combination.

"Are you manipulating my dream?" she asked, her gaze bright with knowledge.

I smiled. "Shade told you Kols has been in your head, too."

She nodded. "Yes."

"Then you already know the answer, pixie flower." I took her mouth again before she could issue a complaint, needing her more than she could possibly know. Biting her breast had quenched some of my thirst and stirred a whole new addiction that required satisfaction. And only she could relieve me now.

My grasp tightened around her throat, my lips curling as she gulped in response. She must have been naked with Shade because she wore nothing now, her gorgeous curves on display for me to explore and taste to completion.

But I started with her mouth, slipping my tongue inside to dominate hers in the manner I favored. Each stroke served as a lesson, teaching her how to receive me, how to welcome me, and how to kiss exactly the way I preferred.

She was a fucking natural, her moans confirming she enjoyed the exploration as well, her body curving into mine in beautiful submission. "You're perfect," I praised, kissing a path along her jaw and tenderly nipping her pulse before pressing my lips to her ear. "I've wanted you since that first night," I admitted softly. "But you've been the forbidden fruit I couldn't taste. All that ended tonight, pixie flower. You're mine now, and I intend to take you thoroughly."

I pulled back to catch her gaze, noting the reddening of her cheeks and the escalation of her breath. All signs of arousal, except for the hint of fear in her eyes, the one I'd placed there earlier with Raph's demonstration.

I didn't like seeing that glimmer in her eyes.

But I could respect it.

"I'm not an easy lover, Aflora," I warned her. "Pain intrigues me, and I favor control. But you're in charge here. Always. You need to tell me if I push you too far. Until I can trust you to do that, we'll go easy on each other. Both in your mind and outside of it. The kind of relationship I prefer takes time." Kols was the only one in my life who had ever truly reached the level of trust I required, which was why we often shared women. He kept me balanced. Told me when I took it too far.

And in turn, I protected him.

Or I tried, anyway.

Two times I'd failed now, the second of which being the female gazing up at me now.

However, I hadn't failed just him this time, but myself, too.

Worse, I couldn't bring myself to regret it. Not this time. Not with Aflora submitting so beautifully beneath me.

She didn't question my preferences.

Didn't balk at them.

Merely accepted them with a slight nod and an adorable little lick of her lips. It wasn't enough but definitely served as a start.

"Tonight I'm just going to taste you," I told her. "But consider this an introductory warning for what I will eventually want from you. Now grab the headboard and don't come until I give you permission."

She shivered but lifted her arms in the perfect display of obedience. I half expected her to fight me, to argue, to say something to the contrary. Yet she seemed completely enthralled, as if I were acting on a fantasy she long harbored. Maybe she did. We were playing in her mind, after all. She could try to take over, if she wanted to. However, she appeared content to let me lead, and I adored her all the more for it.

I sensed Shade slipping into the periphery of her mind, having found a way around my block.

It'd be easy to kick him out, to eject him yet again, but I let him stay this time. It was my job as headmaster to teach, so I'd show him how this was done.

Kols's amusement touched my mind, his years of experience showing as he guessed my motive for allowing Shade to remain on the edge. He knew I loved to taunt, and taunt I would.

"Are you ready for me, Aflora?" I asked softly.

She nodded.

And I shook my head. "Words, pixie flower. Give me words." That was the first lesson in trust—communicating openly and verbally.

"Y-yes, except I'm still not sure if this is real or not."

"It's fantasy," I whispered, nuzzling her. "A joint fantasy."

"In my head."

"Yes."

"With you being in control, like Kols and Shade."

"With me being in control, but I'm nothing like Kols or Shade, Aflora." I sank my teeth into her lower lip, drawing blood in the process and groaning at the exquisite taste of her.

She sucked in a breath in reply, goose bumps pebbling along her arms and spreading to her delicious tits. Her nipples hardened into beautiful little points that begged for my mouth, but I wouldn't indulge in them until I had her full understanding and consent.

"This is a dream," I murmured. "One I'm influencing in your mind."

"Okay."

"We're both aware that this is happening," I added.

She nodded again and repeated, "Okay."

"Do I have your permission to continue?"

She paused, considering me for a long moment before dipping her chin once. "Yes."

"Good." Because I needed this to be mutual, not one-sided.

"Only, I'm confused," she admitted against my mouth just as I was about to kiss her again.

"Confused about what?" I asked her softly, my lips skating over hers with each word.

Her blue eyes held mine, her brow furrowing. Yet her pulse escalated. She clearly wanted me. It was her mind giving us trouble now. "In class earlier, you—"

"No, Aflora," I cut in, knowing what she wanted to discuss. "What I demand of you during a lesson in the classroom will never overlap with what I require from you in the bedroom. They are two different entities, entirely separate. I'm Headmaster Zephyrus during Academy hours. And after them, I'm just Zeph."

She swallowed, her pupils dilating. "Just Zeph."

"Can you handle that?"

Another nod, this one slightly shallower but accompanied by a heated glance that confirmed her yearning rivaled mine. "Yes," she whispered.

"Then I can proceed?"

"Yes," she said again.

I smiled. *Brilliant.* "No more talking unless it's to tell me how good you feel beneath my tongue." I captured her mouth and swallowed the sweet little noise she made in response to my command.

That little noise blossomed into a moan as I ran my palms up her sides, exploring her supple curves.

Aflora was feminine perfection, soft in all the right

places with a warrior's heart underneath. I felt it beat against my hand as I cupped her breast, my thumb flicking her rosy bud and drawing more of those intriguing sounds from her lips.

Fuck, I adored a responsive woman.

And Aflora was definitely that.

She didn't shy away from her pleasure, her nipples tightening in eagerness and invitation. I licked a path down her neck to her collarbone and lower to take one of the stiff peaks into my mouth. She threaded her fingers through my hair in an attempt to hold me there. I bit her hard in response, my gaze capturing her wounded one as I growled low in my throat.

She stiffened, her fuckable mouth parting in confusion.

"Did I give you permission to release the headboard, Aflora?" I asked her.

"N-no," she stammered.

"Then I suggest you grab it again—right now—hold on, and don't let go until I tell you otherwise."

She quickly gripped the wood, her throat working as she managed to reply, "Sorry."

I smiled against her abused breast. "Oh, darling, you're not sorry. Not really. But if you release that headboard again, you will well and truly be sorry."

Orgasm denial was a favorite pastime of mine, and I excelled at it. She'd be in tears before the end of my torment, begging to come, and then I wouldn't stop until she begged me to stop.

Her grip tightened around the headboard, her cheeks going a little white.

The exact opposite of what I wanted to see from her.

And precisely why we would be taking our time getting to know each other.

"I would never injure you," I promised her. "I like pain, but only when mingled with pleasure."

I demonstrated by gently laving the bite mark on her tit, my tongue soothing her wound and seducing her back into the moment.

"Like this," I whispered, closing my mouth around her nipple and sucking her deep while massaging the tip with my tongue.

She bowed off the mattress in reply, her eyes falling shut on a groan as she desperately clung to the headboard.

"Just like that," I praised, switching to her other breast.

She practically panted in response, her heart bouncing wildly against her ribs.

Mmm, her arousal mounted by the second, permeating the air and taunting all my masculine senses. I inhaled deeply, loving the floral scent of her and finding it beautifully appropriate.

While delayed gratification might be a favorite game of mine, I wouldn't do that to her tonight. Mostly because I couldn't. I was dying to taste her, to feel her climax against my tongue, and revel in her pleasure over and over again until sunset.

There would be no sleeping for either of us tonight.

She'd be exhausted and gratified and unable to move later without thinking of me and the memory of my tongue between her thighs.

I slid down, kissing a wet path along her abdomen, pausing to dip my tongue into her navel while studying her reactions.

Parted lips.

Rosy cheeks.

Half-mast eyes.

Absolutely everything I wanted to see in a woman when making this descent. I nibbled her hip bone, smiling when she gasped and bucked in reply. Such a sensitive female, definitely made to be bitten. But I'd save that for our real experience together.

This dream was about satisfaction for us both.

A way to learn more about one another without risk.

Her soft, dark curls teased the hairs along my chin as I pressed a kiss to the top of her mound. I palmed her thighs to push them wide, exposing her slick pussy to my view.

She didn't shy away from me.

Didn't fight, either.

Merely tossed her head back with an eager sound, her excitement palpable and visible in the slickness of her folds.

"You're soaked for me, pixie flower," I whispered, admiring her damp heat. "I can't wait to make you wetter, baby."

She shivered, her lips parting in expectation.

I drew my nose along her seam, inhaling deeply and allowing her sweet nectar to take me completely. My dick throbbed, begging me to rip off my sweatpants and sink myself into her. But this wasn't about me or my needs.

I wanted to do this for her.

And also to fulfill my desire to taste her pleasure.

Something told me she'd be a screamer, unafraid of sharing her ecstasy with the world. Mmm, I bet she'd lock down on my fingers, too, her greedy cunt craving a cock to milk instead. *My* cock.

Soon, I promised us both. *Very soon*.

However, first, I required *this*. I parted her intimately with my tongue, licking upward to her clit and back down to the tight hole that would one day soon hug my shaft. I'd take her ass as well, once we worked up to it. Maybe even while Kols fucked her pussy.

Just thinking about it had my balls tightening in need.

She'd be the perfect puzzle piece between us, writhing in exquisite rapture while we took her to oblivion and back.

All the females we'd shared previously meant nothing, were just passing opportunities we took temporary pleasure from.

Aflora would be different.

Because she belonged to us, as we belonged to her.

Our mate.

Our minds would soon be intertwined—once we bit

her two more times.

I groaned at the very real thought of what that would mean for us, how truly intimate it would be to fuck her while *inside* her. Our souls married as one. Our hearts beating in tandem with the other.

Fuck, who knew that could be so damn sexy?

I never desired a mate because it wasn't meant for me. Kols was my future. Serving as his Guardian my only path.

But now Aflora existed between us.

Having her changed everything.

"Zeph," she whispered, her plea a song I wanted to strum all night. I'd paused just under her clit, tasting without pleasing, and she desired more.

Her knuckles were white around the headboard, her restraint admirable as she held on for dear life. I could see her desire to let go, grab my head, and guide me upward to the place she needed me to touch.

I hummed against her flesh, smiling when she jolted. The reverberations would have given her just a hint of satisfaction, only to pull her deeper into a blanket of despair.

"*Please*," she said, her musical voice a proverbial stroke against my shaft. Because I loved the sound of a female begging, especially her.

"Please what?" I taunted her, studying her face as her eyes clenched shut in pleasurable frustration. Because my words had vibrated her once more. "Do you want me to suck your little clit into my mouth, Aflora? Massage you with my tongue until you explode?"

"Yes," she whimpered, her legs trembling around me.

"Say it," I encouraged her. "Tell me to suck your clit."

She gave an adorable little groan, my demand turning her on even more. It helped that my lips were now brushing her clit when I spoke, the heat of my breath stroking her arousal.

Her tongue slipped from her mouth to dampen her lips, a shuddering exhale escaping her as she quivered.

"Please suck my clit, Zeph. Let me come."

Clever angel, I thought, amused. Not only had she asked nicely, but she'd also added a comment about being allowed to fall apart. "You're perfect, Aflora," I informed her. "Fucking perfect." And she didn't even know why. She was just a natural at submitting to me, her ability to take instruction displaying gorgeously in the bedroom.

I rewarded her with a firm lick, my mouth closing around her sensitive bud and giving her the suction she craved.

She screamed, her body coming off the mattress as she maintained a death grip on the bars of the headboard. Her admirable display of submission required an ample reward, so I gave it to her. "Come for me, pixie flower," I whispered. "Come hard."

I'd barely uttered the last two words when she fell apart on a scream that I would forever remember. Because it was underlined with my name. Never had I enjoyed hearing it more than in this moment as she repeated it over and over, her head thrashing from side to side as she shattered spectacularly beneath my tongue.

Kols stirred beside me in his bed, his mind attuned to mine and Aflora's, his voyeuristic tendencies shining through as he observed us. He stroked his cock in the real world, just outside the dreamscape, his orgasm mounting.

I reached across to stop him from continuing. "No. Time for you to join us."

"What?" Aflora asked, surfacing from her orgasmic state and hearing me speaking out loud and in my mind to Kols.

He didn't hesitate or argue, his powers mingling with mine as he joined us inside her mind.

I smiled as her eyebrows flew upward, her red cheeks showcasing her recent pleasure. Kissing a line up her abdomen, I returned to her mouth as I settled my body alongside hers. "Kols wants to play, too."

"But he hates me," she whispered to me, causing Kols

to chuckle as he settled between her legs.

"This is about fantasy," he told her softly, his lips brushing the same place I just abandoned. "Just lie there and enjoy it, sweetheart." He didn't give her time to protest, his mouth sealing around her clit as he slid two fingers into her tight channel.

She yelped, her hands nearly leaving the headboard to make him stop, but I caught her wrists before she could. "Shh, you'll be all right."

"It's too much," she panted, squirming. "Too much... *sensation.*"

I smiled, knowing exactly what she meant. "Ah, Aflora, but this is a dream," I murmured, kissing her tenderly to silence her continued protests. "Don't you know the best part of dreaming, pixie flower?"

She shook her head. I couldn't tell if it was in response to my question or to the torment Kols was inflicting upon her between her thighs.

Either way, I answered. "The best part about a dream is it can defy reality," I whispered. "Which means we can make you come over and over again, all night, without once having to take a break. Because your body will continue to regenerate to our expectations."

Her eyes widened. "No."

"Oh, yes," I replied, nuzzling her and palming her breast to give her nipple a little squeeze. "It's the worst and best form of torment known to the Midnight Fae. And we're only just getting started."

She began to quake, her next orgasm already mounting, thanks to Kols's expert skill.

"Welcome to my mind, Aflora." I kissed the corner of her mouth and tweaked her peak once more, drawing a shudder from her. "It's a devious, intense place filled with endless ways to pleasure you. Tonight is merely an introduction, a taste of what our future holds."

She whimpered, and I smiled, sensing her mounting rapture.

"Go ahead and scream for us, baby," I said quietly, giving her permission to fall apart. "Once Kols is done, we'll switch places, and I'll drive you to new heights all over again."

And again.

And again.

Which I did.

As did Kols.

Until the sun went down, when I promised her a repeat performance again later.

Only, the moment I opened my eyes, everything went to hell.

And my plans for Aflora disappeared beneath a wave of crushing reality.

The Council knows…

Midnight Fae Academy: Book Two

I'm in purgatory.
Hell.
A Midnight Fae dungeon.
All because my mates betrayed me.

Shade swears he's innocent.
Zeph promises that what he did was for my own best interest.
Meanwhile, Kols isn't apologetic in the slightest, his cocky
arrogance claiming fate intervened at just the right moment.

I hate them all.
Crave them, too.
And now I have to work with them to solve a millennia-old
secret, one that involves my true heritage.

Except our digging has awoken an ancient power and it's
threatening to destroy the Midnight Fae realm with its
vengeance.

If only the Academy offered courses in mediation.
I could use one of those right about now.
Because as it turns out, I'm the only one with the power to
stop this thing from taking over.
And I have to rely on my mates to help guide me.

Welcome to Midnight Fae Academy, where the classes are useless and the male fae are all jackholes. Wish me luck.

Author Note: This is a dark paranormal reverse harem trilogy with bully romance (enemies-to-lovers) elements. Despite Aflora's opinions on the matter, there will definitely be biting. Shadow, aka Shade, guarantees it. This book ends on a cliffhanger.

You met Gina in *Midnight Fae Academy*. Find out what she's really up to in *Fortune Fae Academy*...

I never asked to be an Omega.

I'm a Fortune Fae—I see the future. But I didn't see this coming.
My Alpha will stop at nothing to possess me until he drags me all the way to Fortune Fae Academy to join the other wide-eyed Omegas-in-training. He believes I'm strong enough to survive—and I hope he's right.

He also believes I'll kneel at his feet.

He couldn't be more wrong about that.
I don't need three broody Betas and an asshat Alpha telling me what to do. I'm going to keep running until he realizes he's chasing the wrong girl.

Except there's one slight problem. My Alpha has seen the future too... and he knows something I don't.

Whatever he thinks is going to happen, his cruel smirk says I'm not going anywhere.

Fortune Fae Academy is Book 1 in a Reverse Harem Omegaverse Romance. Be warned there are obsessive males who will stop at nothing to claim their fated mate. Trigger warnings include dub-con, strong language, and violence. As this is a series, book 1 ends on a cliffhanger.

ACKNOWLEDGMENTS

Oh, where to begin? This book wouldn't have been possible without so many factors. First of all, to J.R. Thorn, for helping me create the Fae Realms. It was an absolute pleasure and honor to work on Elemental Fae Academy with you, and I love that we're able to continue playing in this world with other fae characters. I cannot wait to read Fortune Fae Academy! Please hurry up.

A heartfelt thank-you to Katie, for all of your help and guidance along the way. I love working with you and always enjoy your feedback while I'm writing. Zeph sends his love (or his version of it, anyway).

To Bethany, thank you for being an amazing editor and constantly dealing with my moving deadlines/final word counts. One of these days, I will finish a project at the desired word length and on time. Maybe. I blame the voices. In this particular case, the boys are to blame. I hate them all. (Just kidding, guys. I love you. Sort of. Well, really just Shade. Kols and Zeph, you know why I'm annoyed.)

To Vicki, Laura & Matt, thank you for your patience and understanding and for letting me skip brewery/chocolate day to finish Aflora's first book. Next time we go on vacay, I promise not to have a deadline near the travel time!

To Lori, thank you for the seriously **beautiful** cover. It is so incredibly inspiring, as is the entire series. I am so in love with the art and design. Thank you for creating all the little details that match my words.

To Heather, thank you for the gorgeous headers and title

page. I'm so in love with the paperback print. It's amazing; as is my website, which I adore you for creating and maintaining.

To Louise and Diane, thank you for being my figurative backbones and for always being there for me. You both keep me afloat when I need it, tell me to hide and write (when I need to be told to hide and write), and help me in ways you probably don't even realize. I love you both!

To my Essentially Chase PR team, thank you for guiding me and providing your ample expertise in this industry. I adore you both. Please don't ever leave me. I'm not great at running, but I will chase after you!

To my ARC team and Foss's Famous Owls, thank you for your support and for loving on my books! I appreciate you all more than you know.

And to my readers, thank you for being here! I love hearing from you all and adore your reviews, comments, and messages. You all consistently make my days better and provide me with the motivation I need to continue. I share my words because you all convince me to, so thank you for letting me tell the world about the voices in my head.

I'll be back with more Aflora, Kols, Shade, and Zeph soon! <3

ABOUT LEXI C. FOSS

USA Today Bestselling Author Lexi C. Foss loves to play in dark worlds, especially the ones that bite. She lives in Atlanta, Georgia with her husband and their furry children. When not writing, she's busy crossing items off her travel bucket list, or chasing eclipses around the globe. She's quirky, consumes way too much coffee, and loves to swim.

www.LexiCFoss.com
https://www.facebook.com/LexiCFoss
https://www.twitter.com/LexiCFoss